JOYCE CAROL OATES

SMALL AVALANCHES

and

other stories

5c
OAT

HARPERTEMPEST
AN IMPRINT OF HARPERCOLLINS*PUBLISHERS*

Small Avalanches and Other Stories
Copyright © 2003 by The Ontario Review, Inc.

Printed in the United States of America. For information address
HarperCollins Children's Books, a division of HarperCollins
Publishers, 1350 Avenue of the Americas, New York, NY 10019.

Library of Congress Cataloging-in-Publication Data

Oates, Joyce Carol, date.

  Small avalanches and other stories / by Joyce Carol Oates.

    p. cm.

  Summary: A collection of twelve short stories for young people,
including "Where Are You Going, Where Have You Been," "Life
After High School," and "How I Contemplated the World."

  ISBN 0-06-001217-X — ISBN 0-06-001218-8 (lib. bdg.)

  ISBN 0-06-001219-6 (pbk.)

  1. Adolescence—Fiction. 2. Youth—Fiction. [1. Coming of
age—Fiction. 2. Short stories.] 1. Title.

PZ7.O1056 Sm 2003   2002023311

[Fic]—dc21   CIP

                                                      AC

Typography by Alison Donalty

❖

First paperback edition, 2004

Visit us on the World Wide Web!

www.harpertempest.com

for the "bad girls"

CONTENTS

WHERE ARE YOU GOING, WHERE HAVE YOU BEEN?

For Bob Dylan

Her name was Connie. She was fifteen and she had a quick, nervous giggling habit of craning her neck to glance into mirrors or checking other people's faces to make sure her own was all right. Her mother, who noticed everything and knew everything and who hadn't much reason any longer to look at her own face, always scolded Connie about it. "Stop gawking at yourself. Who are you? You think you're so pretty?" she would say. Connie would raise her eyebrows at these familiar old complaints and look right through her mother, into a shadowy vision of herself as she was right at that moment: she knew she was pretty and that was everything. Her mother had been pretty once too, if you could believe those old snapshots in the album, but now her looks were gone and that was why she was always after Connie.

"Why don't you keep your room clean like your sister? How've you got your hair fixed—what the hell stinks? Hair spray? You don't see your sister using that junk."

Her sister, June, was twenty-four and still lived at home. She was a secretary in the high school Connie attended, and if that wasn't bad enough—with her in the same building—she was so plain and chunky and steady that Connie had to hear her praised all the time by her mother and her mother's sisters. June did this, June did that, she saved money and helped clean the house and cooked and Connie couldn't do a thing, her mind was all filled with trashy daydreams. Their father was away at work most of the time and when he came home he wanted supper and he read the newspaper at supper and after supper he went to bed. He didn't bother talking much to them, but around his bent head Connie's mother kept picking at her until Connie wished her mother was dead and she herself was dead and it was all over. "She makes me want to throw up sometimes," she complained to her friends. She had a high, breathless, amused voice that made everything she said sound a little forced, whether it was sincere or not.

There was one good thing: June went places with girl friends of hers, girls who were just as plain and steady as she, and so when Connie wanted to do that her mother had no objections. The father of Connie's best girl friend drove the girls the three miles to town and left them at a shopping plaza so they could walk through the stores or go to a movie, and when he came to pick them up again at eleven he never bothered to ask what they had done.

They must have been familiar sights, walking around the shopping plaza in their shorts and flat ballerina slippers that always scuffed on the sidewalk, with charm bracelets jingling on their thin wrists; they would lean together to whisper and laugh secretly if someone passed who amused or interested them. Connie had long dark blond hair that drew anyone's eye to it, and she wore part of it pulled up on her head and puffed out and the rest of it she let fall down her back. She wore a pullover jersey top that looked one way when she was at home and another way when she was away from home. Everything about her had two sides to it, one for home and one for anywhere that was not home: her walk, which could be childlike and bobbing, or languid enough to make anyone think she was hearing music in her head; her mouth, which was pale and smirking most of the time, but bright and pink on these evenings out; her laugh, which was cynical and drawling at home—"Ha, ha, very funny,"—but high-pitched and nervous anywhere else, like the jingling of the charms on her bracelet.

Sometimes they did go shopping or to a movie, but sometimes they went across the highway, ducking fast across the busy road, to a drive-in restaurant where older kids hung out. The restaurant was shaped like a big bottle, though squatter than a real bottle, and on its cap was a revolving figure of a grinning boy holding a hamburger aloft. One night in midsummer they ran across, breathless with daring, and right away someone leaned out a car window and invited them over, but it was just a boy from high school they didn't like. It made them feel good to be able to ignore him. They went up through the maze of parked and cruising cars to the bright-lit, fly-infested restaurant, their faces pleased and expectant as if they were entering a sacred building that loomed up out of the night to give them what haven and blessing they yearned for. They sat at the counter and crossed their legs at the ankles, their thin shoulders rigid with excitement, and listened to the music that made everything so good: the music was always in the background, like music at a church service; it was something to depend upon.

A boy named Eddie came in to talk with them. He sat backward on his stool, turning himself jerkily around in semicircles and then stopping and turning back again, and after a while he asked Connie if she would like something to eat. She said she would so she tapped her friend's arm on her way out—her friend pulled her face up into a brave, droll look—and Connie said she would meet her at eleven across the way. "I just hate to leave her like that," Connie said earnestly, but the boy said that she wouldn't be alone for long. So they went out to his car, and on the way Connie couldn't help but let her eyes wander over the windshields and faces all around her, her face gleaming with a joy that had nothing to do with Eddie or even this place; it might have been the music. She drew her shoulders up and sucked in her breath with the pure pleasure of being alive, and just at that moment she happened to glance at a face just a few feet away from hers. It was a boy with shaggy black hair, in a convertible jalopy painted gold. He stared at her and then his lips widened into a grin. Connie slit her eyes at him and turned away, but she couldn't help glancing back and there he was, still watching her. He wagged a finger and laughed and said, "Gonna get you, baby," and Connie turned away again without Eddie noticing anything.

She spent three hours with him, at the restaurant where they ate hamburgers and drank Cokes in wax cups that were always sweating, and then down an alley a mile or so away, and when he left her off at five to eleven only the movie house was still open at the plaza. Her girl friend was there, talking with a boy. When Connie came up, the two girls smiled at each other and Connie said, "How was the movie?" and the girl said, "*You* should know." They rode off with the girl's father, sleepy and pleased, and Connie couldn't help but look back at the darkened shopping plaza with its big empty parking lot and its signs that were faded and ghostly now, and over at the drive-in restaurant where cars were still circling tirelessly. She couldn't hear the music at this distance.

Next morning June asked her how the movie was and Connie said, "So-so."

She and that girl and occasionally another girl went out several times a week, and the rest of the time Connie spent around the house—it was summer vacation—getting in her mother's way and thinking, dreaming about the boys she met. But all the boys fell back and dissolved into a single face that was not even a face but an idea, a feeling, mixed up with the urgent insistent pounding of the music and the humid night air of July. Connie's mother kept dragging her back to the daylight by finding things for her to do or saying suddenly, "What's this about the Pettinger girl?"

And Connie would say nervously, "Oh, her. That dope." She always drew thick clear lines between herself and such girls, and her mother was simple and kind enough to believe it. Her mother was so simple, Connie thought, that it was maybe cruel to fool her so much. Her mother went scuffling around the house in old bedroom slippers and complained over the telephone to one sister about the other, then the other called up and the two of them complained about the third one. If June's name was mentioned her mother's tone was approving, and if Connie's name was mentioned it was disapproving. This did not really mean she disliked Connie, and actually Connie thought that her mother preferred her to June just because she was prettier, but the two of them kept up a pretense of exasperation, a sense that they were tugging and struggling over something of little value to either of them. Sometimes, over coffee, they were almost friends, but something would come up—some vexation that was like a fly buzzing suddenly around their heads—and their faces went hard with contempt.

One Sunday Connie got up at eleven—none of them bothered with church—and washed her hair so that it could dry all day long in the sun. Her parents and sister were going to a barbecue at an aunt's house and Connie said no, she wasn't interested, rolling her eyes to let her mother know just what she thought of it. "Stay home alone then," her mother said sharply. Connie sat out back in a lawn chair and watched them drive away, her father quiet and bald, hunched around so that he could back the car out, her mother with a look that was still angry and not at all softened through the windshield, and in the backseat poor old June, all dressed up as if she didn't know what a barbecue was, with all the running yelling kids and the flies. Connie sat with her eyes closed in the sun, dreaming and dazed with the warmth about her as if this were a kind of love, the caresses of love, and her mind slipped over onto thoughts of the boy she had been with the night before and how nice he had been, how sweet it always was, not the way someone like June would suppose but sweet, gentle, the way it was in movies and promised in songs; and when she opened her eyes she hardly knew where she was, the backyard ran off into weeds and a fencelike line of trees and behind it the sky was perfectly blue and still. The asbestos "ranch house" that was now three years old startled her—it looked small. She shook her head as if to get awake.

It was too hot. She went inside the house and turned on the radio to drown out the quiet. She sat on the edge of her bed, barefoot, and listened for an hour and a half to a program called *XYZ Sunday Jamboree*, record after record of hard, fast, shrieking songs she sang along with, interspersed by exclamations from "Bobby King": "An' look here, you girls at Napoleon's—Son and Charley want you to pay real close attention to this song coming up!"

And Connie paid close attention herself, bathed in a glow of slow-pulsed joy that seemed to rise mysteriously out of the music itself and lay languidly about the airless little room, breathed in and breathed out with each gentle rise and fall of her chest.

After a while she heard a car coming up the drive. She sat up at once, startled, because it couldn't be her father so soon. The gravel kept crunching all the way in from the road—the driveway was long—and Connie ran to the window. It was a car she didn't know. It was an open jalopy, painted a bright gold that caught the sunlight opaquely. Her heart began to pound and her fingers snatched at her hair, checking it, and she whispered, "Christ, Christ," wondering how she looked. The car came to a stop at the side door and the horn sounded four short taps, as if this were a signal Connie knew.

She went into the kitchen and approached the door slowly, then hung out the screen door, her bare toes curling down off the step. There were two boys in the car and now she recognized the driver: he had shaggy, shabby black hair that looked crazy as a wig and he was grinning at her.

"I ain't late, am I?" he said.

"Who the hell do you think you are?" Connie said.

"Toldja I'd be out, didn't I?"

"I don't even know who you are."

She spoke sullenly, careful to show no interest or pleasure, and he spoke in a fast, bright monotone. Connie looked past him to the other boy, taking her time. He had fair brown hair, with a lock that fell onto his forehead. His sideburns gave him a fierce, embarrassed look, but so far he hadn't even bothered to glance at her. Both boys wore sunglasses. The driver's glasses were metallic and mirrored everything in miniature.

"You wanta come for a ride?" he said.

Connie smirked and let her hair fall loose over one shoulder.

"Don'tcha like my car? New paint job," he said. "Hey."

"What?"

"You're cute."

She pretended to fidget, chasing flies away from the door.

"Don'tcha believe me, or what?" he said.

"Look, I don't even know who you are," Connie said in disgust.

"Hey, Ellie's got a radio, see. Mine broke down." He lifted his friend's arm and showed her the little transistor radio the boy was holding, and now Connie began to hear the music. It was the same program that was playing inside the house.

"Bobby King?" she said.

"I listen to him all the time. I think he's great."

"He's kind of great," Connie said reluctantly.

"Listen, that guy's *great*. He knows where the action is."

Connie blushed a little, because the glasses made it

impossible for her to see just what this boy was looking at. She couldn't decide if she liked him or if he was a jerk, and so she dawdled in the doorway and wouldn't come down or go back inside. She said, "What's all that stuff painted on your car?"

"Can'tcha read it?" He opened the door very carefully, as if he were afraid it might fall off. He slid out just as carefully, planting his feet firmly on the ground, the tiny metallic world in his glasses slowing down like gelatine hardening, and in the midst of it Connie's bright-green blouse. "This here is my name, to begin with," he said. ARNOLD FRIEND was written in tarlike black letters on the side, with a drawing of a round, grinning face that reminded Connie of a pumpkin, except it wore sunglasses. "I wanta introduce myself. I'm Arnold Friend and that's my real name and I'm gonna be your friend, honey, and inside the car's Ellie Oscar, he's kinda shy." Ellie brought his transistor radio up to his shoulder and balanced it there. "Now, these numbers are a secret code, honey," Arnold Friend explained. He read off the numbers 33, 19, 17 and raised his eyebrows at her to see what she thought of that, but she didn't think much of it. The left rear fender had been smashed and around it was written, on the gleaming gold background: DONE BY CRAZY WOMAN DRIVER. Connie had to laugh at that. Arnold Friend was pleased at her laughter and looked up at her. "Around the other side's a lot more—you wanta come and see them?"

"No."

"Why not?"

"Why should I?"

"Don'tcha wanta see what's on the car? Don'tcha wanta go for a ride?"

"I don't know."

"Why not?"

"I got things to do."

"Like what?"

"Things."

He laughed as if she had said something funny. He slapped his thighs. He was standing in a strange way, leaning back against the car as if he were balancing himself. He wasn't tall, only an inch or so taller than she would be if she came down to him. Connie liked the way he was dressed, which was the way all of them dressed: tight faded jeans stuffed into black, scuffed boots, a belt that pulled his waist in and showed how lean he was, and a white pullover shirt that was a little soiled and showed the hard small muscles of his arms and shoulders. He looked as if he probably did hard work, lifting and carrying things. Even his neck looked muscular. And his face was a familiar face, somehow; the jaw and chin and cheeks slightly darkened because he hadn't shaved for a day or two, and the nose long and hawklike, sniffing as if she was a treat he was going to gobble up and it was all a joke.

"Connie, you ain't telling the truth. This is your day set aside for a ride with me and you know it," he said, still laughing. The way he straightened and recovered from his fit of laughing showed that it had been all fake.

"How do you know what my name is?" she said suspiciously.

"It's Connie."

"Maybe and maybe not."

"I know my Connie," he said, wagging his finger. Now she remembered him even better, back at the restaurant, and her cheeks warmed at the thought of how she had sucked in her breath just at the moment she passed him— how she must have looked to him. And he had remembered her. "Ellie and I come out here especially for you," he said. "Ellie can sit in back. How about it?"

"Where?"

"Where what?"

"Where're we going?"

He looked at her. He took off the sunglasses and she saw how pale the skin around his eyes was, like holes that were not in shadow but instead in light. His eyes were like chips of broken glass that catch the light in an amiable way. He smiled. It was as if the idea of going for a ride somewhere, to someplace, was a new idea to him.

"Just for a ride, Connie sweetheart."

"I never said my name was Connie," she said.

"But I know what it is. I know your name and all about you, lots of things," Arnold Friend said. He had not moved yet but stood still leaning back against the side of his jalopy. "I took a special interest in you, such a pretty girl, and found out all about you—like I know your parents and sister are gone somewheres and I know where and how long they're going to be gone, and I know who you were with last night, and your best girl friend's name is Betty. Right?"

He spoke in a simple lilting voice, exactly as if he was reciting the words to a song. His smile assured her that everything was fine. In the car Ellie turned up the volume on his radio and did not bother to look around at them.

"Ellie can sit in the backseat," Arnold Friend said. He indicated his friend with a casual jerk of his chin, as if Ellie did not count and she should not bother with him.

"How'd you find out all that stuff?" Connie said.

"Listen: Betty Schultz and Tony Fitch and Jimmy Pettinger and Nancy Pettinger," he said in a chant. "Raymond Stanley and Bob Hutter—"

"Do you know all those kids?"

"I know everybody."

"Look, you're kidding. You're not from around here."

"Sure."

"But—how come we never saw you before?"

"Sure you saw me before," he said. He looked down at his boots, as if he was a little offended. "You just don't remember."

"I guess I'd remember you," Connie said.

"Yeah?" He looked up at this, beaming. He was pleased. He began to mark time with the music from Ellie's radio, tapping his fists lightly together. Connie looked away from his smile to the car, which was painted so bright it almost hurt her eyes to look at it. She looked at that name, ARNOLD FRIEND. And up at the front fender was an expression that was familiar—MAN THE FLYING SAUCERS. It was an expression kids had used the year before but didn't use this year. She looked at it for a while as if the words meant something to her that she did not yet know.

"What're you thinking about? Huh?" Arnold Friend demanded. "Not worried about your hair blowing around in the car, are you?"

"No."

"Think I maybe can't drive good?"

"How do I know?"

"You're a hard girl to handle. How come?" he said. "Don't you know I'm your friend? Didn't you see me put my sign in the air when you walked by?"

"What sign?"

"My sign." And he drew an X in the air, leaning out toward her. They were maybe ten feet apart. After his hand fell back to his side the X was still in the air, almost visible. Connie let the screen door close and stood perfectly still inside it, listening to the music from her radio and the boy's blend together. She stared at Arnold Friend. He stood there so stiffly relaxed, pretending to be relaxed, with one hand idly on the door handle as if he was keeping himself up that way and had no intention of ever moving again. She recognized most things about him, the tight jeans that showed his thighs and buttocks and the greasy leather boots and the tight shirt, and even that slippery friendly smile of his, that sleepy dreamy smile that all the boys used to get across ideas they didn't want to put into words. She recognized all this and also the singsong way he talked, slightly mocking, kidding, but serious and a little melancholy, and she recognized the way he tapped one fist against the other in homage to the perpetual music behind him. But all these things did not come together.

She said suddenly, "Hey, how old are you?"

His smile faded. She could see then that he wasn't a kid, he was much older—thirty, maybe more. At this knowledge her heart began to pound faster.

"That's a crazy thing to ask. Can'tcha see I'm your own age?"

"Like hell you are."

"Or maybe a coupla years older. I'm eighteen."

"Eighteen?" she said doubtfully.

He grinned to reassure her and lines appeared at the corners of his mouth. His teeth were big and white. He grinned so broadly his eyes became slits and she saw how thick the lashes were, thick and black as if painted with a black tarlike material. Then, abruptly, he seemed to become embarrassed and looked over his shoulder at Ellie. "*Him*, he's crazy," he said. "Ain't he a riot? He's a nut, a real character." Ellie was still listening to the music. His sunglasses told nothing about what he was thinking. He wore a bright-orange shirt unbuttoned halfway to show his chest, which was a pale, bluish chest and not muscular like Arnold Friend's. His shirt collar was turned up all around and the very tips of the collar pointed out past his chin as if they were protecting him. He was pressing the transistor radio up against his ear and sat there in a kind of daze, right in the sun.

"He's kinda strange," Connie said.

"Hey, she says you're kinda strange! Kinda strange!" Arnold Friend cried. He pounded on the car to get Ellie's attention. Ellie turned for the first time and Connie saw with shock that he wasn't a kid either—he had a fair, hairless face, cheeks reddened slightly as if the veins grew too close to the surface of his skin, the face of a forty-year-old baby. Connie felt a wave of dizziness rise in her at this sight and she stared at him as if waiting for something to change the shock of the moment, make it all right again. Ellie's lips kept shaping words, mumbling along with the words blasting in his ear.

"Maybe you two better go away," Connie said faintly.

"What? How come?" Arnold Friend cried. "We come out here to take you for a ride. It's Sunday." He had the voice of the man on the radio now. It was the same voice, Connie thought. "Don'tcha know it's Sunday all day? And honey, no matter who you were with last night, today you're with Arnold Friend and don't you forget it! Maybe you better step out here," he said, and this last was in a different voice. It was a little flatter, as if the heat was finally getting to him.

"No. I got things to do."

"Hey."

"You two better leave."

"We ain't leaving until you come with us."

"Like hell I am—"

"Connie, don't fool around with me. I mean—I mean, don't fool *around*," he said, shaking his head. He laughed incredulously. He placed his sunglasses on top of his head, carefully, as if he was indeed wearing a wig, and brought the stems down behind his ears. Connie stared at him, another wave of dizziness and fear rising in her so that for a moment he wasn't even in focus but was just a blur standing there against his gold car, and she had the idea that he had driven up the driveway all right but had come from nowhere before that and belonged nowhere and that everything about him and even about the music that was so familiar to her was only half real.

"If my father comes and sees you—"

"He ain't coming. He's at a barbecue."

"How do you know that?"

"Aunt Tillie's. Right now they're—uh—they're drinking. Sitting around," he said vaguely, squinting as if he was staring all the way to town and over to Aunt Tillie's backyard. Then the vision seemed to get clear and he nodded energetically. "Yeah. Sitting around. There's your sister in a blue dress, huh? And high heels, the poor sad bitch—nothing like you, sweetheart! And your mother's helping some fat woman with the corn, they're cleaning the corn—husking the corn—"

"What fat woman?" Connie cried.

"How do I know what fat woman, I don't know every goddamn fat woman in the world!" Arnold Friend laughed.

"Oh, that's Mrs. Hornsby. . . . Who invited her?" Connie said. She felt a little lightheaded. Her breath was coming quickly.

"She's too fat. I don't like them fat. I like them the way you are, honey," he said, smiling sleepily at her. They stared at each other for a while through the screen door. He said softly, "Now, what you're going to do is this: you're going to come out that door. You're going to sit up front with me and Ellie's going to sit in the back, the hell with Ellie, right? This isn't Ellie's date. You're my date. I'm your lover, honey."

"What? You're crazy—"

"Yes. I'm your lover. You don't know what that is but you will," he said. "I know that too. I know all about you. But look: it's real nice and you couldn't ask for nobody better than me, or more polite. I always keep my word. I'll tell you how it is, I'm always nice at first, the first time. I'll hold you so tight you won't think you have to try to get away or pretend anything because you'll know you can't. And I'll come inside you where it's all secret and you'll give in to me and you'll love me—"

"Shut up! You're crazy!" Connie said. She backed away from the door. She put her hands up against her ears as if she'd heard something terrible, something not meant for her. "People don't talk like that, you're crazy," she muttered. Her heart was almost too big now for her chest and its pumping made sweat break out all over her. She looked out to see Arnold Friend pause and then take a step toward the porch, lurching. He almost fell. But, like a clever drunken man, he managed to catch his balance. He wobbled in his high boots and grabbed hold of one of the porch posts.

"Honey?" he said. "You still listening?"

"Get the hell out of here!"

"Be nice, honey. Listen."

"I'm going to call the police—"

He wobbled again and out of the side of his mouth came a fast spat curse, an aside not meant for her to hear. But even this "Christ!" sounded forced. Then he began to smile again. She watched this smile come, awkward as if he was smiling from inside a mask. His whole face was a mask, she thought wildly, tanned down to his throat but then running out as if he had plastered makeup on his face but had forgotten about his throat.

"Honey—? Listen, here's how it is. I always tell the truth and I promise you this: I ain't coming in that house after you."

"You better not! I'm going to call the police if you—if you don't—"

"Honey," he said, talking right through her voice, "honey. I'm not coming in there but you are coming out here. You know why?"

She was panting. The kitchen looked like a place she had never seen before, some room she had run inside but that wasn't good enough, wasn't going to help her. The kitchen window had never had a curtain, after three years, and there were dishes in the sink for her to do—probably—and if you ran your hand across the table you'd probably feel something sticky there.

"You listening, honey? Hey?"

"—going to call the police—"

"Soon as you touch the phone I don't need to keep my promise and can come inside. You won't want that."

She rushed forward and tried to lock the door. Her fingers were shaking. "But why lock it," Arnold Friend said gently, talking right into her face. "It's just a screen door. It's just nothing." One of his boots was at a strange angle, as if his foot wasn't in it. It pointed out to the left, bent at the ankle. "I mean, anybody can break through a screen door and glass and wood and iron or anything else if he needs to, anybody at all, and specially Arnold Friend. If the place got lit up with a fire, honey, you'd come runnin' out into my arms, right into my arms an' safe at home—like you knew I was your lover and'd stopped fooling around. I don't mind a nice shy girl but I don't like no fooling around." Part of those words were spoken with a slight rhythmic lilt, and Connie somehow recognized them—the echo of a song from last year, about a girl rushing into her boyfriend's arms and coming home again—

Connie stood barefoot on the linoleum floor, staring at him. "What do you want?" she whispered.

"I want you," he said.

"What?"

"Seen you that night and thought, that's the one, yes sir. I never needed to look anymore."

"But my father's coming back. He's coming to get me. I had to wash my hair first—" She spoke in a dry, rapid voice, hardly raising it for him to hear.

"No, your daddy is not coming and yes, you had to wash your hair and you washed it for me. It's nice and shining and all for me. I thank you sweetheart," he said with a mock bow, but again he almost lost his balance. He had to bend and adjust his boots. Evidently his feet did not go all the way down; the boots must have been stuffed with something so that he would seem taller. Connie stared out at him and behind him at Ellie in the car, who seemed to be looking off toward Connie's right, into nothing. Then Ellie said, pulling the words out of the air one after another as if he were just discovering them, "You want me to pull out the phone?"

"Shut your mouth and keep it shut," Arnold Friend said, his face red from bending over or maybe from embarrassment because Connie had seen his boots. "This ain't none of your business."

"What—what are you doing? What do you want?" Connie said. "If I call the police they'll get you, they'll arrest you—"

"Promise was not to come in unless you touch that phone, and I'll keep that promise," he said. He resumed his erect position and tried to force his shoulders back. He sounded like a hero in a movie, declaring something important. But he spoke too loudly and it was as if he was speaking to someone behind Connie. "I ain't made plans for coming in that house where I don't belong but just for you to come out to me, the way you should. Don't you know who I am?"

"You're crazy," she whispered. She backed away from the door but did not want to go into another part of the house, as if this would give him permission to come through the door. "What do you . . . you're crazy, you . . ."

"Huh? What're you saying, honey?"

Her eyes darted everywhere in the kitchen. She could not remember what it was, this room.

"This is how it is, honey: you come out and we'll drive away, have a nice ride. But if you don't come out we're gonna wait till your people come home and then they're all going to get it."

"You want that telephone pulled out?" Ellie said. He held the radio away from his ear and grimaced, as if without the radio the air was too much for him.

"I toldja shut up, Ellie," Arnold Friend said, "you're deaf, get a hearing aid, right? Fix yourself up. This little girl's no trouble and's gonna be nice to me, so Ellie keep to yourself, this ain't your date—right? Don't hem in on me, don't hog, don't crush, don't bird dog, don't trail me," he said in a rapid, meaningless voice, as if he were running through all the expressions he'd learned but was no longer sure which of them was in style, then rushing on to new ones, making them up with his eyes closed. "Don't crawl under my fence, don't squeeze in my chipmunk hole, don't sniff my glue, suck my Popsicle, keep your own greasy fingers on yourself!" He shaded his eyes and peered in at Connie, who was backed against the kitchen table. "Don't mind him, honey, he's just a creep. He's a dope. Right? I'm the boy for you and like I said, you come out here nice like a lady and give me your hand, and nobody else gets hurt, I mean, your nice old bald-headed daddy and your mummy and your sister in her high heels. Because listen: why bring them in this?"

"Leave me alone," Connie whispered.

"Hey, you know that old woman down the road, the one with the chickens and stuff—you know her?"

"She's dead!"

"Dead? What? You know her?" Arnold Friend said.

"She's dead—"

"Don't you like her?"

"She's dead—she's—she isn't here anymore—"

"But don't you like her, I mean, you got something against her? Some grudge or something?" Then his voice dipped as if he was conscious of a rudeness. He touched the sunglasses perched up on top of his head as if to make sure they were still there. "Now, you be a good girl."

"What are you going to do?"

"Just two things, or maybe three," Arnold Friend said.

"But I promise it won't last long and you'll like me the way you get to like people you're close to. You will. It's all over for you here, so come on out. You don't want your people in any trouble, do you?"

She turned and bumped against a chair or something, hurting her leg, but she ran into the back room and picked up the telephone. Something roared in her ear, a tiny roaring, and she was so sick with fear that she could do nothing but listen to it—the telephone was clammy and very heavy and her fingers groped down to the dial but were too weak to touch it. She began to scream into the phone, into the roaring. She cried out, she cried for her mother, she felt her breath start jerking back and forth in her lungs as if it was something Arnold Friend was stabbing her with again and again with no tenderness. A noisy sorrowful wailing rose all about her and she was locked inside it the way she was locked inside this house.

After a while she could hear again. She was sitting on the floor with her wet back against the wall.

Arnold Friend was saying from the door, "That's a good girl. Put the phone back."

She kicked the phone away from her.

"No, honey. Pick it up. Put it back right."

She picked it up and put it back. The dial tone stopped.

"That's a good girl. Now, you come outside."

She was hollow with what had been fear but what was now just an emptiness. All that screaming had blasted it out of her. She sat, one leg cramped under her, and deep inside her brain was something like a pinpoint of light that kept going and would not let her relax. She thought, I'm not going to see my mother again. She thought, I'm not going to sleep in my bed again. Her bright-green blouse was all wet.

Arnold Friend said, in a gentle-loud voice that was like a stage voice, "The place where you came from ain't there anymore, and where you had in mind to go is canceled out. This place you are now—inside your daddy's house— is nothing but a cardboard box I can knock down anytime. You know that and always did know it. You hear me?"

She thought, *I have got to think. I have got to know what to do.*

"We'll go out to a nice field, out in the country here where it smells so nice and it's sunny," Arnold Friend said. "I'll have my arms tight around you so you won't need to try to get away and I'll show you what love is like, what it does. The hell with this house! It looks solid all right," he said. He ran his fingernail down the screen and the noise did not make Connie shiver, as it would have the day before. "Now, put your hand on your heart, honey. Feel that? That feels solid too but we know better. Be nice to me, be sweet like you can because what else is there for a girl like you but to be sweet and pretty and give in?—and get away before her people get back?"

She felt her pounding heart. Her hand seemed to enclose it. She thought for the first time in her life that it was nothing that was hers, that belonged to her, but just a pounding, living thing inside this body that wasn't really hers either.

"You don't want them to get hurt," Arnold Friend went on. "Now, get up, honey. Get up all by yourself."

She stood.

"Now, turn this way. That's right. Come over here to me.—Ellie, put that away, didn't I tell you? You dope. You miserable creepy dope," Arnold Friend said. His words were not angry but only part of an incantation. The incantation was kindly. "Now, come out through the kitchen to me, honey, and let's see a smile, try it, you're a brave, sweet little girl and now they're eating corn and hot dogs cooked to bursting over an outdoor fire, and they don't know one thing about you and never did and honey, you're better than them because not a one of them would have done this for you."

Connie felt the linoleum under her feet; it was cool. She brushed her hair back out of her eyes. Arnold Friend let go of the post tentatively and opened his arms for her, his elbows pointing in toward each other and his wrists limp, to show that this was an embarrassed embrace and a little mocking, he didn't want to make her self-conscious.

She put out her hand against the screen. She watched herself push the door slowly open as if she was back safe somewhere in the other doorway, watching this body and this head of long hair moving out into the sunlight where Arnold Friend waited.

"My sweet little blue-eyed girl," he said in a half-sung sigh that had nothing to do with her brown eyes but was taken up just the same by the vast sunlit reaches of the land behind him and on all sides of him—so much land that Connie had never seen before and did not recognize except to know that she was going to it.

THE SKY BLUE BALL

In a long-ago time when I didn't know *Yes I was happy, I was myself and I was happy*. In a long-ago time when I wasn't a child any longer yet wasn't entirely not-a-child. In a long-ago time when I seemed often to be alone, and imagined myself lonely. *Yet this is your truest self: alone, lonely*.

One day I found myself walking beside a high brick wall the color of dried blood, the aged bricks loose and moldering, and over the wall came flying a spherical object so brightly blue I thought it was a bird!—until it dropped a few yards in front of me, bouncing at a crooked angle off the broken sidewalk, and I saw that it was a rubber ball. A child had thrown a rubber ball over the wall, and I was expected to throw it back.

Hurriedly I let my things fall into the weeds, ran to

snatch up the ball, which looked new, smelled new, spongy and resilient in my hand like a rubber ball I'd played with years before as a little girl; a ball I'd loved and had long ago misplaced; a ball I'd loved and had forgotten. "Here it comes!" I called, and tossed the ball back over the wall; I would have walked on except, a few seconds later, there came the ball again, flying back.

A game, I thought. *You can't quit a game.*

So I ran after the ball as it rolled in the road, in the gravelly dirt, and again snatched it up, squeezing it with pleasure, how spongy how resilient a rubber ball, and again I tossed it over the wall; feeling happiness in swinging my arm as I hadn't done for years since I'd lost interest in such childish games. And this time I waited expectantly, and again it came!—the most beautiful sky blue rubber ball rising high, high into the air above my head and pausing for a heartbeat before it began to fall, to sink, like an object possessed of its own willful volition; so there was plenty of time for me to position myself beneath it and catch it firmly with both hands.

"Got it!"

I was fourteen years old and did not live in this neighborhood, nor anywhere in the town of Strykersville, New

York (population 5,600). I lived on a small farm eleven miles to the north and I was brought to Strykersville by school bus, and consequently I was often alone; for this year, ninth grade, was my first at the school and I hadn't made many friends. And though I had relatives in Strykersville these were not relatives close to my family; they were not relatives eager to acknowledge me; for we who still lived in the country, hadn't yet made the inevitable move into town, were perceived inferior to those who lived in town. And, in fact, my family was poorer than our relatives who lived in Strykersville.

At our school teachers referred to the nine farm children bussed there as "North Country children." We were allowed to understand that "North Country children" differed significantly from Strykersville children.

I was not thinking of such things now, I was smiling thinking it must be a particularly playful child on the other side of the wall, a little girl like me; like the little girl I'd been; though the wall was ugly and forbidding with rusted signs EMPIRE MACHINE PARTS and PRIVATE PROPERTY NO TRESPASSING. On the other side of the Chautauqua & Buffalo railroad yard was a street of small wood-frame houses; it must have been in one of these that the little girl, my invisible playmate, lived. She must be much younger than I was; for fourteen-year-old girls didn't play such heedless games with strangers, we grew up swiftly if our families were not well-to-do.

I threw the ball back over the wall, calling, "Hi! Hi, there!" But there was no reply. I waited; I was standing in broken concrete, amid a scrubby patch of weeds. Insects buzzed and droned around me as if in curiosity, yellow butterflies no larger than my smallest fingernail fluttered and caught in my hair, tickling me. The sun was bright as a nova in a pebbled-white soiled sky that was like a thin chamois cloth about to be lifted away and I thought, *This is the surprise I've been waiting for.* For somehow I had acquired the belief that a surprise, a nice surprise, was waiting for me. I had only to merit it, and it would happen. (And if I did not merit it, it would not happen.) Such a surprise could not come from God but only from strangers, by chance.

Another time the sky blue ball sailed over the wall, after a longer interval of perhaps thirty seconds; and at an unexpected angle, as if it had been thrown away from me, from my voice, purposefully. Yet there it came, as if it could not not come: my invisible playmate was obliged to continue the game. I had no hope of catching it but ran blindly into the road (which was partly asphalt and partly gravel and not much traveled except by trucks) and there came a dump truck headed at me, I heard the ugly shriek of brakes and a deafening angry horn and I'd fallen onto my knees, I'd cut my knees that were bare, probably I'd torn my skirt, scrambling quickly to my feet, my cheeks smarting with shame, for wasn't I too grown a girl for such behavior? "Get the hell out of the road!" a man's voice was furious in rectitude, the voice of so many adult men of my acquaintance, you did not question such voices, you did not doubt them, you ran quickly to get out of their way, already I'd snatched up the ball, panting like a dog, trying to hide the ball in my skirt as I turned, shrinking and ducking so the truck driver couldn't see my face, for what if he was someone who knew my father, what if he recognized me, knew my name. But already the truck was thundering past, already I'd been forgotten.

Back then I ran to the wall, though both my knees throbbed with pain, and I was shaking as if shivering, the air had grown cold, a shaft of cloud had pierced the sun. I threw the ball back over the wall again, underhand, so that it rose high, high—so that my invisible playmate would have plenty of time to run and catch it. And it disappeared behind the wall and I waited, I was breathing hard and did not investigate my bleeding knees, my torn skirt. More clouds pierced the sun and shadows moved swift and certain across the earth like predator fish. After a while I called out hesitantly, "Hi? Hello?" It was like a ringing telephone you answer but no one is there. You wait, you inquire again, shyly, "Hello?" A vein throbbed in my forehead, a tinge of pain glimmered behind my eyes, that warning of pain, of punishment, following excitement. The child had drifted away, I supposed; she'd lost interest in our game, if it was a game. And suddenly it seemed silly and contemptible to me, and sad: there I stood, fourteen years old, a long-limbed weed of a girl, no longer a child yet panting and bleeding from the knees, the palms of my hands, too, chafed and scraped and dirty; there I stood alone in front of a moldering brick wall waiting for— what?

It was my school notebook, my several textbooks I'd let fall into the grass and I would afterward discover that my math textbook was muddy, many pages damp and torn; my spiral notebook in which I kept careful notes of the intransigent rules of English grammar and sample sentences diagrammed was soaked in a virulent-smelling chemical and my teacher's laudatory comments in red and my grades of A (for all my grades at Strykersville Junior High were A, of that I was obsessively proud) had become illegible as if they were grades of C, D, F. I should have taken up my books and walked hurriedly away and put the sky blue ball out of my mind entirely but I was not so free, through my life I've been made to realize that I am not free, as others appear to be free, at all. For the "nice" surprise carries with it the "bad" surprise and the two are intricately entwined and they cannot be separated, nor even defined as separate. So though my head pounded I felt obliged to look for a way over the wall. Though my knees were scraped and bleeding I located a filthy oil drum and shoved it against the wall and climbed shakily up on it, dirtying my hands and arms, my legs, my clothes, even more. And I hauled myself over the wall, and jumped down, a drop of about ten feet, the breath knocked out of me as I landed, the shock of the impact reverberating through me, along my spine, as if I'd been struck a sledge-hammer blow to the soles of my feet. At once I saw that there could be no little girl here, the factory yard was surely deserted, about the size of a baseball diamond totally walled in and overgrown with weeds pushing through cracked asphalt, thistles, stunted trees, and clouds of tiny yellow butterflies clustered here in such profusion I was made to see that they were not beautiful creatures, but mere insects, horrible. And rushing at me as if my very breath sucked them at me, sticking against my sweaty face, and in my snarled hair.

Yet stubbornly I searched for the ball. I would not leave without the ball. I seemed to know that the ball must be there, somewhere on the other side of the wall, though the wall would have been insurmountable for a little girl. And at last, after long minutes of searching, in a heat of indignation I discovered the ball in a patch of chicory. It was no longer sky blue but faded and cracked; its dun-colored rubber showed through the venous-cracked surface, like my own ball, years ago. Yet I snatched it up in triumph, and squeezed it, and smelled it—it smelled of nothing: of the earth: of the sweating palm of my own hand.

SMALL AVALANCHES

I kept bothering my mother for a dime, so she gave me a dime, and I went down our lane and took the shortcut to the highway, and down to the gas station. My uncle Winfield ran the gas station. There were two machines in the garage and I had to decide between them: the pop machine and the candy bar machine. No, there were three machines, but the other one sold cigarettes and I didn't care about that.

It took me a few minutes to make up my mind, then I bought a bottle of Pepsi-Cola.

Sometimes a man came to unlock the machines and take out the coins, and if I happened to be there it was interesting—the way the machines could be changed so fast if you just had the right key to open them. This man drove up in a white truck with a license plate from Kansas, a different color from our license plates, and he unlocked the machines and took out the money and loaded the machines up again. When we were younger we liked to hang around and watch. There was something strange about it, how the look of the machines could be changed so fast, the fronts swinging open, the insides showing, just because a man with the right keys drove up.

I went out front where my uncle was working on a car. He was under the car, lying on a thing made out of wood that had rollers on it so that he could roll himself under the car; I could just see his feet. He had on big heavy shoes that were all greasy. I asked him if my cousin Georgia was home—they lived about two miles away and I could walk—and he said no, she was baby-sitting in Stratton for three days. I already knew this but I hoped the people might have changed their minds.

"Is that man coming today to take out the money?"

My uncle didn't hear me. I was sucking at the Pepsi-Cola and running my tongue around the rim of the bottle. I always loved the taste of pop, the first two or three swallows. Then I would feel a little filled up and would have to drink it slowly. Sometimes I even poured the last of it out, but not so that anyone saw me.

"That man who takes care of the machines, is he coming today?"

"Who? No. Sometime next week."

My uncle pushed himself out from under the car. He was my mother's brother, a few years older than my mother. He had bushy brown hair and his face was dirty. "Did you call Georgia last night?"

"No. Ma wouldn't let me."

"Well, somebody was on the line because Betty wanted to check on her and the goddam line was busy all night. So Betty wanted to drive in, all the way to Stratton, drive six miles when probably nothing's wrong. You didn't call her, huh?"

"No."

"This morning Betty called her and gave her hell and she tried to say she hadn't been talking all night, that the telephone lines must have gotten mixed up. Georgia is a goddam little liar and if I catch her fooling around . . ."

He was walking away, into the garage. In the back pocket of his overalls was a dirty rag, stuffed there. He always yanked it out and wiped his face with it, not looking at it, even if it was dirty. I watched to see if he would do this and he did.

I almost laughed at this, and at how Georgia got away with murder. I had a good idea who was talking to her on the telephone.

The pop made my tongue tingle, a strong acid-sweet taste that almost hurt. I sat down and looked out at the road. This was in the middle of Colorado, on the road that goes through, east and west. It was a hot day. I drank one, two, three, four small swallows of pop. I pressed the bottle against my knees because I was hot. I tried to balance the bottle on one knee and it fell right over; I watched the pop trickle out onto the concrete.

I was too lazy to move my feet, so my bare toes got wet.

Somebody came along the road in a pickup truck, Mr. Watkins, and he tapped on the horn to say hello to me and my uncle. He was on his way to Stratton. I thought, *Damn it, I could have hitched a ride with him.* I don't know why I bothered to think this because I had to get home pretty soon, anyway, my mother would kill me if I went to town without telling her. Georgia and I did that once, back just after school let out in June, we went down the road a ways and hitched a ride with some guy in a beat-up car we thought looked familiar, but when he stopped to let us in we didn't know him and it was too late. But nothing happened, he was all right. We walked all the way back home again because we were scared to hitch another ride. My parents didn't find out, or Georgia's, but we didn't try it again.

I followed my uncle into the gas station. The building was made of ordinary wood, painted white a few years ago but starting to peel. It was just one room. The floor was concrete, all stained with grease and cracked. I knew the whole place by heart: the ceiling planks, the black rubber things hanging on the wall, looped over big rusty spikes, the Marlboro cigarettes ad that I liked, and the other ads for beer and cigarettes on shiny pieces of cardboard that stood up. To see those things you wouldn't guess how they came all flat, and you could unfold them and fix them yourself, like fancy things for under the Christmas tree. Inside the candy machine, behind the little windows, the candy bars stood up on display: Milky Way, Oh Henry!, Junior Mints, Mallow Cup, Three Musketeers, Hershey's. I liked them all. Sometimes Milky Way was my favorite, other times I only bought Mallow Cup for weeks in a row, trying to get enough of the cardboard letters to spell out

Mallow Cup. One letter came with each candy bar, and if you spelled out the whole name you could send away for a prize. But the letter *w* was hard to find. There were lots of *l*'s, it was rotten luck to open the wrapper up and see another *l* when you already had ten of them.

"Could I borrow a nickel?" I asked my uncle.

"I don't have any change."

Like hell, I thought. My uncle was always stingy.

I pressed the "return coin" knob but nothing came out. I pulled the knob out under Mallow Cup but nothing came out.

"Nancy, don't fool around with that thing, okay?"

"I don't have anything to do."

"Yeah, well, your mother can find something for you to do."

"She can do it herself."

"You want me to tell her that?"

"Go right ahead."

"Hey, did your father find out any more about that guy in Polo?"

"What guy?"

"Oh, I don't know, some guy who got into a fight and was arrested—he was in the Navy with your father, I don't remember his name."

"I don't know."

My uncle yawned. I followed him back outside and he stretched his arms and yawned. It was very hot. You could see the fake water puddles on the highway that were so mysterious and always moved back when you approached them. They could hypnotize you. Across from the garage was the mailbox on a post and then just scrub land, nothing to look at, pastureland and big rocky hills.

I thought about going to check to see if my uncle had any mail, but I knew there wouldn't be anything inside. We only got a booklet in the mail that morning, some information about how to make money selling jewelry door-to-door that I had written away for, but now I didn't care about. "Georgia has all the luck," I said. "I could use a few dollars myself."

"Yeah," my uncle said. He wasn't listening.

I looked at myself in the outside mirror of the car he was fixing. I don't know what kind of car it was, I never memorized the makes like the boys did. It was a dark maroon color with big heavy fenders and a bumper that had little bits of rust in it, like sparks. The runningboard had old, dried mud packed down inside its ruts. It was covered with black rubber, a mat. My hair was blown-looking. It was a big heavy mane of hair the color everybody called dishwater blond. My baby pictures showed that it used to be light blond.

"I wish I could get a job like Georgia," I said.

"Georgia's a year older than you."

"Oh hell. . . ."

I was thirteen but I was Georgia's size, all over, and I was smarter. We looked alike. We both had long bushy flyaway hair that frizzed up when the air was wet, but kept curls in very well when we set it, like for church. I forgot about my hair and leaned closer to the mirror to look at my face. I made my lips shape a little circle, noticing how wrinkled they got. They could wrinkle up into a small space. I poked the tip of my tongue out.

There was the noise of something on gravel, and I looked around to see a man driving in. Out by the highway my uncle just had gravel, then around the gas pumps he had concrete. This man's car was white, a color you don't see much, and his license plate was from Kansas.

He told my uncle to fill up the gas tank and he got out of the car, stretching his arms.

He looked at me and smiled. "Hi," he said.

"Hi."

He said something to my uncle about how hot it was, and my uncle said it wasn't too bad. Because that's the way he is—always contradicting you. My mother hates him for this. But then he said, "You read about the dry spell coming up?—right into September?" My uncle meant the ranch bureau thing but the man didn't know what he was talking about. He meant the "Bureau News & Forecast." This made me mad, that my uncle was so stupid, thinking that a man from out of state and probably from a city would know about that, or give a damn. It made me mad. I saw my pop bottle where it fell and I decided to go home, not to bother putting it in the case where you were supposed to.

I walked along on the edge of the road, on the pavement, because there were stones and prickles and weeds with bugs in them off the side that I didn't like to walk in barefoot. I felt hot and mad about something. A yawn started in me, and I felt it coming up like a little bubble of gas from the pop. There was my cousin Georgia in town, and all she had to do was watch a little girl who wore thick glasses and was sort of strange, but very nice and quiet and no trouble, and she'd get two dollars. I thought angrily that if anybody came along I'd put out my thumb and hitch a ride to Stratton, and the hell with my mother.

Then I did hear a car coming but I just got over to the side and waited for him to pass. I felt stubborn and wouldn't look around to see who it was, but then the car didn't pass and I looked over my shoulder—it was the man in the white car who had stopped for gas. He was driving very slow. I got farther off the road and waited for him to pass. But he leaned over to this side and said out the open window, "You want a ride home? Get in."

"No, that's okay," I said.

"Come on, I'll drive you home. No trouble."

"No, it's okay. I'm almost home," I said.

I was embarrassed and didn't want to look at him. People didn't do this, a grown-up man in a car wouldn't bother to do this. Either you hitched for a ride or you didn't, and if you didn't, people would never slow down to ask you. *This guy is crazy,* I thought. I felt very strange. I tried to look over into the field but there wasn't anything to look at, not even any cattle, just land and scrubby trees and a barbed-wire fence half falling down.

"Your feet will get all sore, walking like that," the man said.

"I'm okay."

"Hey, watch out for the snake!"

There wasn't any snake and I made a noise like a laugh to show that I knew it was a joke but didn't think it was very funny.

"Aren't there rattlesnakes around here? Rattlers?"

"Oh I don't know," I said.

He was still driving right alongside me, very slow. You are not used to seeing a car slowed-down like that, it seems very strange. I tried not to look at the man. But there was nothing else to look at, just the country and the road and the mountains in the distance and some clouds.

"That man at the gas station was mad, he picked up the bottle you left."

I tried to keep my lips pursed shut, but they were dry and came open again. I wondered if my teeth were too big in front.

"How come you walked away so fast? That wasn't friendly," the man said. "You forgot your pop bottle and the man back there said somebody could drive over it and get a flat tire, he was a little mad."

"He's my uncle," I said.

"What?"

He couldn't hear or was pretending he couldn't hear, so I had to turn toward him. He was all-right-looking, he was smiling. "He's my uncle," I said.

"Oh, is he? You don't look anything like *him*. Is your home nearby?"

"Up ahead." I was embarrassed and started to laugh, I don't know why.

"I don't see any house there."

"You can't see it from here," I said, laughing.

"What's so funny? My face? You know, when you smile you're a very pretty girl. You should smile all the time. . . ." He was paying so much attention to me it made me laugh. "Yes, that's a fact. Why are you blushing?"

I blushed fast, like my mother; we both hated to blush and hated people to tease us. But I couldn't get mad.

"I'm worried about your feet and the rattlers around here. Aren't there rattlers around here?"

"Oh I don't know."

"Where I come from there are streets and sidewalks and no snakes, of course, but it isn't interesting. It isn't dangerous. I think I'd like to live here, even with the snakes— this is very beautiful, hard country, isn't it? Do you like the mountains way over there? Or don't you notice them?"

I didn't pay any attention to where he was pointing, I looked at him and saw that he was smiling. He was my father's age but he wasn't stern like my father, who had a line between his eyebrows like a knife cut, from frowning. This man was wearing a shirt, a regular white shirt, out in the country. His hair was dampened and combed back from his forehead; it was damp right now, as if he had just combed it.

"Yes, I'd like to take a walk out here and get some exercise," he said. His voice sounded very cheerful. "Snakes or no snakes! You turned me down for a free ride so maybe I'll join you in a walk."

That really made me laugh: *join you in a walk.*

"Hey, what's so funny?" he said, laughing himself.

People didn't talk like that, but I didn't say anything. He parked the car on the shoulder of the road and got out and I heard him drop the car keys in his pocket. He was scratching at his jaw. "Well, excellent! This is excellent, healthy, divine country air! Do you like living out here?"

I shook my head, no.

"You wouldn't want to give all this up for a city, would you?"

"Sure. Any day."

I was walking fast to keep ahead of him, I couldn't help but giggle, I was so embarrassed—this man in a white shirt was really walking out on the highway, he was really going to leave his car parked like that! You never saw a car parked on the road around here, unless it was by the creek, fishermen's cars, or unless it was a wreck. All this made my face get hotter.

He walked fast to catch up with me. I could hear coins and things jingling in his pockets.

"You never told me your name," he said. "That isn't friendly."

"It's Nancy."

"Nancy what?"

"Oh I don't know." I laughed.

"Nancy I-Don't-Know?" he said.

I didn't get this. He was smiling hard. He was shorter than my father and now that he was out in the bright sun I could see he was older. His face wasn't tanned, and his mouth kept going into a soft smile. Men like my father and my uncles and other men never bothered to smile like that at me, they never bothered to look at me at all. Some men did, once in a while, in Stratton, strangers waiting for Greyhound buses to Denver or Kansas City, but they weren't friendly like this, they didn't keep on smiling for so long.

When I came to the path I said, "Well, good-bye, I'm going to cut over this way. This is a shortcut."

"A shortcut where?"

"Oh I don't know," I said, embarrassed.

"To your house, Nancy?"

"Yeah. No, it's to our lane, our lane is half a mile long."

"Is it? That's very long. . . ."

He came closer. "Well, good-bye," I said.

"That's a long lane, isn't it?—it must get blocked up with snow in the winter, doesn't it? You people get a lot of snow out here—"

"Yeah."

"So your house must be way back there . . . ?" he said, pointing. He was smiling. When he stood straight like this, looking over my head, he was more like the other men. But then he looked down at me and smiled again, so friendly. I waved good-bye and jumped over the ditch and climbed the fence, clumsy as hell just when somebody was watching me, wouldn't you know it. Some barbed wire caught at my shorts and the man said, "Let me get that loose—" but I jerked away and jumped down again. I waved good-bye again and started up the path. But the man said something and when I looked back he was climbing over the fence himself. I was so surprised that I just stood there.

"I like shortcuts and secret paths," he said. "I'll walk a little way with you."

"What do you—" I started to say. I stopped smiling because something was wrong. I looked around and there was just the path behind me that the kids always took, and some boulders and old dried-up manure from cattle, and some scrubby bushes. At the top of the hill was the big tree that had been struck by lightning so many times. I was looking at all this and couldn't figure out why I was looking at it.

"You're a brave little girl to go around barefoot," the man said, right next to me. "Or are your feet tough on the bottom?"

I didn't know what he was talking about because I was worried; then I heard his question and said vaguely, "I'm all right," and started to walk faster. I felt a tingling all through me like the tingling from the Pepsi-Cola in my mouth.

"Do you always walk so fast?" The man laughed.

"Oh I don't know."

"Is that all you can say? Nancy I-Don't-Know! That's a funny name—is it foreign?"

This made me start to laugh again. I was walking fast, then I began to run a few steps. Right away I was out of breath. That was strange—I was out of breath right away.

"Hey, Nancy, where are you going?" the man cried.

But I kept running, not fast. I ran a few steps and looked back and there he was, smiling and panting, and I happened to see his foot come down on a loose rock. I knew what would happen—the rock rolled off sideways and he almost fell, and I laughed. He glanced up at me with a surprised grin. "This path is a booby trap, huh? Nancy has all sorts of little traps and tricks for me, huh?"

I didn't know what he was talking about. I ran up the side of the hill, careful not to step on the manure or anything sharp, and I was still out of breath but my legs felt good. They felt as if they wanted to run a long distance. "You're going off the path," he said, pretending to be mad. "Hey. That's against the rules. Is that another trick?"

I giggled but couldn't think of any answer.

"Did you make this path up by yourself?" the man

asked. But he was breathing hard from the hill. He stared at me, climbing up, with his hands pushing on his knees as if to help him climb. "Little Nancy, you're like a wild colt or a deer, you're so graceful—is this your own private secret path? Or do other people use it?"

"Oh, my brother and some other kids, when they're around," I said vaguely. I was walking backward up the hill now, so that I could look down at him. The top of his hair was thin, you could see the scalp. The very top of his forehead seemed to have two bumps, not big ones, but as if the bone went out a little, and this part was a bright pink, sunburned, but the rest of his face and his scalp were white.

He stepped on another loose rock, and the rock and some stones and mud came loose. He fell hard onto his knee. "Jesus!" he said. The way he stayed down like that looked funny. I had to press my hand over my mouth. When he looked up at me his smile was different. He got up, pushing himself up with his hands, grunting, and then he wiped his hands on his trousers. The dust showed on them. He looked funny.

"Is my face amusing? Is it a good joke?"

I didn't mean to laugh, but now I couldn't stop. I pressed my hand over my mouth hard.

He stared at me. "What do you see in my face, Nancy? What do you see—anything? Do you see my soul, do you see *me*, is that what you're laughing at?" He took a fast step toward me, but I jumped back. It was like a game. "Come on, Nancy, slow down, just slow down," he said. "Come on, Nancy. . . ."

I didn't know what he was talking about, I just had to laugh at his face. It was so tense and strange; it was so *important*.

I noticed a big rock higher up, and I went around behind it and pushed it loose—it rolled right down toward him and he had to scramble to get out of the way. "Hey! Jesus!" he yelled. The rock came loose with some other things and a mud chunk got him in the leg.

I laughed so hard my stomach started to ache.

He laughed too, but a little different from before.

"This is a little trial for me, isn't it?" he said. "A little preliminary contest. Is that how the game goes? Is that your game, Nancy?"

I ran higher up the hill, off to the side where it was steeper. Little rocks and things came loose and rolled back down. My breath was coming so fast it made me wonder if something was wrong. Down behind me the man was following, stooped over, looking at me, and his hand was pressed against the front of his shirt. I could see his hand moving up and down because he was breathing so hard. I could even see his tongue moving around the edge of his dried-out lips. . . . I started to get afraid, and then the tingling came back into me, beginning in my tongue and going out through my whole body, and I couldn't help giggling.

He said something that sounded like "—won't be laughing—" but I couldn't hear the rest of it. My hair was all wet in back where it would be a job for me to unsnarl it with the hairbrush. The man came closer, stumbling, and just for a joke I kicked out at him, to scare him—and he jerked backward and tried to grab onto a branch of a bush, but it slipped through his fingers and he lost his balance and fell. He grunted. He fell so hard that he just lay there for a minute. I wanted to say I was sorry, or ask him if he was all right, but I just stood there grinning.

He got up again; the fleshy part of his hand was bleeding. But he didn't seem to notice it and I turned and ran up the rest of the hill, going almost straight up the last part, my legs were so strong and felt so good. Right at the top I paused, just balanced there, and a gust of wind would have pushed me over—but I was all right. I laughed aloud, my legs felt so springy and strong.

I looked down over the side where he was crawling, down on his hands and knees again. "You better go back to Kansas! Back home to Kansas!" I laughed. He stared up at me and I waited for him to smile again but he didn't. His face was very pale. He was staring at me but he seemed to be seeing something else, his eyes were very serious and strange. I could see his belt creasing his stomach, the bulge of his white shirt. He pressed his hand against his chest again. "Better go home, go home, get in your damn old car and go home," I sang, making a song of it. He looked so serious, staring up at me. I pretended to kick at him again and he flinched, his eyes going small.

"Don't leave me—" he whimpered.

"Oh go on," I said.

"Don't leave—I'm sick—I think I—"

His face seemed to shrivel. He was drawing in his breath very slowly, carefully, as if checking to see how much it hurt, and I waited for this to turn into another joke. Then I got tired of waiting and just rested back on my heels. My smile got smaller and smaller, like his.

"Good-bye, I'm going," I said, waving. I turned and he

said something—it was like a cry—but I didn't want to bother going back. The tingling in me was almost noisy.

I walked over to the other side, and slid back down to the path and went along the path to our lane. I was very hot. I knew my face was flushed and red. "Damn old nut," I said. But I had to laugh at the way he had looked, the way he kept scrambling up the hill and was just crouched there at the end, on his hands and knees. He looked so funny, bent over and clutching at his chest, pretending to have a heart attack or maybe having one, a little one, for all I knew. *This will teach you a lesson,* I thought.

By the time I got home my face had dried off a little, but my hair was like a haystack. I stopped by the old car parked in the lane, just a junker on blocks, and looked in the outside rearview mirror—the mirror was all twisted around because people looked in it all the time. I tried to fix my hair by rubbing my hands down hard against it, but no luck. "Oh damn," I said aloud, and went up the steps to the back, and remembered not to let the screen door slam so my mother wouldn't holler at me.

She was in the kitchen ironing, just sprinkling some clothes on the ironing board. She used a pop bottle painted blue and fitted out with a sprinkler top made of rubber, that I fixed for her at grade school a long time ago for a Christmas present; she shook the bottle over the clothes and stared at me. "Where have you been? I told you to come right back."

"I did come right back."

"You're all dirty, you look like hell. What happened to you?"

"Oh I don't know," I said. "Nothing."

She threw something at me—it was my brother's shirt—and I caught it and pressed it against my hot face.

"You get busy and finish these," my mother said. "It must be ninety-five in here and I'm fed up. And you do a good job, I'm really fed up. Are you listening, Nancy? Where the hell is your mind?"

I liked the way the damp shirt felt on my face. "Oh I don't know," I said.

HAUNTED

Haunted houses, forbidden houses. The old Medlock farm. The Erlich farm. The Minton farm on Elk Creek. NO TRESPASSING the signs said but we trespassed at will. NO TRESPASSING NO HUNTING NO FISHING UNDER PENALTY OF LAW but we did what we pleased because who was there to stop us?

Our parents warned us against exploring these abandoned properties: the old houses and barns were dangerous, they said. We could get hurt, they said. I asked my mother if the houses were haunted and she said, *Of course not, there aren't such things as ghosts, you know that.* She was irritated with me; she guessed how I pretended to believe things I didn't believe, things I'd grown out of years before. It was a habit of childhood—pretending I was younger, more childish, than in fact I was. Opening my eyes wide and looking puzzled, worried. Girls are prone to such trickery, it's a form of camouflage, when every other thought you think is a forbidden thought and with your eyes open staring sightless you can sink into dreams that leave your skin clammy and your heart pounding—dreams that don't seem to belong to you that must have come to you from somewhere else from someone you don't know who knows *you*.

There weren't such things as ghosts, they told us. That was just superstition. But we could injure ourselves tramping around where we weren't wanted—the floorboards and the staircases in old houses were likely to be rotted, the roofs ready to collapse, we could cut ourselves on nails and broken glass, we could fall into uncovered wells—and you never knew who you might meet up with, in an old house or barn that's supposed to be empty. "You mean a bum?— like somebody hitchhiking along the road?" I asked. "It could be a bum, or it could be somebody you know," Mother told me evasively. "A man, or a boy—somebody you know. . . ." Her voice trailed off in embarrassment and I knew enough not to ask another question.

There were things you didn't talk about, back then. I

never talked about them with my own children, there weren't the words to say them.

We listened to what our parents said, we nearly always agreed with what they said, but we went off on the sly and did what we wanted to do. When we were little girls: my neighbor Mary Lou Siskin and me. And when we were older, ten, eleven years old, tomboys, roughhouses our mothers called us. We liked to hike in the woods and along the creek for miles, we'd cut through farmers' fields, spy on their houses—on people we knew, kids we knew from school—most of all we liked to explore abandoned houses, boarded-up houses if we could break in, we'd scare ourselves thinking the houses might be haunted though really we knew they weren't haunted, there weren't such things as ghosts. Except—

I am writing in a dime-store notebook with lined pages and a speckled cover, a notebook of the sort we used in grade school. *Once upon a time* as I used to tell my children when they were tucked safely into bed and drifting off to sleep. *Once upon a time* I'd begin, reading from a book because it was safest so: the several times I told them my own stories they were frightened by my voice and couldn't sleep and afterward I couldn't sleep either and my husband would ask what was wrong and I'd say, *Nothing,* hiding my face from him.

I write in pencil, so that I can erase easily, and I find that I am constantly erasing, wearing holes in the paper. Mrs. Harding, our fifth-grade teacher, disciplined us for handing in messy notebooks: she was a heavy, toad-faced woman, her voice was deep and husky and gleeful when she said, "You, Melissa, what have you to say for yourself?" and I stood there mute, my knees trembling. My friend Mary Lou laughed behind her hand, wriggled in her seat she thought I was so funny. *Tell the old witch to go to hell,* she'd say, *she'll respect you then,* but of course no one would ever say such a thing to Mrs. Harding. Not even Mary Lou. "What have you to say for yourself, Melissa? Handing in a notebook with a ripped page?" My grade for the homework assignment was lowered from A to B, Mrs. Harding grunted with satisfaction as she made the mark, a big swooping B in red ink, creasing the page. "More is expected of you, Melissa, so you disappoint me more," Mrs. Harding always said. So many years ago and I remember those words more clearly than words I heard the other day.

One morning there was a pretty substitute teacher in Mrs. Harding's classroom. "Mrs. Harding is unwell, I'll be taking her place today," she said, and we saw the nervousness in her face, we guessed there was a secret she wouldn't tell and we waited and a few days later the principal himself came to tell us that Mrs. Harding would not be back, she had died of a stroke. He spoke carefully as if we were much younger children and might be upset and Mary Lou caught my eye and winked and I sat there at my desk feeling the strangest sensation, something flowing into the top of my head, honey-rich and warm making its way down my spine. *Our Father Who art in Heaven* I whispered in the prayer with the others my head bowed and my hands clasped tight together but my thoughts were somewhere else leaping wild and crazy somewhere else and I knew Mary Lou's were too.

On the school bus going home she whispered in my ear, "That was because of us, wasn't it!—what happened to that old bag Harding. But we won't tell anybody."

Once upon a time there were two sisters, and one was very pretty and one was very ugly. . . . Though Mary Lou Siskin wasn't my sister. And I wasn't ugly, really: just sallow-skinned, with a small pinched ferrety face. With dark almost lashless eyes that were set too close together and a nose that didn't look right. A look of yearning, and disappointment.

But Mary Lou *was* pretty, even rough and clumsy as she sometimes behaved. That long silky blond hair everybody remembered her for afterward, years afterward. . . . How, when she had to be identified, it was the long silky white-blond hair that was unmistakable. . . .

Sleepless nights but I love them. I write during the nighttime hours and sleep during the day; I am of an age when you don't require more than a few hours' sleep. My husband has been dead for nearly a year and my children are scattered and busily absorbed in their own selfish lives like all children and there is no one to interrupt me no one to pry into my business no one in the neighborhood who dares come knocking at my door to see if I am all right. Sometimes out of a mirror floats an unexpected face, a strange face, lined, ravaged, with deep-socketed eyes always damp, always blinking in shock or dismay or simple bewilderment—but I adroitly look away. I have no need to stare.

It's true, all you have heard of the vanity of the old.

Believing ourselves young, still, behind our aged faces—mere children, and so very innocent!

Once when I was a young bride and almost pretty my color up when I was happy and my eyes shining we drove out into the country for a Sunday's excursion and he wanted to make love I knew, he was shy and fumbling as I but he wanted to make love and I ran into a cornfield in my stockings and high heels, I was playing at being a woman I never could be, Mary Lou Siskin maybe, Mary Lou whom my husband never knew, but I got out of breath and frightened, it was the wind in the cornstalks, that dry rustling sound, that dry terrible rustling sound like whispering like voices you can't quite identify and he caught me and tried to hold me and I pushed him away sobbing and he said, *What's wrong? My God what's wrong?* as if he really loved me as if his life was focused on me and I knew I could never be equal to it, that love, that importance, I knew I was only Melissa the ugly one the one the boys wouldn't give a second glance, and one day he'd understand and know how he'd been cheated. I pushed him away, I said, *Leave me alone! Don't touch me! You disgust me!* I said.

He backed off and I hid my face, sobbing.

But later on I got pregnant just the same. Only a few weeks later.

Always there were stories behind the abandoned houses and always the stories were sad. Because farmers went bankrupt and had to move away. Because somebody died and the farm couldn't be kept up and nobody wanted to buy it—like the Medlock farm across the creek. Mr. Medlock died aged seventy-nine and Mrs. Medlock refused to sell the farm and lived there alone until someone from the county health agency came to get her. *Isn't it a shame,* my parents said. *The poor woman,* they said. They told us never, never to poke around in the Medlocks' barns or house—the buildings were ready to cave in, they'd been in terrible repair even when the Medlocks were living there.

It was said that Mrs. Medlock had gone off her head after she'd found her husband dead in one of the barns, lying flat on his back his eyes open and bulging, his mouth open, tongue protruding, she'd gone to look for him and found him like that and she'd never gotten over it they said, never got over the shock. They had to commit her to the state hospital for her own good (they said) and the house and the barns were boarded up, everywhere tall grass and thistles grew wild, dandelions in the spring, tiger lilies in the summer, and when we drove by I stared and stared narrowing my eyes so I wouldn't see someone looking out one of the windows—a face there, pale and quick—or a dark figure scrambling up the roof to hide behind the chimney—

Mary Lou and I wondered was the house haunted, was the barn haunted where the old man had died, we crept around to spy, we couldn't stay away, coming closer and closer each time until something scared us and we ran away back through the woods clutching and pushing at each other until one day finally we went right up to the house to the back door and peeked in one of the windows. Mary Lou led the way, Mary Lou said not to be afraid, nobody lived there anymore and nobody would catch us, it didn't matter that the land was posted, the police didn't arrest kids our ages.

We explored the barns, we dragged the wooden cover off the well and dropped stones inside. We called the cats but they wouldn't come close enough to be petted. They were barn cats, skinny and diseased-looking, they'd said at the county bureau that Mrs. Medlock had let a dozen cats live in the house with her so that the house was filthy from their messes. When the cats wouldn't come we got mad and threw stones at them and they ran away hissing— nasty dirty things, Mary Lou said. Once we crawled up on the tarpaper roof over the Medlocks' kitchen, just for fun, Mary Lou wanted to climb up the big roof too to the very top but I got frightened and said, *no, no please don't, no Mary Lou please,* and I sounded so strange Mary Lou looked at me and didn't tease or mock as she usually did. The roof was so steep, I'd known she would hurt herself. I could see her losing her footing and slipping, falling, I could see her astonished face and her flying hair as she fell, knowing nothing could save her. *You're no fun,* Mary Lou said, giving me a hard little pinch. But she didn't go climbing up the big roof.

Later we ran through the barns screaming at the top of our lungs just for fun for the hell of it as Mary Lou said, we tossed things in a heap, broken-off parts of farm imple- ments, leather things from the horses' gear, handfuls of straw. The farm animals had been gone for years but their smell was still strong. Dried horse and cow droppings that looked like mud. Mary Lou said, "You know what—I'd like to burn this place down." And she looked at me and I said, "Okay—go on and do it, burn it down." And Mary Lou said, "You think I wouldn't?—just give me a match." And I said, "You know I don't have a match." And a look passed between us. And I felt something flooding at the top of my head, my throat tickled as if I didn't know would I laugh or cry and I said, "You're crazy—" and Mary Lou said with a sneering little laugh, "*You're* crazy, dumbbell—I was just testing you."

By the time Mary Lou was twelve years old Mother had got to hate her, was always trying to turn me against her so I'd make friends with other girls. Mary Lou had a fresh mouth, she said. Mary Lou didn't respect her elders—not even her own parents. Mother guessed that Mary Lou laughed at her behind her back, said things about all of us. She was mean and snippy and a smart-ass, rough sometimes as her brothers. Why didn't I make other friends? Why did I always go running when she stood out in the yard and called me? The Siskins weren't a whole lot better than white trash, the way Mr. Siskin worked that land of his.

In town, in school, Mary Lou sometimes ignored me

when other girls were around, girls who lived in town, whose fathers weren't farmers like ours. But when it was time to ride home on the bus she'd sit with me as if nothing was wrong and I'd help her with her homework if she needed help, I hated her sometimes but then I'd forgive her as soon as she smiled at me, she'd say, "Hey 'Lissa are you mad at me?" and I'd make a face and say no as if it was an insult, being asked. Mary Lou was my sister I sometimes pretended, I told myself a story about us being sisters and looking alike, and Mary Lou said sometimes she'd like to leave her family her goddamned family and come live with me. Then the next day or the next hour she'd get moody and be nasty to me and get me almost crying. All the Siskins had mean streaks, bad tempers, she'd tell people. As if she was proud.

Her hair was a light blond, almost white in the sunshine, and when I first knew her she had to wear it braided tight around her head—her grandmother braided it for her, and she hated it. Like Gretel or Snow White in one of those damn dumb picture books for children, Mary Lou said. When she was older she wore it down and let it grow long so that it fell almost to her hips. It was very beautiful—silky and shimmering. I dreamed of Mary Lou's hair sometimes but the dreams were confused and I couldn't remember when I woke up whether I was the one with the long blond silky hair, or someone else. It took me a while to get my thoughts clear lying there in bed and then I'd remember Mary Lou, who was my best friend.

She was ten months older than I was, and an inch or so taller, a bit heavier, not fat but fleshy, solid and fleshy, with hard little muscles in her upper arms like a boy. Her eyes were blue like washed glass, her eyebrows and lashes were almost white, she had a snub nose and Slavic cheekbones and a mouth that could be sweet or twisty and smirky depending upon her mood. But she didn't like her face because it was round—a moon face she called it, staring at herself in the mirror though she knew damned well she was pretty—didn't older boys whistle at her, didn't the bus driver flirt with her?—calling her "Blondie" while he never called me anything at all.

Mother didn't like Mary Lou visiting with me when no one else was home in our house: she didn't trust her, she said. Thought she might steal something, or poke her nose into parts of the house where she wasn't welcome. *That girl is a bad influence on you,* she said. But it was all the same old crap I heard again and again so I didn't even listen. I'd have told her she was crazy except that would only make things worse.

Mary Lou said, "Don't you just hate them?—your mother, and mine? Sometimes I wish—"

I put my hands over my ears and didn't hear.

The Siskins lived two miles away from us, farther back the road where it got narrower. Those days, it was unpaved, and never got plowed in the winter. I remember their barn with the yellow silo, I remember the muddy pond where the dairy cows came to drink, the muck they churned up in the spring. I remember Mary Lou saying she wished all the cows would die—they were always sick with something—so her father would give up and sell the farm and they could live in town in a nice house. I was hurt, her saying those things as if she'd forgotten about me and would leave me behind. *Damn you to hell,* I whispered under my breath.

I remember smoke rising from the Siskins' kitchen chimney, from their wood-burning stove, straight up into the winter sky like a breath you draw inside you deeper and deeper until you begin to feel faint.

Later on, that house was empty too. But boarded up

only for a few months—the bank sold it at auction. (It turned out the bank owned most of the Siskin farm, even the dairy cows. So Mary Lou had been wrong about that all along and never knew.)

As I write I can hear the sound of glass breaking, I can feel glass underfoot. *Once upon a time there were two little princesses, two sisters, who did forbidden things.* That brittle terrible sensation under my shoes—slippery like water— "Anybody home? Hey—anybody home?" and there's an old calendar tacked to a kitchen wall, a faded picture of Jesus Christ in a long white gown stained with scarlet, thorns fitted to His bowed head. Mary Lou is going to scare me in another minute making me think that someone is in the house and the two of us will scream with laughter and run outside where it's safe. Wild frightened laughter and I never knew afterward what was funny or why we did these things. Smashing what remained of windows, wrenching at stairway railings to break them loose, running with our heads ducked so we wouldn't get cobwebs in our faces.

One of us found a dead bird, a starling, in what had been the parlor of the house. Turned it over with a foot—

there's the open eye looking right up calm and matter-of-fact. *Melissa,* that eye tells me, silent and terrible, *I see you.*

That was the old Minton place, the stone house with the caved-in roof and the broken steps, like something in a picture book from long ago. From the road the house looked as if it might be big but when we explored it we were disappointed to see that it wasn't much bigger than my own house, just four narrow rooms downstairs, another four upstairs, an attic with a steep ceiling, the roof partly caved in. The barns had collapsed in upon themselves; only their stone foundations remained solid. The land had been sold off over the years to other farmers, nobody had lived in the house for a long time. The old Minton house, people called it. On Elk Creek where Mary Lou's body was eventually found.

In seventh grade Mary Lou had a boyfriend she wasn't supposed to have and no one knew about it but me—an older boy who'd dropped out of school and worked as a farmhand. I thought he was a little slow—not in his speech which was fast enough, normal enough, but in his way of thinking. He was sixteen or seventeen years old. His name was Hans; he had crisp blond hair like the bristles of a brush, a coarse blemished face, derisive eyes. Mary Lou was crazy for him she said, aping the older girls in town who said they were "crazy for" certain boys or young men. Hans and Mary Lou kissed when they didn't think I was watching, in an old ruin of a cemetery behind the Minton house, on the creek bank, in the tall marsh grass by the end of the Siskins' driveway. Hans had a car borrowed from one of his brothers, a battered old Ford, the front bumper held up by wire, the running board scraping the ground. We'd be out walking on the road and Hans would come along tapping the horn and stop and Mary Lou would climb in but I'd hang back knowing they didn't want me and the hell with them: I preferred to be alone.

"You're just jealous of Hans and me," Mary Lou said, unforgivably, and I hadn't any reply. "Hans is sweet. Hans is nice. He isn't like people say," Mary Lou said in a quick bright false voice she'd picked up from one of the older, popular girls in town. "He's—" And she stared at me blinking and smiling not knowing what to say as if in fact she didn't know Hans at all. "He isn't *simple*," she said angrily, "—he just doesn't like to talk a whole lot."

When I try to remember Hans Meunzer after so many decades I can see only a muscular boy with short-trimmed blond hair and protuberant ears, blemished skin, the shadow of a mustache on his upper lip—he's looking at me, eyes narrowed, crinkled, as if he understands how I fear him, how I wish him dead and gone, and he'd hate me too if he took me that seriously. But he doesn't take me that seriously, his gaze just slides right through me as if nobody's standing where I stand.

There were stories about all the abandoned houses but the worst story was about the Minton house over on the Elk Creek Road about three miles from where we lived. For no reason anybody ever discovered Mr. Minton had beaten his wife to death and afterward killed himself with a .12-gauge shotgun. He hadn't even been drinking, people said. And his farm hadn't been doing at all badly, considering how others were doing.

Looking at the ruin from the outside, overgrown with trumpet vine and wild rose, it seemed hard to believe that anything like that had happened. Things in the world even those things built by man are so quiet left to themselves. . . .

The house had been deserted for years, as long as I could remember. Most of the land had been sold off but the heirs didn't want to deal with the house. They didn't want to sell it and they didn't want to raze it and they certainly didn't want to live in it so it stood empty. The property was posted with NO TRESPASSING signs layered one atop another but nobody took them seriously. Vandals had broken into the house and caused damage, the McFarlane boys had tried to burn down the old hay barn one Halloween night. The summer Mary Lou started seeing Hans she and I climbed in the house through a rear window—the boards guarding it had long since been yanked away—and walked through the rooms slow as sleepwalkers our arms around each other's waists our eyes staring waiting to see Mr. Minton's ghost as we turned each corner. The inside smelled of mouse droppings, mildew, rot, old sorrow. Strips of wallpaper torn from the walls, plasterboard exposed, old furniture overturned and smashed, old yellowed sheets of newspaper underfoot, and broken glass, everywhere broken glass. Through the ravaged windows sunlight spilled in tremulous quivering bands. The air was afloat, alive: dancing dust atoms. "I'm afraid," Mary Lou whispered. She squeezed my waist and I felt my mouth go dry for hadn't I been hearing something upstairs, a low persistent murmuring like quarreling like one person trying to convince another going on and on and on but when I stood very still to listen the sound vanished and there were only the comforting summer sounds of birds, crickets, cicadas.

I knew how Mr. Minton had died: he'd placed the barrel of the shotgun beneath his chin and pulled the trigger with his big toe. They found him in the bedroom upstairs, most of his head blown off. They found his wife's body in the cistern in the cellar where he'd tried to hide her. "Do you think we should go upstairs?" Mary Lou asked, worried. Her fingers felt cold; but I could see tiny sweat beads on her forehead. Her mother had braided her hair in one thick clumsy braid, the way she wore it most of the summer, but the bands of hair were loosening. "No," I said, frightened. "I don't know." We hesitated at the bottom of the stairs—just stood there for a long time. "Maybe not," Mary Lou said. "Damn stairs'd fall in on us."

In the parlor there were bloodstains on the floor and on the wall—I could see them. Mary Lou said in derision, "They're just water stains, dummy."

I could hear the voices overhead, or was it a single droning persistent voice. I waited for Mary Lou to hear it but she never did.

Now we were safe, now we were retreating, Mary Lou

said as if repentant, "Yeah—this house *is* special."

We looked through the debris in the kitchen hoping to find something of value but there wasn't anything—just smashed chinaware, old battered pots and pans, more old yellowed newspaper. But through the window we saw a garter snake sunning itself on a rusted water tank, stretched out to a length of two feet. It was a lovely coppery color, the scales gleaming like perspiration on a man's arm; it seemed to be asleep. Neither one of us screamed, or wanted to throw something—we just stood there watching it for the longest time.

Mary Lou didn't have a boyfriend any longer, Hans had stopped coming around. We saw him driving the old Ford now and then but he didn't seem to see us. Mr. Siskin had found out about him and Mary Lou and he'd been upset—acting like a damn crazy man Mary Lou said, asking her every kind of nasty question then interrupting her and not believing her anyway, then he'd put her to terrible shame by going over to see Hans and carrying on with him. "I hate them all," Mary Lou said, her face darkening with blood. "I wish—"

We rode our bicycles over to the Minton farm, or

tramped through the fields to get there. It was the place we liked best. Sometimes we brought things to eat, cookies, bananas, candy bars, sitting on the broken stone steps out front, as if we lived in the house really, we were sisters who lived here having a picnic lunch out front. There were bees, flies, mosquitoes, but we brushed them away. We had to sit in the shade because the sun was so fierce and direct, a whitish heat pouring down from overhead.

"Would you ever like to run away from home?" Mary Lou said. "I don't know," I said uneasily. Mary Lou wiped at her mouth and gave me a mean narrow look. "'I don't know,'" she said in a falsetto voice, mimicking me. At an upstairs window someone was watching us—was it a man or was it a woman—someone stood there listening hard and I couldn't move feeling so slow and dreamy in the heat like a fly caught on a sticky petal that's going to fold in on itself and swallow him up. Mary Lou crumpled up some wax paper and threw it into the weeds. She was dreamy too, slow and yawning. She said, "Shit—they'd just find me. Then everything would be worse."

I was covered in a thin film of sweat but I'd begun to shiver. Goose bumps were raised on my arms. I could see us sitting on the stone steps the way we'd look from the second floor of the house, Mary Lou sprawled with her legs apart, her braided hair slung over her shoulder, me sitting with my arms hugging my knees my backbone tight and straight knowing I was being watched. Mary Lou said, lowering her voice, "Did you ever touch yourself in a certain place, Melissa?" "No," I said, pretending I didn't know what she meant. "Hans wanted to do that," Mary Lou said. She sounded disgusted. Then she started to giggle. "I wouldn't let him, then he wanted to do something else—started unbuttoning his pants—wanted me to touch *him*. And—"

I wanted to hush her, to clap my hand over her mouth. But she just went on and I never said a word until we both started giggling together and couldn't stop. Afterward I didn't remember most of it or why I'd been so excited my face burning and my eyes seared as if I'd been staring into the sun.

On the way home Mary Lou said, "Some things are so sad you can't say them." But I pretended not to hear.

A few days later I came back by myself. Through the ravaged cornfield: the stalks dried and broken, the tassels burned, that rustling whispering sound of the wind I can hear now if I listen closely. My head was aching with excitement. I was telling myself a story that we'd made plans to run away and live in the Minton house. I was carrying a willow switch I'd found on the ground, fallen from a tree but still green and springy, slapping at things with it as if it was a whip. Talking to myself. Laughing aloud. Wondering was I being watched.

I climbed in the house through the back window and brushed my hands on my jeans. My hair was sticking to the back of my neck.

At the foot of the stairs I called up, "Who's here?" in a voice meant to show it was all play, I knew I was alone.

My heart was beating hard and quick, like a bird caught in the hand. It was lonely without Mary Lou so I walked heavy to let them know I was there and wasn't afraid. I started singing, I started whistling. Talking to myself and slapping at things with the willow switch. Laughing aloud, a little angry. Why was I angry, well I didn't know, someone was whispering telling me to come upstairs, to walk on the inside of the stairs so the steps wouldn't collapse.

The house was beautiful inside if you had the right

eyes to see it. If you didn't mind the smell. Glass underfoot, broken plaster, stained wallpaper hanging in shreds.
Tall narrow windows looking out onto wild weedy patches
of green. I heard something in one of the rooms but when
I looked I saw nothing much more than an easy chair lying
on its side. Vandals had ripped stuffing out of it and tried
to set it afire. The material was filthy but I could see that it
had been pretty once—a floral design—tiny yellow flowers
and green ivy. A woman used to sit in the chair, a big
woman with sly staring eyes. Knitting in her lap but she
wasn't knitting just staring out the window watching to see
who might be coming to visit.

Upstairs the rooms were airless and so hot I felt my
skin prickle like shivering. I wasn't afraid!—I slapped at the
walls with my springy willow switch. In one of the rooms
high in a corner wasps buzzed around a fat wasps' nest. In
another room I looked out the window leaning out the
window to breathe thinking this was my window, I'd come
to live here. She was telling me I had better lie down and
rest because I was in danger of heatstroke and I pretended
not to know what heatstroke was but she knew I knew
because hadn't a cousin of mine collapsed haying just last
summer, they said his face had gone blotched and red and

he'd begun breathing faster and faster not getting enough oxygen until he collapsed. I was looking out at the over-grown apple orchard, I could smell the rot, a sweet winy smell, the sky was hazy like something you can't get clear in your vision, pressing in close and warm. A half mile away Elk Creek glittered through a screen of willow trees moving slow glittering with scales like winking.

Come away from that window, someone told me sternly.

But I took my time obeying.

In the biggest of the rooms was an old mattress pulled off rusty bedsprings and dumped on the floor. They'd torn some of the stuffing out of this too, there were scorch marks on it from cigarettes. The fabric was stained with something like rust and I didn't want to look at it but I had to. Once at Mary Lou's when I'd gone home with her after school there was a mattress lying out in the yard in the sun and Mary Lou told me in disgust that it was her youngest brother's mattress—he'd wet his bed again and the mattress had to be aired out. As if the stink would ever go away, Mary Lou said.

Something moved inside the mattress, a black-glittering thing, it was a cockroach but I wasn't allowed

to jump back. Suppose you have to lie down on that mattress and sleep, I was told. Suppose you can't go home until
you do. My eyelids were heavy, my head was pounding
with blood. A mosquito buzzed around me but I was too
tired to brush it away. Lie down on that mattress, Melissa,
she told me. You know you must be punished.

I knelt down, not on the mattress, but on the floor
beside it. The smells in the room were close and rank but I
didn't mind, my head was nodding with sleep. Rivulets of
sweat ran down my face and sides, under my arms, but I
didn't mind. I saw my hand move out slowly like a
stranger's hand to touch the mattress and a shiny black
cockroach scuttled away in fright, and a second cockroach,
and a third—but I couldn't jump up and scream.

Lie down on that mattress and take your punishment.

I looked over my shoulder and there was a woman
standing in the doorway—a woman I'd never seen before.

She was staring at me. Her eyes were shiny and dark.
She licked her lips and said in a jeering voice, "What are
you doing here in this house, miss?"

I was terrified. I tried to answer but I couldn't speak.

"Have you come to see me?" the woman asked.

She was no age I could guess. Older than my mother

but not old-seeming. She wore men's clothes and she was tall as any man, with wide shoulders, and long legs, and big sagging breasts like cows' udders loose inside her shirt not harnessed in a brassiere like other women's. Her thick wiry gray hair was cut short as a man's and stuck up in tufts that looked greasy. Her eyes were small, and black, and set back deep in their sockets; the flesh around them looked bruised. I had never seen anyone like her before— her thighs were enormous, big as my body. There was a ring of loose soft flesh at the waistband of her trousers but she wasn't fat.

"I asked you a question, miss. Why are you here?"

I was so frightened I could feel my bladder contract. I stared at her, cowering by the mattress, and couldn't speak.

It seemed to please her that I was so frightened. She approached me, stooping a little to get through the doorway. She said, in a mock-kindly voice, "You've come to visit with me—is that it?"

"No," I said.

"No!" she said, laughing. "Why, of course you have."

"No. I don't know you."

She leaned over me, touched my forehead with her fingers. I shut my eyes waiting to be hurt but her touch was cool. She brushed my hair off my forehead where it was sticky with sweat. "I've seen you here before, you and that other one," she said. "What is her name? The blond one. The two of you, trespassing."

I couldn't move, my legs were paralyzed. Quick and darting and buzzing my thoughts bounded in every which direction but didn't take hold. "Melissa is *your* name, isn't it," the woman said. "And what is your sister's name?"

"She isn't my sister," I whispered.

"What is her name?"

"I don't know."

"You don't know!"

"—don't know," I said, cowering.

The woman drew back half sighing half grunting. She looked at me pityingly. "You'll have to be punished, then."

I could smell ashes about her, something cold. I started to whimper started to say I hadn't done anything wrong, hadn't hurt anything in the house, I had only been exploring—I wouldn't come back again—

She was smiling at me, uncovering her teeth. She could read my thoughts before I could think them.

The skin of her face was in layers like an onion, like she'd been sunburned, or had a skin disease. There were patches that had begun to peel. Her look was wet and gloating. *Don't hurt me,* I wanted to say. *Please don't hurt me.*

I'd begun to cry. My nose was running like a baby's. I thought I would crawl past the woman I would get to my feet and run past her and escape but the woman stood in my way blocking my way leaning over me breathing damp and warm her breath like a cow's breath in my face. *Don't hurt me,* I said, and she said, "You know you have to be punished—you and your pretty blond sister."

"She isn't my sister," I said.

"And what is her name?"

The woman was bending over me, quivering with laughter.

"Speak up, miss. What is it?"

"I don't know—" I started to say. But my voice said, "Mary Lou."

The woman's big breasts spilled down onto her belly, I could feel her shaking with laughter. But she spoke sternly saying that Mary Lou and I had been very bad girls and we knew it her house was forbidden territory and we knew it hadn't we known all along that others had come to grief beneath its roof?

"No," I started to say. But my voice said, "Yes."

The woman laughed, crouching above me. "Now, miss, 'Melissa' as they call you—your parents don't know where you are at this very moment, do they?"

"I don't know."

"Do they?"

"No."

"They don't know anything about you, do they?—what you do, and what you think? You and 'Mary Lou.'"

"No."

She regarded me for a long moment, smiling. Her smile was wide and friendly.

"You're a spunky little girl, aren't you, with a mind of your own, aren't you, you and your pretty little sister. I bet your bottoms have been warmed many a time," the woman said, showing her big tobacco-stained teeth in a grin, ". . . your tender little asses."

I began to giggle. My bladder tightened.

"Hand that here, miss," the woman said. She took the willow switch from my fingers—I had forgotten I was holding it. "I will now administer punishment: take down your jeans. Take down your panties. Lie down on that mattress. Hurry." She spoke briskly now, she was all business. "Hurry, Melissa! *And* your panties! Or do you want me to pull them down for you?"

She was slapping the switch impatiently against the palm of her left hand, making a wet scolding noise with her lips. Scolding and teasing. Her skin shone in patches, stretched tight over the big hard bones of her face. Her eyes were small, crinkling smaller, black and damp. She was so big she had to position herself carefully over me to give herself proper balance and leverage so that she wouldn't fall. I could hear her hoarse eager breathing as it came to me from all sides like the wind.

I had done as she told me. It wasn't me doing these things but they were done. *Don't hurt me,* I whispered, lying on my stomach on the mattress, my arms stretched above me and my fingernails digging into the floor. The coarse wood with splinters pricking my skin. *Don't don't hurt me O please* but the woman paid no heed her warm wet breath louder now and the floorboards creaking beneath her weight. "Now, miss, now 'Melissa' as they call you—this will be our secret won't it—"

When it was over she wiped at her mouth and said she would let me go today if I promised never to tell anybody if I sent my pretty little sister to her tomorrow.

She isn't my sister, I said, sobbing. When I could get my breath.

I had lost control of my bladder after all, I'd begun to pee even before the first swipe of the willow switch hit me on the buttocks, peeing in helpless spasms, and sobbing, and afterward the woman scolded me saying wasn't it a poor little baby wetting itself like that. But she sounded repentant too, stood well aside to let me pass, *Off you go! Home you go! And don't forget!*

And I ran out of the room hearing her laughter behind me and down the stairs running running as if I hadn't any weight my legs just blurry beneath me as if the air was water and I was swimming I ran out of the house and through the cornfield running in the cornfield sobbing as the corn stalks slapped at my face *Off you go! Home you go! And don't forget!*

I told Mary Lou about the Minton house and something that had happened to me there that was a secret and she didn't believe me at first saying with a jeer, "Was it a ghost? Was it Hans?" I said I couldn't tell. Couldn't tell what? she said. Couldn't tell, I said. Why not? she said.

"Because I promised."

"Promised who?" she said. She looked at me with her wide blue eyes like she was trying to hypnotize me. "You're a goddamned liar."

Later she started in again asking me what had happened what was the secret was it something to do with Hans? did he still like her? was he mad at her? and I said it didn't have anything to do with Hans not a thing to do with him. Twisting my mouth to show what I thought of him.

"Then who—?" Mary Lou asked.

"I told you it was a secret."

"Oh shit—what kind of a secret?"

"A secret."

"A secret *really*?"

I turned away from Mary Lou, trembling. My mouth kept twisting in a strange hurting smile. "Yes. A secret *really*," I said.

The last time I saw Mary Lou she wouldn't sit with me on the bus, walked past me holding her head high giving me a mean snippy look out of the corner of her eye. Then when she left for her stop she made sure she bumped me going by my seat, she leaned over to say, "I'll find out for myself, I hate you anyway," speaking loud enough for everybody on the bus to hear, "—I always have."

Once upon a time the fairy tales begin. But then they end and often you don't know really what has happened, what was meant to happen, you only know what you've been told, what the words suggest. Now that I have completed my story, filled up half my notebook with my handwriting that disappoints me, it is so shaky and childish—now the story is over I don't understand what it means. I know what happened in my life but I don't know what has happened in these pages.

Mary Lou was found murdered ten days after she said those words to me. Her body had been tossed into Elk Creek a quarter mile from the road and from the old Minton place. Where, it said in the paper, nobody had lived for fifteen years.

It said that Mary Lou had been thirteen years old at the time of her death. She'd been missing for seven days, had been the object of a county-wide search.

It said that nobody had lived in the Minton house for

years but that derelicts sometimes sheltered there. It said that the body was unclothed and mutilated. There were no details.

This happened a long time ago.

The murderer (or murderers as the newspaper always said) was never found.

Hans Meunzer was arrested of course and kept in the county jail for three days while police questioned him but in the end they had to let him go, insufficient evidence to build a case it was explained in the newspaper though everybody knew he was the one wasn't he the one?—everybody knew. For years afterward they'd be saying that. Long after Hans was gone and the Siskins were gone, moved away nobody knew where.

Hans swore he hadn't done it, hadn't seen Mary Lou for weeks. There were people who testified in his behalf said he couldn't have done it for one thing he didn't have his brother's car any longer and he'd been working all that time. Working hard out in the fields—couldn't have slipped away long enough to do what police were saying he'd done. And Hans said over and over he was innocent. Sure he was innocent. Son of a bitch ought to be hanged my father said, everybody knew Hans was the one unless it was a derelict or a fisherman—fishermen often drove out to Elk Creek to fish for black bass, built fires on the creek bank and left messes behind—sometimes prowled around the Minton house too looking for things to steal. The police had records of automobile license plates belonging to some of these men, they questioned them but nothing came of it. Then there was that crazy man that old hermit living in a tarpaper shanty near the Shaheen dump that everybody'd said ought to have been committed to the state hospital years ago. But everybody knew really it was Hans and Hans got out as quick as he could, just disappeared and not even his family knew where unless they were lying which probably they were though they claimed not.

Mother rocked me in her arms crying, the two of us crying, she told me that Mary Lou was happy now, Mary Lou was in Heaven now, Jesus Christ had taken her to live with Him and I knew that didn't I? I wanted to laugh but I didn't laugh. Mary Lou shouldn't have gone with boys, not a nasty boy like Hans, Mother said, she shouldn't have been sneaking around the way she did—I knew that didn't I? Mother's words filled my head flooding my head so there was no danger of laughing.

Jesus loves you too you know that don't you Melissa? Mother asked, hugging me. I told her yes. I didn't laugh because I was crying.

They wouldn't let me go to the funeral, said it would scare me too much. Even though the casket was closed.

It's said that when you're older you remember things that happened a long time ago better than you remember things that have just happened and I have found that to be so.

For instance I can't remember when I bought this notebook at Woolworth's whether it was last week or last month or just a few days ago. I can't remember why I started writing in it, what purpose I told myself. But I remember Mary Lou stooping to say those words in my ear and I remember when Mary Lou's mother came over to ask us at suppertime a few days later if I had seen Mary Lou that day—I remember the very food on my plate, the mashed potatoes in a dry little mound. I remember hearing Mary Lou call my name standing out in the driveway cupping her hands to her mouth the way Mother hated her to do, it was white trash behavior.

"'Lissa!" Mary Lou would call, and I'd call back, "Okay I'm coming!" *Once upon a time.*

BAD GIRLS

That last year of the four of us—Marietta Murchison and her three teenaged daughters—if we'd known it was to be the last we'd have done things differently. But we didn't know, nor did we have a clue how happy (in spite of all our squabbling!) we were. So what came out was, I guess you could say, what had to.

Nor did we set out to destroy our mother's man friend Isaak Drumm, exactly.

How Icy, Orchid, and Crystal, sixteen years old, fifteen, and thirteen, confirmed the neighborhood's and our own relatives' judgment of us, that we were *bad*. And not only *bad* in ourselves but the cause of somebody else being *bad*, too.

But who would have thought we had that much power?

For in our lives, Momma with two ex-husbands and no child support let alone alimony, living on the south side of Yewville on Niagara Street where the old wood-frame ratty-rotted houses look like they're about to slide downhill into the railroad yard and the river—we didn't have any power, at all. If what's meant by *power* is to control your own life and the lives of people you love and make them turn out well and happy. *That*, we sure didn't have.

Seeing us downtown after school, though, or at the East Hills Mall where the kids hang out, the three of us swinging along with our arms around one another's waists, in tight jeans and tank tops in summer, metal-stud jackets in cold weather and clattery boots, purple, maroon, and bright-green dye streaks in our hair—Icy with her gold nose ring and a half dozen studs in each ear, and Orchid with her heavy-broody eyebrows and sassy mouth, and baby-girl Crystal in skintight jeans looking from the rear like a juicy honeydew melon sliced in half—people cut their eyes at us like we were threats to public safety. *Bad girls* you could almost hear them thinking. *Bad girls!* some old pain-in-the-ass aunt of Momma's once hissed at us 'cause we were doing something she didn't like. Which is what adults mean by *bad*—you're doing something they don't like.

It's to hurt your feelings, too. Like Momma's aunt meaning to make a judgment on Momma as a mother. But look—anybody wants to hurt your feelings the smartest strategy is just to laugh in their face. That, Crystal and I learned from Icy. And it works.

Every time our mother fell in love it was like whichever apartment or house we lived in, the actual floors and walls would begin to lurch. Like the four of us were in a boat we weren't aware of in calm waters and then a storm comes up pitching and tossing us—causing seasickness, or worse. You're desperate clutching for something to keep from being thrown overboard. To keep from being drowned.

Momma's men! On the telephone asking for her they'd sound okay then she'd bring them home and it was all we could do, Icy, Orchid, and Crystal, to keep from laughing in their faces—even their names were weird. There was "John Calvin Penny" who was Momma's boss at Penny Realtors where she answered phones and did bookkeeping for a while till working conditions became, in Momma's words, "too tense." There was "Dr. Kenneth Nutt" who was our dentist—he first asked Momma for a date in the dentist's chair!—till Momma broke up with him. There was "Corky Silver" who passed himself off as a freelance investment banker and who drove a lipstick-red MG and wore a wavy blond toupee so fake it was embarrassing— this creep in his fifties at least pretending to be Momma's age (thirty-six) and calling us all *"girls."* And for a while there was this class-A jerk we called "The Hulk." And this serial-killer type "Mouse Ears." And there was "Isaak Drumm."

The way Momma spoke of Drumm, only informing us after they'd gone out three times, almost stammering his name and her eyes clouding up not looking at us exactly, a single thought rushed through us like a warning—*This one might be serious.* Isaak Drumm, Momma informed us, worked for O'Mara's Construction Co., which was a well-known local name, and he'd been a U.S. Army sergeant for seven years having served—the goofy way Momma said "served"!—in Beirut, Lebanon. (Which was where? And who gives a damn?) "Isaak" had a Silver Star medal, Momma said, like she expected us to be impressed. He was thirty-nine years old and long ago married and divorced with no children—here Momma spoke rapidly not inviting questions—and a volunteer in the Niagara Christian

Youth Aid which was one of those do-good organizations you yawn just to hear the name of. And "Isaak" was courteous, Momma said. And kind. And warm. And *funny*—a wonderful sense of humor. Momma talking fast trying not to see the three of us staring deadpan at her, taking all this in like it was gospel truth and not a variation of the crap we'd been hearing, in different words, a dozen times already. *Yeah sure Momma, we know this guy is terrific! Sure! We'll be real nice to him we'll be good girls you can trust us!*

What Momma neglected to tell us, and it's the first thing anybody would notice about Isaak Drumm, as soon as he approached us smiling and squinting and shifting his shoulders like his coat's too tight—and *limping* from his "war wound" in his left knee—is the guy's *weird-looking*. Not ugly because actually Isaak Drumm wasn't ugly, you could almost see how somebody hopeful like our mother might imagine he was handsome, sort of—just *weird-looking*. His eyes were shiny black like beetles' shells, staring at us so hard we all felt queasy. His skin was coarse and the cheeks pitted from old acne scars and a queer radish color like it'd been stewed. His head looked like a concrete block, so square, the jaw especially, and he had a bushy-droopy mustache that looked like it'd been soaked in peanut oil, and his thick black hair was oily too, a little pompadour up front then matted down with a full tube of Brylcreem. Probably he'd been in great condition when he was younger, a bodybuilder maybe, but now he was thickset in the torso and neck like a bull going to fat. Six feet tall and weighing, I'd guess, two hundred fifteen pounds. He was wearing a sport coat with a silvery sheen like plastic and a black silk shirt open at the neck showing frizzy iron-gray hairs and trousers flared at the knees and he was clumsy on his feet with that limp he tried to disguise, not walking so much as plunging forward, in a way that was swaggering but also self-conscious—like his sharp eyes were taking in the fact that the three of us were surprised by him, we were judging him and not too positively. And when he shook hands with us and repeated our names as Momma pronounced them—"Isabel!" (for Momma refused to call Icy "Icy")—"Orchid!"—"Crystal!"—we had all we could do not to duck away from this latest man friend of our mother's looming over us breathing hot in our faces and doused with enough cologne to kill mosquitoes on the wing and practically breaking our hands in his big ham hand. That first evening Isaak Drumm emitted such a heat, he was so pushy and *hopeful* himself, like a car salesman on TV, we girls could hardly think of anything to say to him that didn't sound weak and stumbling. Even Icy, who'd gone against Momma's wishes and was wearing her nose ring, had to admit afterward Isaak Drumm sort of swept her away.

That night Drumm took us all out to the Friday All-You-Can-Eat Buffet at the Ramada Inn and the more he and Momma talked, the quieter Icy, Orchid, and Crystal were. Though hitting the buffet like starving refugees and nudging one another giggling at the attention we drew— what's there about teenagers with dye-streaked hair, not to mention ear studs and nose rings, that freaks "normal" people out? Wild! We basked in the attention and liked it fine but turned sullen when Momma scolded us for sampling so many desserts, and Isaak Drumm defended us saying, "Marietta, these are growing girls—" or some similar asshole remark. And him twirling his mustache around his fork, and laughing this phony-happy laugh like he was our favorite uncle or somebody, or our own dad. Icy terminated the scene by reaching for a spoon and accidentally spilling The Mustache's beer stein into his lap.

That night we're undressing for bed, Crystal and Orchid in one room and Icy next door but hanging out with us peering out our window at the street where, in Drumm's car (a Mazda, creamy yellow, looking like it was washed and simonized for tonight), Drumm and Momma were sitting and talking, and Icy said, " 'Isaak Drumm'!— he's the scariest yet. You notice those eyes? I know psycho eyes when I see them. *Rapist* eyes. *Pederast*."

In a single amazed voice Orchid and Crystal said, " 'Pederast'?—"

The words Icy came up with, sometimes you'd wonder if she invented them herself. Or flipped through the dictionary seeking strangeness.

Walking out of our room Icy tossed back over her shoulder, with a sneer, "Ask 'Isaak.' "

Three bad girls. In the neighborhoods we'd lived in on the south side of Yewville—Momma had to move a lot, one dumpy rental to another—and among our relatives, us Murchison girls were tough characters. This was a joke applied to Crystal who'd burst into tears if some asshole teacher made a sarcastic remark to her, but, with Icy and Orchid as models, she learned to hide the fact.

I'm Orchid. Momma always claimed she named me this because "it was the prettiest name I could think of" and I'd say, making a face, since if you're ugly the only strategy is to make yourself uglier by your own effort, "Geez Momma, too bad you couldn't make *me* pretty, not just my name." And Momma, being Momma, would protest, "Orchid, you *are* pretty!" like her words, earnest enough, could make it so.

Momma hadn't anything solid to trust in beyond the words she'd say to us all the time, with her bright forced smile and upturned eyes—"We'll be just fine, as long as we're *together*." Icy said Momma's faith was like trying to keep warm in a freezing wind by calling to mind the memory of a heated, sheltered place.

Also, not to be critical of her, Marietta Murchison was so *hopeful* it brought out the sadist in you. And she'd contradict herself like her tongue got twisted and things came out the opposite of what she wanted to say—like insisting she was "fine" returning from the gynecologist, then adding, with that smile that meant she was scared stiff, "if God wills!" The kind of behavior you see a lot on TV and in the movies, good-looking woman not overly bright but *sexy*. I guess you could say, sort of, Marietta Murchison was *sexy*. With curly auburn hair, eyes a deeper green than Icy's, a smooth almost-unlined skin. And except when she got depressed, and overate, and drank, and could put on ten pounds in a week, her eyes seeming to shrink in her puffy face, she had a nice figure. Men did glance after her in the street, and in stores—we noticed that, all the time. And her man friends would smile at her indulging her dumb-bimbo remarks saying, "Just like a woman!"—like it was praise, and not an insult.

Icy used to say contemptuously, "Well, what can you expect?—our mother was born in a retrograde era."

Weird to think how long ago that was: Momma a little girl, and videos hadn't been invented yet! or VCRs! or computers! and Elvis Presley still living, and Marilyn Monroe! They'd invented the atomic bomb by then, and dropped it in Japan, but no nuclear warheads or space stations—Momma said when she was growing up the big question was, would the Russians blow us up, or would we blow them up first?

Like Icy said, *retrograde*.

Icy's actual name was "Isabel" which she hated, it was so prissy and *nice*. The one thing you don't want to be, the world's gonna walk over you if you are, is *nice*, Icy said. In ninth grade she named herself "Icy" because it suited her. Probably still does.

Icy was sort of pretty and might have been popular at school but we moved around a lot and it was hard to get settled and even so, as Icy said, you can't trust other people—even the "nice" ones, the girls who invite you home with them, and want to be friends, betray your secrets. She did okay in school but her teachers never liked her—the deadpan way she'd stare at them, and refuse to laugh at their jokes, and wouldn't let herself be, as she said, "co-opted" by the Establishment. She'd started dyeing purple streaks in her hair, her junior year in high school, and got Orchid and Crystal to dye theirs; went to the mall to get her nose pierced, without informing Momma—*that* was a wild scene, like something on TV when Momma came home.

Momma, said, "My own daughter, looking like a *cannibal*!"

Crystal was named by her own mother, not Momma. She'd come to live with us when she was nine and her mother died of some terrible quick cancer when Momma and her second husband Wayne Murchison (who was Crystal's father) had only been married about a year. For a while she wouldn't talk, or couldn't. Nor could she go to school, where she was supposed to be in fourth grade. But

Momma was real nice to her, and in a few months she got better, though she was always shy. (Shyest around her own father, for good reason as we learned.) Unlike Icy and Orchid who were apt to take their mother for granted, Crystal never did. So she was the most anxious about Momma's man friends. After Momma and Crystal's father were divorced (that's another story) there was a calm quiet interlude of eighteen months when Momma lost fifteen pounds to fit into a size 9 dress, switched to a new receptionist job and started dating men again and each one of them she brought home, poor Crystal would go into a panic thinking he'd take Momma away from us.

Even so, we were *not* jealous of Momma's man friends. Even Crystal could see the logic of, how, if Momma married again, this time a man who was worthy of her, we'd all be better off. A hell of a lot better off. We'd move from the south side of Yewville uptown, transfer to new schools where nobody knew us. We'd get a new car—maybe two new cars. Momma could quit work if she wanted and anyway would never again be made to grovel applying for county assistance when she was between jobs.

Except—Momma never seemed to bring home a man who was worthy. For sure, The Mustache wasn't him.

• • •

Like each of Momma's man friends she was serious about, Isaak Drumm came to possess a mysterious power. Us girls could see this clearly, and we didn't like it. Momma's emotional life was surrendered to this guy we scarcely knew, this "U.S. Army sergeant" with the goofy mustache and bad knee and gleaming black eyes like Dracula. *He* had the power of making her happy like a little girl, hugging and kissing us for no reason, or plunging her into worry and self-doubt. First thing in the morning Momma might be singing, or she might be padding around heavyhearted and distracted squinting at her own daughters like for a moment she didn't know who we were. As Icy observed, "It's goddamned *insulting.*"

Isaak Drumm did make Momma cry, sometimes. Maybe he was seeing another woman, or women?—we'd hear Momma on the phone saying quietly, "Whatever you think is best, Isaak. I understand." Or, "I was needing a little time to myself this weekend, too. As a matter of fact."

Then, a few days later, The Mustache would "happen to be in the neighborhood" around six P.M. bringing some dead-looking scentless red hothouse flowers "for all my girls"—except, in his mouth, the word came out "gur-rls."

And every time, to our disgust, Momma's face lit up in welcome and she'd insist he eat supper with us.

Most times Drumm took Momma out, and always on her late night at work, which was Fridays, and they'd be gone for hours. No regular dinner and movie date but obviously they were at his place—for hours. It was clear that Momma was *in love* with this latest man friend but not clear that he was *in love* with her and this hurt our pride, beyond just the fact of disliking him. Icy said, "Momma has become a desperate woman. Somebody's got to save her." We vowed we'd never be *women* if *women* means *weakness*.

Watching a cop show on TV one night when Momma and Drumm were out, Icy came up with her plan. "This is what we'll do: break in his place and collect the evidence."

Orchid and Crystal just stared at Icy. We'd been eating cold slices of pizza and a rubbery string of mozzarella hung down from Crystal's lip like a broken tusk. "'Evidence'—?"

"To use against him."

"Use against him *how*?"

Icy smiled pityingly at us, the way she would when she solved my algebra problems in her head without needing any steps to get the answer, or the way she'd finish Crystal's slow sentences for her. Like it was the most obvious thing in the world we should've thought of ourselves. "To make our deluded mother realize what a slimy bastard she's gotten involved with. Again."

Icy's and my father's name was Marvin H. Wilmer and he left us when I was two years old and I didn't remember him at all, it was like a blank whitewashed wall if I tried to remember him, and it still is.

Icy said, "Lucky you."

The Mustache was always making such a big deal of how his boss Mr. O'Mara counted on him to work long hours so we believed we'd be safe breaking into his place after school. Meaning after four P.M. which was the earliest we could get to where he lived—this "condominium village" called Brookside Manor, about three miles away, we had to take a city bus to get to. We'd seen the place from the outside once when Momma drove by saying in her moony voice, "That's where Isaak lives"—like it was the White House or something not some dumpy apartment building covered in aluminum siding glaring like tin. Nine Brookside Manor was Drumm's address, lucky for us at the far end of the building practically in a woods. Each of the units had its own front and rear entrance and a balcony that would've been cramped for a dwarf overlooking the "brook"—a greasy little ditch down a ravine littered with debris. So's not to be seen by anyone Icy led us along this route and it was depressing on a drizzly-windy day and the clouds overhead like bread mold and Icy saying, to spook Orchid and Crystal, "Brrr! This is the exact kind of place, the caption says 'Where the bodies were discovered, partly decomposed.'"

No cars were parked behind 9 Brookside. We crept up behind the garbagey-smelling Dumpster, trying to avoid broken glass; tried the back door but naturally it was locked. Icy led the way up onto the balcony and that door was locked, too, but—this was Icy's luck!—beside the door was one of those narrow windows operated by a crank, and this Icy discovered was loose enough to pry open so she could force her hand, then her arm, inside, and crank it open as far as it would go. You'd see such a small window and figure nobody could squeeze through it, but this wasn't so.

Afterward we'd be asked if we broke in places habitu-ally—if we were thieves, shoplifters—but I swear this wasn't so. Maybe a few things lifted from the 7-Eleven near

our house, and Discount Drugs and Woolworth's, sometimes. Nothing major.

Icy crawled through the window supple and squirmy
as a snake, nor had Orchid any trouble, being rail-thin too
and wiry; Crystal with her soft hips might've gotten stuck,
and panicked, if we hadn't tugged at her arms to yank her
free. Poor Crystal flush-faced and panting like a dog and
terrified clutching at her sisters' hands so we slapped her
away, laughing and giddy. "Control yourself," Icy whispered. "This is it." But she was trembling, too. *For now we
were in Isaak Drumm's apartment. In the place of the enemy.*

For the first ten minutes or so we drifted around staring like this was a weird dream. We'd bump into each
other, like sleepwalkers. Not that The Mustache's living
quarters were anything special, they were not. "Luxury
units" the sign out front said but that was an exaggeration.
The rooms were small and there wasn't much furniture and
it was all cheap-slick and impersonal like in a motel room.
Drawers and cupboards in the kitchen open, plates in
the sink, burned crud on the stove and a mixed smell of
cooking odors and cologne—no mistaking who lived here.
One of us collided with a chair and the others went
"Shhh!" not knowing if we were scared to death or about

the most excited we'd ever been, the three of us. Breaking into somebody's place there's a way your heart beats, like a hummingbird's whirring wings, and a sharp taste in your mouth you don't get anywhere anytime else!

On top of the TV set in the living room were framed photos of Drumm's family. Lots of them. We tried to pick Drumm out but weren't too sure, he had brothers, or cousins; all of them with those deep dark glistening eyes and thick black hair and square-built faces. Orchid said in surprise, "The Mustache has a *family*!" and Icy said, sneering, "So what? So's a rat." Of course, this was so.

If Isaak Drumm had been expecting visitors today, he'd have picked up a little. Or maybe, when Momma came over, *she* picked up for him—that'd be just like Momma. There were soiled T-shirts tossed around, and a pair of what looked like size XXX jogging shoes under the coffee table in the living room, and lots of old newspapers, magazines, *TV Guide*s, paperback books, videos. Why anybody buys videos, not just rents them, *I* don't know. Drumm's taste was for sappy macho-action films—sci-fi horror—some of the stuff, in video stores, classified as "cult." Momma's taste was for romantic comedy—you had to wonder, if they watched videos together here, what they watched. Or maybe Momma pretended she liked Drumm's choices? That's part of being *sexy*, being a *hypocrite*.

The bedroom at the rear was the room we needed to search but we seemed reluctant to go into it. Even Icy. The thought came to us all—*what if he's in there, hiding? waiting for us?*

Crystal went suddenly into the kitchen where she opened the refrigerator and snatched up a can of Miller's Ale and, before we could stop her, opened it and took a large gulping swallow. "Crystal! Shit!" Icy grabbed the can from her but took a swallow herself, and so did Orchid. We shared the ale and it was gone in possibly thirty seconds. Then—*three bad girls* wiping our mouths and panting, shivering with excitement.

Ale or beer, drunk fast, when you're in a state of nerves, generates a glowing buzz at the back of the skull you can just about feel *vibrate*.

We took another Miller's figuring The Mustache wouldn't miss it, he had plenty in reserve. Or maybe we took two.

We felt braver poking around next in the bathroom noting the sink, the toilet, the shower stall weren't any too clean. Soap scum in the sink, and tiny black hairs from shaving. And more hairs in the shower drain. "Look!" Icy pointed at the two shampoos side by side on the shower ledge: one of them Head & Shoulders Dandruff Control and the other Finesse for Fine, Thin, Permed Hair— Momma's shampoo. And in the medicine cabinet, the first thing we saw was Lady Speed Stick Deodorant—Momma's deodorant. The three of us just staring not saying anything.

Was *this* evidence?

We pushed into the bedroom where the smell of Drumm was strongest. Cologne, hair oil, used sheets and clothes. And that low-grade stink of shoes in an unaired closet. At least, the bed was made—a shiny pumpkin-colored spread carelessly yanked up over the pillows. There was another TV on a bureau, and more paperbacks and videos. This room was darker than the front rooms over-looking the "brook"—though mainly the Dumpster. The horrible thought came to us *Momma has been here, in that bed? is that possible!* but somehow it did not seem possible. We scared ourselves seeing our reflections in a mirror— how pale and *young* we looked. Those bright dye streaks of color in our hair like somebody had swathed us with paint as a cruel joke.

We poked around in the closet, sniffing and giggling at Drumm's clothes. For a guy who worked construction he sure owned a lot of sport coats and fancy shirts. And shoes, including more jogging shoes. But what stopped us cold was a baby-blue flannel bathrobe of Momma's we'd given her for Christmas a few years before and we hadn't even realized it was missing from home! Crystal made a little mewing-hurt sound and we just stood there, staring. Like it was Momma herself, her body, we'd discovered, hidden in Isaak Drumm's closet.

Evidence.

More evidence: in a drawer of Drumm's bedside table, a broken-open packet of condoms. And a much-squeezed tube of Vaseline.

"Dis-gusting!" Icy said, her nostrils pinched, shutting the drawer quick.

"Well, what'd you think they did," Orchid asked meanly, "—watch videos every night?"

Crystal rushed off to be sick in the bathroom. We heard her choking and coughing, and the toilet flush. When she reappeared, wiping her mouth, her eyes were brimming with tears. "Oh, Icy, I want to go home, I'm *scared*."

Icy and Orchid had checked into the kitchen again, came away with two more ales and a box of Frosties— sugary cereal you can eat in handfuls like candy. Crystal was moaning but shared the ale and ate Frosties anyway. Scared and excited, you eat like it's your last meal. There's no real taste but your jaws take pleasure in *grinding*.

Icy was searching Drumm's bureau drawers. No interrupting Icy. And whatever time it was we'd sort of lost awareness. As, in a dream, you have no awareness of time nor even that, like a fast-running river, time is rushing out of your control. "Look!"—Icy drew out from under a bunch of balled-up socks a snub-nosed bluish-gleaming handgun.

From TV and movies you see so many guns the real, actual thing doesn't seem much different. Except there's a part of your brain clicking *Yes this is different! You can die!*

After this, things get confused.

The more we were questioned afterward, and talked about it again, again, again among ourselves, the more confused it was. But, for sure: Orchid and Crystal were so scared they practically wet themselves seeing this *gun* out of nowhere in Icy's hand—and her hand visibly trembling, though she tried to hide it.

Icy lifted the gun and stared at it, weighed it reverently in her hand, frowned at herself in the mirror, aimed it at the mirror. While Orchid begged, "Icy, no! It might be loaded!" Icy teased, "Y' want me to pull the trigger, and see?" It was like she was hypnotized. Her cheeks were warm and splotched and her glassy-green eyes were shining like cat's eyes.

Icy murmuring, with a level gaze at herself in the mirror, "I'm holding Death in my hand." Swinging the gun in a slow arc, always watching herself in the mirror, as Orchid and Crystal ducked. "This is Death I'm holding in my hand."

Crystal was whimpering, "Oh Icy, please!" and Orchid was saying, "Hey, Icy, you're scaring us!" and Icy ignored them preening in front of the mirror and how long, how many actual minutes, this craziness went on, I don't know. Finally we got Icy to put back the gun, she made a fuss wiping her fingerprints off, the drawer was messed up so we tried to straighten it and we were laughing and hiccuping and getting in one another's way and we could tell it was getting darker outside, or a storm was coming up, and we were jumpy even before hearing a car pull up at the rear, and suddenly *the worst that can happen is happening: Isaak Drumm is home.*

We were frozen in place. Hearing a car door slam, and a few seconds later somebody is whistling at the back door, fitting a key in the lock.

What I believed happened was: Icy quick-shoved the gun back into the drawer. And herded us ahead of her, back to the window we'd crawled through. Except evidently Icy hadn't put the gun back at all, but shoved it into the belt of her jeans.

First went Crystal, panting and whimpering like a sick baby—her sisters saw to that, hoisting her up when she slipped, and pushing her hips through the narrow space; then Orchid, flushed with adrenaline, wiry-quick and unhesitating, though she would have fallen onto her head on the balcony if Crystal hadn't managed to catch her. Next was Icy at the window with a look of fierce concentration, biting her lower lip to draw blood, squeezing through too, almost she was going to make it—we had hold of her wrists—but this nightmare thing happens: Isaak Drumm comes up yelling behind her and grabs her ankles, her thighs, her shoulders, and yanks her back inside. Icy is screaming, and Drumm is cursing, and Orchid and Crystal freak out completely jumping off the balcony and running to hide behind the Dumpster.

Where, panting, crouched like hunted animals, staring terrified at each other and gripping each other's hand, they hear the gun go off, a single *crack!* of a shot, inside Isaak Drumm's apartment.

Afterward there would be so much confusion about what happened that day at 9 Brookside Manor, so many rumors!—what was truth, and what wasn't, soon got lost, like pieces of a shattered vase swept up with all kinds of other debris. But: taking in both Icy's and Drumm's testimonies, before they diverged, it's clear they were struggling at the window, and Icy had the gun (which was a .38-caliber Smith & Wesson holding six bullets), and Drumm tried to wrestle it from her, and Icy pulled the trigger or the trigger went off, and a bullet just missed Drumm's head—so close his scalp was singed!—and lodged in the ceiling.

Of course, out behind the Dumpster, Orchid and Crystal didn't know this. We believed one of them was killed. Knowing Icy, how wired she'd been, we thought it would be Isaak Drumm. And Icy, our sister, would be arrested for murder!

We hugged each other, crying. Hiding there behind the smelly Dumpster in the rain with no clue what was happening until, a while later, a Yewville city cop discovered us, as surprised to see us there as we were surprised to see him.

Nobody knew it at the time but that was the end, right then, of Momma and Isaak Drumm. Immediately when the gun went off, and the gunshot was heard, and a neighbor called the police.

If the police hadn't been called, and all of us questioned, and so much attention paid, things might have gone differently. Sure, Isaak Drumm was furious about us breaking into his apartment, and shocked at how Icy seemed to hate him, but he and Momma might have smoothed things out between them. And maybe they'd be together now—Momma might be Mrs. Isaak Drumm. Who knows?

Poor Momma. Her rotten luck with men. And us *bad girls* breaking her heart.

But there was so much fuss, fuss, fuss! and naturally Momma kept after Icy with questions, and finally after about forty-eight hours Icy freaked out and started sobbing like a little, hurt girl, lifting her shirt to show Momma the bruises on her breasts, midriff, and back, and lowering her jeans to show even uglier bruises on her thighs and buttocks. She was crying, choked, "You know what he did, Momma?—he assaulted me. Sexual assault! Tried to rape me!"

Momma almost fainted. Later she'd say this was her worst, her very worst nightmare come true: one of her daughters would be injured by a man she'd brought into our lives.

Right away Momma drove Icy who was hysterical now to the emergency room of the Yewville General Hospital. And there Icy was treated for her bruises, and given a pelvic examination, no she had not been raped but she repeated her story of how Isaak Drumm had assaulted her when he'd caught her in his apartment, and the hospital informed the police, and two police officers, one of them a woman, came to question Icy, and Icy repeated her story, and expanded it, encouraged to describe in detail how Drumm grabbed her and yanked her from the window, how he'd sworn at her, how he'd fondled her breasts, squeezed and pinched and slapped her, yanked her by the hair, pulled down her jeans and panties and spanked her as hard as he could, and kneaded her buttocks, and opened his pants and jabbed his penis against her like a maniac—"He said he'd strangle me if I told anyone," Icy said, "—so when the police came I didn't say anything. But now I'm scared he'll kill me anyway!"

There was no trace of semen on Icy's body for by then she'd taken several baths. And her clothes—thrown into the washer, and laundered.

Orchid and Crystal, when they heard their sister's story, which was an *official testimony* filed with the county district attorney's office, had to wonder—was this true? In the weeks that followed, sometimes they'd think one way; sometimes another. What was certain was, for Icy, once she found the words to tell the story and saw how adults believed her, not just Momma but strangers, people in authority, and how they felt such sympathy for her, it *was* true, for her.

Momma must have made a decision, like throwing a bolt to lock a door forever—*she* believed Icy. She would never waver in believing Icy. Saying, "Nobody hurts my girls and gets away with it. Nobody so much as *touches* my girls and gets away with it."

Sure, Isaak Drumm tried to talk to her. In person, and, when she refused to let him in, over the phone. But she never would speak with him. Never again.

That very day Momma took Icy to the hospital, Drumm was served with a warrant for a "sexual felony committed against a minor" and arrested at a construction site, hauled off in a squad car handcuffed and astonished, his picture in the Yewville *Journal*, publicly shamed. Already Drumm was in trouble with the law for possession of an unlicensed handgun, and the kindness he'd done us—declining to press charges against us for unlawful entry of his home, passing off the incident as "just some kids playing around"—seemed to backfire on him. At police headquarters, Drumm lost his temper insisting he hadn't touched Icy at all; refused to call a lawyer because he didn't want to pay any goddamned lawyer when he was innocent; threatened the police with false arrest charges— which, I'm told, you don't want to do. And later he changed his story admitting yes maybe he'd spanked Icy, but not hard. But he hadn't pulled down her jeans and panties, no he had *not*.

SUSPECT ADMITS SPANKING GIRL got in the *Journal*, and it was all anybody talked about! In the end, the lawyer Isaak Drumm finally hired advised him to plead guilty to a reduced charge—a "sexual misdemeanor." If Drumm insisted he was innocent, and went to trial, he'd risk being found guilty of the more serious charge and wind up going to prison for as long as seven years. As it was, he was given two years' suspended sentence, and put on probation.

After this upset to all our lives, which was sort of like a death in the family, Momma has never regained her old, hopeful spirits. Nor her desire to meet the right man and remarry. So much rumor and gossip, she'd had to move from Niagara Street, and she'd gained so much weight so fast, she lost her job as a receptionist; right now she's working checkout at a 7-Eleven. She's gotten religious, joined the Methodist Church. She tells me, "You get to feel God is testing you, and watching how you react. *That's* the important thing."

Icy soon left home. Quit high school, quarreled with her mother and her sisters and moved away. It's been four years since she left Yewville and at least a year since any of us, even Momma, have heard from her. The last was a postcard from Pensacola, Florida—saying she loves us, and misses us, but she's okay, she's planning to sign up with the U.S. Navy and would Momma make a copy of her birth certificate? But no further word.

Crystal is seventeen, still in school, and Momma's worried sick about *her*—Crystal and the guys she hangs out with.

As for Orchid—I'm nineteen, a second-year nursing student in Rochester. I'm not a *bad girl* now except sometimes in my thoughts.

What I think about a lot, and I'll never tell Momma, is: a few weeks ago I ran into Isaak Drumm here in Rochester. He'd just parked his car at a curb and I noticed him looking at me not recognizing him at first, then he got out, car keys in hand, and stared—and I stared back—neither of us sure who the other was. Isaak Drumm had changed a lot in four years, his hair not in a pompadour now but flat and graying, and his mustache vanished so his face looked raw and exposed, the skin coarser than I remembered, yet the eyes so *intense*. I realized I've been seeing those eyes, feeling that hurt liquidy *intense* stare, for a long time.

Hesitantly Drumm called out, "Orchid—?"

So seeing he recognized me, and there's no danger in

it, out here on a public sidewalk, I admitted yes, I was Orchid Murchison. My face going hot, and my heart pounding so hard I believed I would faint.

But I didn't faint, I was okay. Though this conversation, the next five or ten minutes, passed by me in a roar.

I believe Isaak Drumm asked me would I like to have a cup of coffee with him and I must have said no thank you. He saw how nervous I was so he didn't press it and tried to smile to indicate he had no grudge against me, raising his voice to be heard over the street noises asking after Momma and I told him Momma was fine, he asked was she married and I said yes in fact she was, and he took that news sort of squinting and smiling harder. It was strange—he wasn't all that tall, only two or three inches taller than me. The limp wasn't that noticeable, or he was better practiced at disguising it. He was asking after Crystal, and me, and I told him we were fine, too, keeping it brief and polite as possible. I was surprised he remembered our names! I could see he was reluctant to ask after Icy—"Isabel"—so I volunteered she was in the Navy and doing okay, we were proud of her. To all this Isaak Drumm listened inclining his head, as if he'd become hard of hearing in his left ear; or it pained him, to look me full in the face.

Then suddenly he was looking at me, and his eyes were shiny with tears, he was saying, "—I was hurt so bad, Orchid, the way it ended—like I was kicked in the stomach"—actually rubbing his stomach and his chest beneath his heart, wincing—"it took me a long time to get over it—except I'm not, I guess. I had to leave Yewville, I was so shamed. I live here in Rochester now, I'm looking for work. Sometimes even now I can't believe it—how my life changed, in one hour. The way you all dumped me—so fast. Your mother—who I loved—believed that girl, the story that girl told, not even giving me a chance to talk to her. Your sister *was* lying—didn't you all know? You must've known! Didn't you *care*? Didn't any of you like me, or trust me? Jesus, I loved you so much. I was crazy about you all. I wanted to—you know—marry your mother, and—"

I just stood there, stunned. Here's the man we'd so feared would take Momma from us, and he's standing in front of me on a street corner just about crying confiding in me the most amazing thing I have ever heard. My thoughts are all in a buzz. I don't know what to think. *Can a man have such feelings, like a woman? Can a man be hurt? Is that possible?* My eyes were brimming with tears like Isaak Drumm's and I was in a panic I'd start crying, and how would that end, right out here on the street where people were glancing at us. I hate being emotional, I'm not good at emotions and I avoid things I don't do well. So I mumbled something vague and apologetic and said I had to leave, I had a class to get to, and Isaak Drumm followed after me a bit but not too forcibly so it wouldn't look like here's a guy harassing this girl right out on the street, he was saying maybe we could get together sometime? maybe we could talk? would I pass along hello and best wishes to my mother?—"You remember my name, Orchid? 'Isaak Drumm'—I'm in the Rochester directory—if you could call me sometime—" I was walking quickly away. My head ached, and my eyes were stinging so I was in a fury wiping them with my fists. *Can a man love you? Can a man tell the truth?* I walked away without looking back and Isaak Drumm's voice was fading, lost in the traffic noises, becoming more and more remote like a voice inside my head or like the memory of something that once held my life together, that, now I'm grown up, I can't remember—like the one thing you vow you'll never lose turns into, in time, the one thing too painful to recall.

No, I'll never tell Momma. Even if I telephone Isaak Drumm, and hear more of this. Which I don't know if I want to do, exactly—I'm still debating.

HOW I CONTEMPLATED
THE WORLD FROM THE DETROIT
HOUSE OF CORRECTIONS
AND BEGAN MY LIFE OVER AGAIN

Notes for an essay for an English class at Baldwin Country Day School; poking around in debris; disgust and curiosity; a revelation of the meaning of life; a happy ending . . .

I EVENTS

1. The girl (myself) is walking through Branden's, that excellent store. Suburb of a large famous city that is a symbol for large famous American cities. The event sneaks up on the girl, who believes she is herding it along with a small fixed smile, a girl of fifteen, innocently experienced. She dawdles in a certain style by a counter of costume

jewelry. Rings, earrings, necklaces. Prices from $5 to $50, all within reach. All ugly. She eases over to the glove counter, where everything is ugly too. In her close-fitted coat with its black fur collar she contemplates the luxury of Branden's, which she has known for many years: its many mild pale lights, easy on the eye and the soul, its elaborate tinkly decorations, its women shoppers with their excellent shoes and coats and hairdos, all dawdling gracefully, in no hurry.

2. The girl seated at home. A very small library, paneled walls of oak. Someone is talking to me. An earnest, husky, female voice drives itself against my ears, nervous, frightened, groping around my heart, saying, "If you wanted gloves, why didn't you say so? Why didn't you ask for them?" That store, Branden's, is owned by Raymond Forrest who lives on Du Maurier Drive. We live on Sioux Drive. Raymond Forrest. A handsome man? An ugly man? A man of fifty or sixty, with gray hair, or a man of forty with earnest, courteous eyes, a good golf game; who is Raymond Forrest, this man who is my salvation? Father has been talking to him. Father is not his physician; Dr. Berg is his physician. Father and Dr. Berg refer patients to

each other. There is a connection. Mother plays bridge with . . . On Mondays and Wednesdays our maid Billie works at . . . The strings draw together in a cat's cradle, making a net to save you when you fall. . . .

3. *Harriet Arnold's.* A small shop, better than Branden's. Mother in her black coat, I in my close-fitted blue coat. Shopping. Now look at this, isn't this cute, do you want this, why don't you want this, try this on, take this with you to the fitting room, take this also, what's wrong with you, what can I do for you, why are you so strange . . . ? "I wanted to steal but not to buy," I don't tell her. The girl droops along in her coat and gloves and leather boots, her eyes scan the horizon, which is pastel pink and decorated like Branden's, tasteful walls and modern ceilings with graceful glimmering lights.

4. Weeks later, the girl at a bus stop. Two o'clock in the afternoon, a Tuesday; obviously she has walked out of school.

5. The girl stepping down from a bus. Afternoon, weather changing to colder. Detroit. Pavement and closed-

up stores; grillwork over the windows of a pawnshop. What is a pawnshop, exactly?

II CHARACTERS

1. The girl stands five feet five inches tall. An ordinary height. Baldwin Country Day School draws them up to that height. She dreams along the corridors and presses her face against the Thermoplex glass. No frost or steam can ever form on that glass. A smudge of grease from her forehead . . . could she be boiled down to grease? She wears her hair loose and long and straight in suburban teenage style. Eyes smudged with pencil, dark brown. Brown hair. Vague green eyes. A pretty girl? An ugly girl? She sings to herself under her breath, idling in the corridor, thinking of her many secrets (the thirty dollars she once took from the purse of a friend's mother, just for fun, the basement window she smashed in her own house just for fun) and thinking of her brother who is at Susquehanna Boys' Academy, an excellent preparatory school in Maine, remembering him unclearly . . . he has long manic hair and a squeaking voice and he looks like one of the popular teenage singers, one of those in a group, The Splats, Hunger Hunger, Hot Rats. The girl in her turn looks like

one of those fieldsful of girls who listen to the boys' singing, dreaming and mooning restlessly, breaking into high sullen laughter, innocently experienced.

2. The mother. A Midwestern woman of Detroit and suburbs. Belongs to the Detroit Athletic Club. Also the Detroit Golf Club. Also the Bloomfield Hills Country Club. The Village Women's Club at which lectures are given each winter on Genet and Sartre and James Baldwin, by the Director of the Adult Education Program at Wayne State University. . . . The Bloomfield Art Association. Also the Founders Society of the Detroit Institute of Arts. Also . . . Oh, she is in perpetual motion, this lady, hair like blown-up gold and finer than gold, hair and fingers and body of inestimable grace. Heavy weighs the gold on the back of her hairbrush and hand mirror. Heavy heavy the candlesticks in the dining room. Very heavy is the big car, a Lincoln, long and black, that on one cool autumn day split a squirrel's body in two unequal parts.

3. The father. Dr.   . He belongs to the same clubs as #2. A player of squash and golf; he has a golfer's umbrella of stripes. Candy stripes. In his mouth nothing turns to sugar,

however; saliva works no miracles here. His doctoring is of the slightly sick. The sick are sent elsewhere (to Dr. Berg?), the deathly sick are sent back for more tests and their bills are sent to their homes, the unsick are sent to Dr. Coronet (Isabel, a lady), an excellent psychiatrist for unsick people who angrily believe they are sick and want to do something about it. If they demand a male psychiatrist, the unsick are sent by Dr.   (my father) to Dr. Lowenstein, a male psychiatrist, excellent and expensive, with a limited practice.

4. Clarita. She is twenty, twenty-five, she is thirty or more? Pretty, ugly, what? She is a woman lounging by the side of the road, in jeans and a sweater, hitchhiking, or she is slouched on a stool at a counter in some roadside diner. A hard line of jaw. Curious eyes. Amused eyes. Behind her eyes processions move, funeral pageants, cartoons. She says, "I never can figure out why girls like you bum around down here. What are you looking for anyway?" An odor of tobacco about her. Unwashed underclothes, or no underclothes, unwashed skin, gritty toes, hair long and falling into strands, not recently washed.

5. Simon. In this city the weather changes abruptly, so

Simon's weather changes abruptly. He sleeps through the afternoon. He sleeps through the morning. Rising, he gropes around for something to get him going, for a cigarette or a pill to drive him out to the street, where the temperature is hovering around thirty-five degrees. Why doesn't it drop? Why, why doesn't the cold clean air come down from Canada; will he have to go up into Canada to get it? will he have to leave the Country of his Birth and sink into Canada's frosty fields . . . ? Will the F.B.I. (which he dreams about constantly) chase him over the Canadian border on foot, hounded out in a blizzard of broken glass and horns . . . ?

"Once I was Huckleberry Finn," Simon says, "but now I am Roderick Usher." Beset by frenzies and fears, this man who makes my spine go cold, he takes green pills, yellow pills, pills of white and capsules of dark blue and green . . . he takes other things I may not mention, for what if Simon seeks me out and climbs into my girl's bedroom here in Bloomfield Hills and strangles me, what then . . . ? (As I write this I begin to shiver. Why do I shiver? I am now sixteen and sixteen is not an age for shivering. It comes from Simon, who is always cold.)

III WORLD EVENTS
Nothing.

IV PEOPLE AND CIRCUMSTANCES CONTRIBUTING TO THIS DELINQUENCY
Nothing.

V SIOUX DRIVE

George, Clyde G. 240 Sioux. A manufacturer's representative; children, a dog, a wife. Georgian with the usual columns. You think of the White House, then of Thomas Jefferson, then your mind goes blank on the white pillars and you think of nothing. Norris, Ralph W. 246 Sioux. Public relations. Colonial. Bay window, brick, stone, concrete, wood, green shutters, sidewalk, lantern, grass, trees, blacktop drive, two children, one of them my classmate Esther (Esther Norris) at Baldwin. Wife, cars. Ramsey, Michael D. 250 Sioux, Colonial. Big living room, thirty by twenty-five, fireplaces in living room, library, recreation room, paneled walls wet bar five bathrooms five bedrooms two lavatories central air conditioning automatic sprinkler automatic garage door three children one wife two cars a breakfast room a patio a large fenced lot fourteen trees a front door with a brass knocker never knocked. Next is our house. Classic contemporary. Traditional modern. Attached garage, attached Florida room, attached patio, attached pool and cabana, attached roof. A front-door mail slot through which pour *Time* magazine, *Fortune*, *Life*, *Business Week*, *The Wall Street Journal*, *The New York Times*, *The New Yorker*, the *Saturday Review*, *M.D.*, *Modern Medicine*, *Disease of the Month* . . . and also. . . . And in addition to all this, a quiet sealed letter from Baldwin saying: *Your daughter is not doing work compatible with her performance on the Stanford-Binet.* . . . And your son is not doing well, not well at all, very sad. Where is your son anyway? Once he stole trick-or-treat candy from some six-year-old kids, he himself being a robust ten. The beginning. Now your daughter steals. In the Village Pharmacy she made off with, yes she did, don't deny it, she made off with a copy of *Pageant* magazine for no reason, she swiped a roll of Life Savers in a green wrapper and was in no need of saving her life or even in need of sucking candy; when she was no more than eight years old she stole, don't blush, she stole a package of Tums only because it was out on the counter and available, and the nice lady behind the counter (now dead) said nothing. . . . Sioux Drive. Maples, oaks, elms. Diseased elms cut down. Sioux Drive runs into Roosevelt Drive. Slow, turning lanes, not streets, all drives and lanes and ways and passes. A private police force. Quiet private police, in unmarked cars. Cruising on Saturday evenings with paternal smiles for the residents who are streaming in and out of houses, going to and from parties, a thousand parties, slightly staggering, the women in their furs alighting from automobiles bought of Ford and General Motors and Chrysler, very heavy automobiles. No foreign cars. Detroit. In 275 Sioux, down the block in that magnificent French-Normandy mansion, lives X   himself, who has the C   account itself, imagine that! Look at where he lives and look at the enormous trees and chimneys, imagine his many fireplaces, imagine his wife and children, imagine his wife's hair, imagine her finger-nails, imagine her bathtub of smooth clean glowing pink, imagine their embraces, his trouser pockets filled with odd coins and keys and dust and peanuts, imagine their ecstasy on Sioux Drive, imagine their income tax returns, imagine their little boy's pride in his experimental car, a scaled-down C   , as he roars around the neighborhood on the sidewalks frightening dogs and maids, oh imagine all these things, imagine everything, let your mind roar out all over

Sioux Drive and Du Maurier Drive and Roosevelt Drive and Ticonderoga Pass and Burning Bush Way and Lincolnshire Pass and Lois Lane.

When spring comes, its winds blow nothing to Sioux Drive, no odors of hollyhocks or forsythia, nothing Sioux Drive doesn't already possess, everything is planted and performing. The weather vanes, had they weather vanes, don't have to turn with the wind, don't have to contend with the weather. There is no weather.

VI DETROIT

There is always weather in Detroit. Detroit's temperature is always thirty-two degrees. Fast-falling temperatures. Slow-rising temperatures. Wind from the north-northeast four to forty miles an hour, small-craft warnings, partly cloudy today and Wednesday changing to partly sunny through Thursday . . . small warnings of frost, soot warnings, traffic warnings, hazardous lake conditions for small craft and swimmers, restless black gangs, restless cloud formations, restless temperatures aching to fall out the very bottom of the thermometer or shoot up over the top and boil everything over in red mercury.

Detroit's temperature is thirty-two degrees. Fast-falling

temperatures. Slow-rising temperatures. Wind from the north-northeast four to forty miles an hour. . . .

VII EVENTS

1. The girl's heart is pounding. In her pocket is a pair of gloves! In a plastic bag! Airproof breathproof plastic bag, gloves selling for twenty-five dollars on Branden's counter! In her pocket! Shoplifted! . . . In her purse is a blue comb, not very clean. In her purse is a leather billfold (a birthday present from her grandmother in Philadelphia) with snap-shots of the family in clean plastic windows, in the billfold are bills, she doesn't know how many bills. . . . In her purse is an ominous note from her friend Tykie *What's this about Joe H. and the kids hanging around at Louise's Sat. night? You heard anything?* . . . passed in French class. In her purse is a lot of dirty yellow Kleenex, her mother's heart would break to see such very dirty Kleenex, and at the bottom of her purse are brown hairpins and safety pins and a broken pencil and a ballpoint pen (blue) stolen from somewhere forgotten and a purse-size compact of Cover Girl makeup, Ivory Rose. . . . Her lipstick is Broken Heart, a corrupt pink; her fingers are trembling like crazy; her teeth are beginning to chatter; her insides are alive; her eyes glow in

her head; she is saying to her mother's astonished face *I wanted to steal but not to buy.*

2. At Clarita's. Day or night? What room is this? A bed, a regular bed, and a mattress on the floor nearby. Wallpaper hanging in strips. Clarita says she tore it like that with her teeth. She was fighting a barbaric tribe that night, high from some pills; she was battling for her life with men wearing helmets of heavy iron and their faces no more than Christian crosses to breathe through, every one of those bastards looking like her lover Simon, who seems to breathe with great difficulty through the slits of mouth and nostrils in his face. Clarita has never heard of Sioux Drive. Raymond Forrest cuts no ice with her, nor does the C account and its millions; Harvard Business School could be at the corner of Vernor and Twelfth Street for all she cares, and Vietnam might have sunk by now into the Dead Sea under its tons of debris, for all the amazement she could show . . . her face is overworked, overwrought, at the age of twenty (thirty?) it is already exhausted but fanciful and ready for a laugh. Clarita says mournfully to me *Honey somebody is going to turn you out let me give you warning.* In a movie shown on late-night television Clarita

is not a mess like this but a nurse, with short neat hair and a dedicated look, in love with her doctor and her doctor's patients and their diseases, enamored of needles and sponges and rubbing alcohol. . . . Or no: she is a private secretary. Robert Cummings is her boss. She helps him with fantastic plots, the canned audience laughs, no, the audience doesn't laugh because nothing is funny, instead her boss is Robert Taylor and they are not boss and secretary but husband and wife, she is threatened by a young starlet, she is grim, handsome, wifely, a good companion for a good man. . . . She is Claudette Colbert. Her sister too is Claudette Colbert. They are twins, identical. Her husband Charles Boyer is a very rich handsome man and her sister, Claudette Colbert, is plotting her death in order to take her place as the rich man's wife, no one will know because they are *twins*. . . . All these marvelous lives Clarita might have lived, but she fell out the bottom at the age of thirteen. At the age when I was packing my overnight case for a slumber party at Toni Deshield's she was tearing filthy sheets off a bed and scratching up a rash on her arms. . . . "Thirteen is young for a Caucasian/suburban girl of the Detroit area," Miss Brock of the Detroit House of Corrections said in an interview for the *Detroit News*:

fifteen and sixteen are more common. Yet such "young ages" as eleven and twelve are not uncommon in black girls . . . they are "more precocious." What can we do? Whose fault is it? Taxes are rising even as the city's tax base is falling. The temperature rises slowly but falls rapidly. Everything is falling out the bottom, Woodward Avenue is filthy, Livernois Avenue is filthy! Scraps of paper flutter in the air like pigeons, dirt flies up and hits you right in the eye, oh Detroit is breaking up into dangerous bits of newspaper and dirt, watch out. . . .

Clarita's apartment is over a restaurant. Simon her lover emerges from the cracks at dark. Mrs. Olesko, a neighbor of Clarita's, an aged white wisp of a woman, doesn't complain but sniffs with contentment at Clarita's noisy life and doesn't tell the cops, hating cops, when the cops arrive. I should give more fake names, more blanks, instead of telling all these secrets. I myself am a secret; I am a minor.

3. My father reads a paper at a medical convention in Los Angeles. There he is, on the edge of the North American continent when the unmarked detective put his hand so gently on my arm in the aisle of Branden's and

said, "Miss, would you like to step over here for a minute?"

And where was he when Clarita put her hand on my arm, that wintry dark sulphurous aching day in Detroit, in the company of closed-down barbershops, closed-down diners, closed-down movie houses, homes, windows, basements, faces . . . she put her hand on my arm and said, "Honey, are you looking for somebody down here?"

And was he home worrying about me, gone for two weeks solid, when they carried me off . . . ? It took three of them to get me in the police cruiser, so they said, and they put more than their hands on my arm.

4.   I work on this lesson. My English teacher is Mr. Forest, who is from Michigan State. Not handsome, Mr. Forest, and his name is plain, unlike Raymond Forrest's, but he is sweet and rodentlike, he has conferred with the principal and my parents, and everything is fixed . . . treat her as if nothing has happened, a new start, begin again, only sixteen years old, what a shame, how did it happen?—nothing happened, nothing could have happened, a slight physiological modification known only to a gynecologist or to Dr. Coronet. I work on my lesson. I sit in my pink room. I look around the room with my sad

pink eyes. I sigh, I dawdle, I pause, I eat up time, I am limp and happy to be home, I am sixteen years old suddenly, my head hangs heavy as a pumpkin on my shoulders, and my hair has just been cut by Mr. Faye at the Crystal Salon and is said to be very becoming.

(Simon too put his hand on my arm and said, "Honey, you have got to come with me," and in his six-by-six room we got to know each other. Would I go back to Simon again? Would I lie down with him in all that filth and craziness? Over and over again

a Clarita is being betrayed as in front of a Cunningham Drug Store she is nervously eying a black man who may or may not have money, or a nervous white boy of twenty with sideburns and an Appalachian look, who may or may not have a knife hidden in his jacket pocket, or a husky red-faced man of friendly countenance who may or may not be a member of the vice squad out for an early twilight walk.)

I work on my lesson for Mr. Forest. I have filled up eleven pages. Words pour out of me and won't stop. I want to tell everything . . . what was the song Simon was always humming, and who was Simon's friend in a very new trench coat with an old high school graduation ring on his finger . . . ? Simon's bearded friend? When I was down too low for him, Simon kicked me out and gave me to him for three days, I think, on Fourteenth Street in Detroit, an airy room of cold cruel drafts with newspapers on the floor. . . . Do I really remember that or am I piecing it together from what they told me? Did they tell the truth? Did they know much of the truth?

VIII CHARACTERS

1. Wednesdays after school, at four; Saturday mornings at ten. Mother drives me to Dr. Coronet. Ferns in the office, plastic or real, they look the same. Dr. Coronet is queenly, an elegant nicotine-stained lady who would have studied with Freud had circumstances not prevented it, a bit of a Catholic, ready to offer you some mystery if your teeth will ache too much without it. Highly recommended by Father! Progress! Looking up! Looking better! That new haircut is so becoming, says Dr. Coronet herself, showing how normal she is for a woman with an I.Q. of 180 and many advanced degrees.

2. Mother. A lady in a brown suede coat. Boots of

shiny black material, black gloves, a black fur hat. She would be humiliated could she know that of all the people in the world it is my ex-lover Simon who walks most like her . . . self-conscious and unreal, listening to distant music, a little bowlegged with craftiness. . . .

3.   Father. Tying a necktie. In a hurry. On my first evening home he put his hand on my arm and said, "Honey, we're going to forget all about this."

4.   Simon. Outside, a plane is crossing the sky, in here we're in a hurry. Morning. It must be morning. The girl is half out of her mind, whimpering and vague; Simon her dear friend is wretched this morning . . . he is wretched with morning itself . . . he forces her to give him an injection with that needle she knows is filthy, she has a dread of needles and surgical instruments and the odor of things that are to be sent into the blood, thinking somehow of her father. . . . This is a bad morning, Simon says that his mind is being twisted out of shape, and so he submits to the needle that he usually scorns and bites his lip with his yellowish teeth, his face going very pale. *Ah baby!* he says in his soft mocking voice, which with all women is a mockery

of love, *do it like this—slowly*—and the girl, terrified, almost drops the precious needle but manages to turn it up to the light from the window . . . is it an extension of herself then? She can give him this gift then? *I wish you wouldn't do this to me,* she says, wise in her terror, because it seems to her that Simon's danger—in a few minutes he may be dead—is a way of pressing her against him that is more powerful than any other embrace. She has to work over his arm, the knotted corded veins of his arm, her forehead wet with perspiration as she pushes and releases the needle, staring at that mixture of liquid now stained with Simon's bright blood. . . . When the drug hits him she can feel it herself, she feels that magic that is more than any woman can give him, striking the back of his head and making his face stretch as if with the impact of a terrible sun. . . . She tries to embrace him but he pushes her aside and stumbles to his feet. *Jesus Christ,* he says. . . .

5. Princess, a black girl of eighteen. What is her charge? She is closemouthed about it, shrewd and silent, you know that no one had to wrestle her to the sidewalk to get her in here; she came with dignity. In the recreation room she sits reading *Nancy Drew and the Jewel Box*

Mystery, which inspires in her face tiny wrinkles of alarm and interest: what a face! Light-brown skin, heavy shaded eyes, heavy eyelashes, a serious sinister dark brow, graceful fingers, graceful wristbones, graceful legs, lips, tongue, a sugar-sweet voice, a leggy stride more masculine than Simon's and my mother's, decked out in a dirty white blouse and dirty white slacks; vaguely nautical is Princess's style. . . . At breakfast she is in charge of clearing the table and leans over me, saying, *Honey you sure you ate enough?*

6. The girl lies sleepless, wondering. Why here, why not there? Why Bloomfield Hills and not jail? Why jail and not her pink room? Why downtown Detroit and not Sioux Drive? What is the difference? Is Simon all the difference? The girl's head is a parade of wonders. She is nearly sixteen, her breath is marvelous with wonders, not long ago she was coloring with crayons and now she is smearing the landscape with paints that won't come off and won't come off her fingers either. She says to the matron *I am not talking about anything,* not because everyone has warned her not to talk but because, because she will not talk; because she won't say anything about Simon, who is her secret. And she says to the matron, *I won't go*

home, up until that night in the lavatory when everything was changed. . . . "No, I won't go home I want to stay here," she says, listening to her own words with amazement thinking that weeds might climb everywhere over that marvelous custom-designed house and dinosaurs might return to muddy the beige carpeting, but never never will she reconcile four o'clock in the morning in Detroit with eight-o'clock breakfasts in Bloomfield Hills. . . . oh, she aches still for Simon's hands and his caressing breath, though he gave her little pleasure, he took everything from her (five-dollar bills, ten-dollar bills, passed into her numb hands by men and taken out of her hands by Simon) until she herself was passed into the hands of other men, police, when Simon evidently got tired of her and her hysteria. . . . *No, I won't go home, I don't want to be bailed out.* The girl thinks as a *Stubborn and Wayward Child* (one of several charges lodged against her), and the matron understands her crazy white-rimmed eyes that are seeking out some new violence that will keep her in jail, should someone threaten to let her out. Such children try to strangle the matrons, the attendants, or one another . . . they want the locks locked forever, the doors nailed shut . . . and this girl is no different up until that night her mind is changed for her. . . .

IX THAT NIGHT

Princess and Dolly, a little white girl of maybe fifteen, hardy however as a sergeant and in the House of Corrections for armed robbery, corner her in the lavatory at the farthest sink and the other girls look away and file to bed, leaving her. God, how she is beaten up! Why is she beaten up? Why do they pound her, why such hatred? Princess vents all the hatred of a thousand silent Detroit winters on her body, this girl whose body belongs to me, fiercely she rides across the Midwestern plains on this girl's tender bruised body . . . revenge on the oppressed minorities of America! revenge on the slaughtered Indians! revenge on the female sex, on the male sex, revenge on Bloomfield Hills, revenge revenge. . . .

X DETROIT

In Detroit, weather weighs heavily upon everyone. The sky looms large. The horizon shimmers in smoke. Downtown the buildings are imprecise in the haze. Perpetual haze. Perpetual motion inside the haze. Across the choppy river is the city of Windsor, in Canada. Part of the continent has bunched up here and is bulging outward, at the tip of Detroit; a cold hard rain is forever falling on the expressways. . . . Shoppers shop grimly, their cars are not parked in safe places, their windshields may be smashed and graceful ebony hands may drag them out through their shatterproof smashed windshields, crying, *Revenge for the Indians!* Ah, they all fear leaving Hudson's and being dragged to the very tip of the city and thrown off the parking roof of Cobo Hall, that expensive tomb, into the river. . . .

XI CHARACTERS WE ARE FOREVER ENTWINED WITH

1. Simon drew me into his tender rotting arms and breathed gravity into me. Then I came to earth, weighed down. He said, *You are such a little girl,* and he weighed me down with his delight. In the palms of his hands were teeth marks from his previous life experiences. He was thirty-five, they said. Imagine Simon in this room, in my pink room; he is about six feet tall and stoops slightly, in a feline cautious way, always thinking, always on guard, with his scuffed light suede shoes and his clothes that are anyone's clothes, slightly rumpled ordinary clothes that ordinary

men might wear to not-bad jobs. Simon has fair long hair, curly hair, spent languid curls that are like . . . exactly like the curls of wood shavings to the touch, I am trying to be exact . . . and he smells of unheated mornings and coffee and too many pills coating his tongue with a faint green-white scum . . . Dear Simon, who would be panicked in this room and in this house (right now Billie is vacuuming next door in my parents' room; a vacuum cleaner's roar is a sign of all good things), Simon who is said to have come from a home not much different from this, years ago, flee-ing all the carpeting and the polished banisters . . . Simon has a deathly face, only desperate people fall in love with it. His face is bony and cautious, the bones of his cheeks prominent as if with the rigidity of his ceaseless thinking, plotting, for he has to make money out of girls to whom money means nothing, they're so far gone they can hardly count it, and in a sense money means nothing to him either except as a way of keeping on with his life. *Each Day's Proud Struggle*, the title of a novel we could read at jail. . . . Each day he needs a certain amount of money. He devours it. It wasn't love he uncoiled in me with his hollowed-out eyes and his courteous smile, that remnant of a prosperous past, but a dark terror that needed to press itself against him, or against another man . . . but he was the first, he came over to me and took my arm, a claim. We struggled on the stairs and I said, *Let me loose, you're hurting my neck, my face,* it was such a surprise that my skin hurt where he rubbed it, and afterward we lay face to face and he breathed everything into me. In the end I think he turned me in.

2. Raymond Forrest. I just read this morning that Raymond Forrest's father, the chairman of the board at   , died of a heart attack on a plane bound for London. I would like to write Raymond Forrest a note of sympathy. I would like to thank him for not pressing charges against me one hundred years ago, saving me, being so generous . . . well, men like Raymond Forrest are generous men, not like Simon. I would like to write him a letter telling of my love, or of some other emotion that is positive and healthy. Not like Simon and his poetry, which he scrawled down when he was high and never changed a word . . . but when I try to think of something to say, it is Simon's language that comes back to me, caught in my head like a bad song, it is always Simon's language:

There is no reality only dreams
Your neck may get snapped when you wake
My love is drawn to some violent end
She keeps wanting to get away
My love is heading downward
And I am heading upward
She is going to crash on the sidewalk
And I am going to dissolve into the clouds

XII EVENTS

1. Out of the hospital, bruised and saddened and converted, with Princess's grunts still tangled in my hair . . . and Father in his overcoat looking like a prince himself, come to carry me off. Up the expressway and out north to home. Jesus Christ, but the air is thinner and cleaner here. Monumental houses. Heartbreaking sidewalks, so clean.

2. Weeping in the living room. The ceiling is two stories high and two chandeliers hang from it. Weeping, weeping, though Billie the maid is *probably listening*. I will never leave home again. Never. Never leave home. Never leave this home again, never.

3. Sugar doughnuts for breakfast. The toaster is very shiny and my face is distorted in it. Is that my face?

4. The car is turning in the driveway. Father brings me home. Mother embraces me. Sunlight breaks in movie-land patches on the roof of our traditional-contemporary home, which was designed for the famous automotive stylist whose identity, if I told you the name of the famous car he designed, you would all know, so I can't tell you because my teeth chatter at the thought of being sued . . . or having someone climb into my bedroom window with a rope to strangle me. . . . The car turns up the blacktop drive. The house opens to me like a doll's house, so lovely in the sunlight, the big living room beckons to me with its walls falling away in a delirium of joy at my return, Billie the maid is *no doubt* listening from the kitchen as I burst into tears and the hysteria Simon got so sick of. Convulsed in Father's arms, I say I will never leave again, never, why did I leave, where did I go, what happened, my mind is gone wrong, my body is one big bruise, my backbone was sucked dry, it wasn't the men who hurt me and Simon never hurt me but only those girls . . . my God, how they hurt me . . . I will never leave home again. . . . The car is

perpetually turning up the drive and I am perpetually breaking down in the living room and we are perpetually taking the right exit from the expressway (Lahser Road) and the wall of the rest room is perpetually banging against my head and perpetually are Simon's hands moving across my body and adding everything up and so too are Father's hands on my shaking bruised back, far from the surface of my skin on the surface of my good blue cashmere coat (dry-cleaned for my release). . . . I weep for all the money here, for God in gold and beige carpeting, for the beauty of chandeliers and the miracle of a clean polished gleaming toaster and faucets that run both hot and cold water, and I tell them, *I will never leave home, this is my home, I love everything here, I am in love with everything here. . . .*

I am home.

"SHOT"

Loneliness sharpens the senses. In this new place where her parents had come to work the girl slept poorly and woke each morning at dawn, or before dawn, to a strange noise in the near distance—shouting, or loud singing, or a dog's repetitive hysterical barking. She lay in bed without moving or breathing and without thinking, listening to the sound with its serrated edges, the texture of mica-studded rusty earth, yet there was something moist and eager about it too, a shameless percussive rhythm that could belong to no machine, only to life. The sound called to her, tugged at her bowels. She dreaded it entering her sleep.

Gradually, with morning, other noises intervened. Diesel trucks on the highway bounding the suburban sub-division to the east, construction crews engaged in build-ing new homes close by, bulldozers, chain saws, garbage trucks, jet bombers from the Joshua Tree Air Force Base at the edge of the desert. In the girl's own household there was likely to be uninterrupted quiet since neither her mother nor her father believed in television or radio news or inconsequential chatter in the crucial hour before they left for work but when, the single time the girl inquired of them if they'd heard that strange noise, "off in the distance, like someone calling for help," the noise had faded or ceased or been drowned out by other noises, so her mother said, after listening, or seeming to listen, for perhaps five seconds, that she couldn't hear anything out of the ordinary, and her father, annoyed by the question, but making an effort to be polite, merely smiled, and shook his head no, not having made much of an effort to listen at all. As always his thoughts were elsewhere where no one, not even his wife, was encouraged to follow.

One morning in midsummer when the family had been living in the new house for about a month and the girl was again wakened by the strange sound she decided to track it to its source. Barefoot, in her pajamas, she went downstairs, and stood on the bare concrete terrace at the rear of the house, listening intently, and fixing the sound at approximately eleven o'clock in terms of her position. It could not have been more than a mile away, probably less. That was to the northeast, for the sky was reddening there, quickened with light like an opening eye beyond the dun-colored foothills of the San Bernardino Mountains. This morning the sound was a harsh careless sobbing that grated against the girl's nerves. She thought, *I don't really want to know what it is!*

Her parents left for work at eight o'clock: though they were not assigned to the same project they worked in the same complex of government buildings known locally as the Institute, and they drove together in the same car. Shortly afterward the girl bicycled out of the subdivision, along the coyly curving asphalt drives past stucco ranch houses with Spanish-style roofs and grassless lawns seemingly held in place by spindly trees and shrubs, houses virtually identical with the one the girl's father had bought for them except in color, the positioning of the garage, and the degree of newness and rawness, and as she approached the highway where, now, the diesel trucks were in full force, she could hear the sound only intermittently, like a radio station fading, and returning, and fading again, but she knew she was going in the right direction.

She left San Jacinto Estates and after a little difficulty

crossed the busy highway and pedaled for about a quarter mile along the shoulder until she came to an unpaved road where instinct told her to turn: she hadn't heard the sound for a few minutes but guessed it might be coming from this direction. To her left was a deep irrigation ditch in which, as if grudgingly, brackish water glinted; to her right were shabby little bungalows and tar-paper shanties, places at which it seemed rude to stare, debris strewn about the burned-out yards, hulks of old automobiles and pickup trucks in fields, small children playing in the dirt oblivious of her passing. It was early but the desert-dry air was warming minute by minute. Unlike the light to which the girl had been accustomed, three thousand miles to the east, filtered and softened by pollutants in the air, this light seemed to emanate whitish and glaring from all directions; it rose from the mineral-glinting earth to strike sparks in her eyes. The girl knew that the world through which she moved was composed of structural fictions—ideograms of a kind, her father would have said—for where she saw light, color, texture, solid shapes, where indeed she felt the physicality of solid shapes, and experienced herself as one, there existed nothing but a cascade of ever-shifting and -changing atoms and molecules, substanceless as hieroglyphics on a computer screen, in some mysterious way linked to the rhythms of the human brain; yet, for all her knowing, for all her having been trained to know, she did not somehow believe. You reach out to touch a phantasmal world and your hand goes right through it—*except your hand does not go through it.* That was the small stubborn fact only a baby could utter and the girl, no longer a baby, no longer dared utter it.

Now the sound resumed and the girl heard it for what it was, distinctly: a dog's barking.

A dog's barking!—so commonplace after all.

But there was a special urgency to it. A sound as of words in a nightmare scramble. Where you hear, but can't understand—you understand but you don't *know.*

The girl bicycled to the dead end of the road, drawn by the dog. And there, in the front yard of a clapboard bungalow, in a mean grassless space littered with human debris and dog feces, a dog that might have been a German shepherd, or a husky, or a mixture of each, was tied by a chain leash to a stake: straining at the leash and barking frantically at the girl who had come to stare at him. So this was it! This! The dog was thick-bodied, ungainly, clearly old; with silver-tipped fur covered in dust and grime; wild rheumy-red eyes, a slavering muzzle, sharp yellowed teeth bared in a ferocious grin. He had been a handsome dog once but now suffered from a bad case of the mange, especially around his ears, and there was something raw and red and terrible about his neck. The iron stake to which his chain was affixed had been driven into the ground beside the bungalow's semirotted front stoop, and in the desperate radius of this ten feet the dog had worn the earth into grooves and ruts with his toenails. There was the evidence here of numberless weeks of captivity by night and by day.

"Nice dog! Good dog! Nobody's going to hurt you!" the girl called out weakly. In truth she was frightened that the dog would tear himself loose from his chain and attack her. No more than fifteen feet separated them and there appeared to be no one home in the bungalow—no car in the rutted driveway, no face at any of the windows.

A phrase of the girl's father's came to mind—*The intersection of certain sets is surely empty.*

The girl stared; the dog barked. Where at a distance the barking had had an almost mechanical sound, up close it seemed alive, as sound, twisting and writhing invisibly in the air, wave upon wave of furious indecipherable speech washing against the girl; buffeting her, rocking her with its violence. An immolation of sheer light and noise was about to explode in her brain but the girl could not break away—stood hunched, straddling her bicycle, hands pressed over her ears.

She had traced the mystery to its source but, at its source, the mystery had deepened. Why would a dog's owners, who presumably loved him, or in any case wished him well, tie him up so brutally, and go away, and forget him?—leave him to his animal misery? Did he bark with such fury for hours of the day? With so little provocation? And the neighbors didn't hear, or didn't care, or were reluctant to complain? In the residential neighborhoods the girl knew city police would be called at once if a dog barked this loudly and continuously; in particular, the girl's parents could not have borne it. But a grove of shabby palm trees separated this bungalow from the bungalow next door and maybe, in such a neighborhood, that was sufficient; maybe nobody did hear. In the wide radius of those presumably within earshot—and there must have been many—the girl might have been the only person who heard.

What did it mean, the girl wondered—that a living creature, animal or human, should make such sounds? and that no one cared enough to interfere?

The little one-story house in which the dog's owner or owners lived had been worn to a gray, neutral, weather-ravaged shade. Blinds had been drawn over its windows, some of its clapboards were hanging loose. It was shabby but not one of the shabbier dwellings on the road. The yard was littered with trash, especially in back, as if it was a dumping ground—cartons, food packages, bottles, tin cans—particularly beer cans—but there were several new-looking brightly striped canvas lawn chairs in the shade of the palm trees and a portable aluminum barbecue as splendid as any in San Jacinto Estates.

As if exhausted the dog lay down suddenly in the dirt. He was panting hard; he continued to bark in brief cough-like spasms, but less excitedly; it must have been impressed upon his consciousness, however dim and suspicious, that the girl was no threat. "Nice dog!" she called out, heartened. He *was* an old dog, and clearly in poor health. His long loose wet tongue lolled, dripping saliva; his shoulder and back muscles rippled beneath his coarse, matted fur; his scabby ears were in constant agitation from flies circling his head. There were flies too around the plastic dishes set out for him and in hazy glittering clouds around the feces scattered in the yard—some of the feces dried and desiccated, others fresh. The girl sniffed the air and her face crinkled.

The dog gave a heaving little shudder, stretching out his forelegs as if settling in for sleep, lowering his head, and the girl saw to her horror that the chain had been fastened directly—and tightly—around the dog's neck, not attached to a collar; and that the fur there was eaten away. It looked almost as if the chain had grown into the dog's flesh. . . . There were scabs, ugly-looking wounds, the glisten of fresh blood.

The girl looked quickly away as if she had seen something forbidden but the shock of it ran through her like an electrical charge.

"Hey there—hel*lo!* You looking for me?"

A woman in a housedress had opened the screen door at the side of the bungalow and was leaning out, blinking in the sunshine like a nocturnal animal. Her skin looked white and moist as bread dough and the housedress was wrapped so loosely around her, tied with a sash, that her pale thighs showed, and the shadowy crevice between her breasts. She was staring at the girl and both frowning and smiling. She might have been any age from thirty to fifty.

"You looking for me?" she repeated.

"No," said the girl shyly. "I just—"

"You live up the road, huh? But I don't guess I know your name?"

The girl stood straddling her bicycle, smiling in confusion. She wanted badly to escape but feared it would seem rude, with the woman looking so intently at her, and now smiling, as if they were indeed neighbors. And there was the dog.

"You live up the road? Where d'you live?" the woman asked, stepping outside. She was attractive, with long untidy glistening black hair like an Indian's or a Mexican's; her face shone as if it had been scrubbed with steel wool and her eyes too shone, with an unnatural, alert brightness, like chunks of charcoal embedded in her white face. "What's your name?"

"Donna."

"Oh yes? Donna, is it? Did I maybe know that?"

The girl continued to smile, perplexed. "Donna" was the name of a girl friend of hers, back east. "I don't know," she said.

"I see you and Shot have been making friends," the woman said. "That's nice." In the direct sunshine it looked as if an older, finely wrinkled face had been pressed atop a young, harshly good-looking face like that of a Hollywood actress of the old days. She smiled repeatedly, strangely, with an elastic sort of enthusiasm. "C'mon closer, Donna! You can pet him. Pet poor Shot."

"Oh—is that his name? 'Shot'?" the girl asked.

The woman picked her way barefoot—her stubby-toed feet were very white, like her face—through the dog droppings and broken glass and pebbles, and squatted dramatically beside the dog, hugging him suddenly with feeling and crooning to him. The dog yipped and whimpered with pleasure and licked her hands and face with his tongue, his body quivered with joy. His long dirt-encrusted tail thumped against the packed earth. The girl stared and felt a small stab of envy. She asked again, "His name is 'Shot'?"

"*Buck*shot!" The woman laughed. "My husband's weird idea. But—it got shortened."

"What kind of a dog is he? A German shepherd?"

"He sure ain't a cocker spaniel or one of them little tiny wiener dogs, are you, Shot?" The woman clumsily straddled the dog's back, hugging him around the neck and playing at riding him. "Giddyup, Shot! Hey!

Giddyup!" She was in a mood bright and electric and way-ward such as the girl had never witnessed in an adult. "Want to pet Shot, Donna? Want to *ride* him? He won't bite, I promise."

"Oh, I don't think so," the girl said, smiling uncertainly.

"He won't bite—he's crazy about kids. Just give him a little pet on the head." The woman rubbed the dog's skull rather brusquely with her knuckles. He whimpered and thrashed about with pleasure. *"C'mon!"*

Summoned thus, the girl had no choice but to obey. She laid her bicycle down carefully in the driveway and approached the woman and the dog and reached out shyly to touch the dog's alert, quivering, high-held head. Did she hear growling?—a sound as of tiny pebbles grating deep in the dog's throat? "Shot, be *good*," the woman scolded. "Donna's a neighbor from up the road. She's a friend!"

The dog's fur was coarser than the girl would have imagined, like wire beneath her fingertips; and without warmth. The raw strip like a necklace around the dog's neck glistened with fresh blood. The girl felt slightly ill, seeing it. She did not understand why the woman took no notice. She said, "His neck—it's hurt?"

The woman said, "Oh—that's nothing. That's 'cause he's a bad boy pulling at his leash all the time." She kissed the dog's nose with a bit of fuss and got to her feet, swaying. A close stale powdery odor wafted from her. Through the opening of the rayon housedress the girl could see, without wishing to see, one of the woman's loose heavy vein-riddled breasts.

The girl said uncertainly, "It must hurt him, though—where it's bleeding? He might get blood poisoning, or gangrene?"

"Naw!" the woman said contemptuously.

The dog was staring up alertly at the girl, his lips drawn back from his yellow teeth. He barked loudly once, twice, then made a whimpering noise and busily licked the girl's fingers. Never in her life had a dog licked her fingers: how wet, how loose and soft, like a chamois cloth, that tongue! It was a shock too to see, close up, the dog's eyes. They were reddened and filmed over with moisture, there were clots of mucus in the corners, but, still, they were beautiful eyes—you could see it, up close. Brimming with passion, with something like thinking, yearning, willing.

The girl said, "But it must hurt him, around the neck there. He must feel pain."

"Naw, dogs don't feel pain," the woman said. Then laughed, relenting, "Or if they do they don't *say*."

The girl swallowed hard and persisted. "You keep him tied up all the time too I guess and he's lonely and barks and—"

"You wouldn't be the party up the road who's trying to make trouble for us, would you?" the woman asked pleasantly.

"Oh no," the girl said. "Actually I don't live—"

"Threatening to call the police and like that? The SPC fucking A?"

"Oh no."

"Look: this dog is my heart," the woman said feelingly, as if there might be some doubt. "When my husband left the last thing he said was, 'You keep Shot for protection,' and I said, 'Protection from what?' and he said, 'Protection from me.'" She laughed loudly and squeezed the girl's hand as if urging her to laugh, too. "You have to hand it to the sons of bitches—men! They always get the last word."

The girl smiled, embarrassed. She could think of no reply.

"You're maybe the daughter of those people?" the woman asked, peering into the girl's face. She was still squeezing the girl's hand and showed no inclination to release it.

"What people?"

"You know."

"What—what people?"

The woman continued to peer into the girl's face, for a long unnerving moment. Her eyes were very black and shiny but appeared to have no pupil, nor had she lashes, or eyebrows except for a thin stubbly arch—it looked as if she'd plucked them out. Excitement like phosphoresence played about her damp fleshy lips. "A person has got to have her dignity. If you take away a person's dignity you know what you got left? A pile of shit."

The girl tugged discreetly at her hand but the woman did not release it.

"Telling other people what to do—that's dangerous," the woman said. She spoke now in surges, quickly, and then slowly, as if she was making an effort to hold herself back. "That's how you get your head blowed off, some places. Say I know I got some problems but I don't need nobody else to tell me about them. Say I know Shot barks a lot 'cause he's excitable and the kids in the neighborhood tease him, throwing stones and shit, and he's tied up like he is 'cause I work, I work weird hours, I'm a beautician by profession and the only work I can get is part-time around here 'cause this is where I fucking ended up 'cause I made a wrong decision I didn't know was a wrong decision at the time so what do you want me to do about it—cut my throat? He left and that isn't enough he takes the car and he says he's coming back and I'm asshole enough to believe him but in the meantime like you can see I don't have no car which means I have to take the fucking bus or get a ride with somebody and now the telephone's out too for back payments and there's these self-righteous fuckers like your mommy and daddy I guess who think I got money to throw around?—money to burn?—money grows on trees and I just reach up and pick it?—like taking Shot to the vet when I fucking need the vet *myself* and I can't afford it and there's these things I need from the drugstore I can't afford and before the phone went out I got these weird calls keeping me up half the night and somebody broke glass all out front here and stuck razor blades in the dirt so I'd walk on them barefoot like I'm so trusting like I am—" Her voice had been spiraling like a singer's and now she broke off, breathing hard, considering. Her eyes were narrowed in shrewdness. She was leaning so close to the girl that the girl could feel her warm moist panting breath and taste its rankness. "Like I said—Shot's my *heart*. He's all I *got*. He forgives me anything 'cause he loves me. He doesn't judge! If I gave the command you know what he'd do, you stupid little cunt? He'd tear out your throat."

The girl stood perfectly still. The dog, nudging at her knees, was alternately barking and whining, snarling and whimpering. His long tail thumped from side to side. The woman said slyly, "D'you know what that command is, Donna?"

The girl licked her cold lips. "No."

"Huh? *Don't* you?"

"No."

"D'you want me to tell you, then?" the woman asked. "'Cause if I say it out loud—!"

Sick with fear the girl shut her eyes. She was trembling violently, thinking, *This is a mistake—this can't be happening. How do I know that this is me? How do I know that this is—now?*

"No," the girl whispered.

"Say what?"

"No, *please*."

"'No, *please!*' That's how it is, huh? Stupid little cunt

butting your nose in other people's business!" With a little shove the woman released the girl, but the girl did not dare make a move to escape. The dog was nudging against their legs in a display of frantic energy; doing a little dance in the dirt. He yipped, he whined, short staccato barks burst from him like bronchial coughing. In dreamlike terror the girl felt his damp nose and slavering mouth against her bare knees, nudged into the crotch of her shorts. How passionately he sniffed, as if sniffing were eyesight, or a kind of speech. . . . The woman was saying, in derision, "Go on, little girl—*go*. Get the hell back home."

The girl backed away. Her knees nearly buckled beneath her. The dog sprang forward, almost knocking her over, standing urgently on his hind legs, barking, whimpering, seeming to plead with her to take him with her. Until finally the girl was safely out of the radius of his chain and free of him, and the woman, hands on her thighs, looked her up and down in mean delight and said, "You know what? You're not even pretty. *You'll have to make your way somehow else.*"

She fled, she returned home.
And she did telephone the SPCA. And the local police.

And whether they came to the woman's house at the end of the dirt road and saved Shot from his misery, or made any difference at all in the dog's life, she didn't know; she kept her windows closed in the morning and kept her air-conditioning unit on. It was hot weather, in any case.

Often, she heard dogs barking. In the distance.

Any number of dogs. For the world was filled with barking dogs after all.

WHY DON'T YOU
COME LIVE WITH ME
IT'S TIME

The other day, it was a sunswept windy March morning, I saw my grandmother staring at me, those deep-socketed eyes, that translucent skin, a youngish woman with very dark hair as I hadn't quite remembered her, who had died while I was in college, years ago, in 1966. Then I saw—of course it was virtually in the same instant—I saw the face was my own, my own eyes in that face floating there not in a mirror but in a metallic mirrored surface, teeth bared in a startled smile, and seeing my face that was not my face I laughed; I think that was the sound.

You're an insomniac, you tell yourself: there are profound truths revealed only to the insomniac by night like those phosphorescent minerals veined and glimmering in the dark but coarse and ordinary otherwise; you have to examine such minerals in the absence of light to discover their beauty, you tell yourself.

Maybe because I was having so much trouble sleeping at the time, twelve or thirteen years old, no one would have called the problem insomnia, that sounds too clinical, too adult, and anyway they'd said, "You can sleep if you try," and I'd overheard, "She just wants attention—you know what she's like," and I was hurt and angry but hopeful too, wanting to ask, But what am I like, are you the ones to tell me?

In fact, Grandmother had insomnia too—"suffered from insomnia" was the somber expression—but no one made the connection between her and me. Our family was that way: worrying that one weakness might find justification in another and things would slip out of containment and control.

In fact, I'd had trouble sleeping since early childhood but I had not understood that anything was wrong. Not secrecy nor even a desire to please my parents made me pretend to sleep; I thought it was what you do: I thought when Mother put me to bed I had to shut my eyes so she could leave and that was the way of releasing her, though immediately afterward when I was alone my eyes opened wide and sleepless. Sometimes it was day, sometimes night. Often by night I could see, I could discern the murky shapes of objects, familiar objects that had lost their names by night, as by night lying motionless with no one to observe me it seemed I had no name and my body was shapeless and undefined. The crucial thing was to lie motionless, scarcely breathing, until at last—it might be minutes or it might be hours; if there were noises in the house or out on the street (we lived on a busy street for most of my childhood in Hammond) it would be hours— a dark pool of warm water would begin to lap gently over my feet, eventually it would cover my legs, my chest, my face. . . . What adults called "sleep," this most elusive and strange and mysterious of experiences, a cloudy trans- parency of ever-shifting hues and textures surrounded tense islands of wakefulness, so during the course of a night I would sleep and wake and sleep and wake a dozen times, as the water lapped over my face and retreated from it; this seemed altogether natural, it was altogether desir- able, for when I slept another kind of sleep, heavily, deeply, plunged into a substance not water and not a transparency but an oozy lightless muck, when I plunged down into that sleep and managed to wake from it shivering and sweating with a pounding heart and a pounding head as if my brain trapped inside my skull (but "brain" and "skull" were not concepts I would have known, at that time) had been racing feverishly like a small machine gone berserk, it was to a sense of total helplessness and an exhaustion so profound it felt like death: sheer nonexistence, oblivion; and I did not know, nor do I know now, decades later, which sleep is preferable, which sleep is normal, how is one defined by sleep, from where in fact does "sleep" arise.

When I was older, a teenager, with a room at a little distance from my parents' bedroom, I would often, those sleepless nights, simply turn on my bedside lamp and read; I'd read until dawn and day and the resumption of daytime routine in a state of complete concentration, or sometimes I'd switch on the radio close beside my bed—I was cautious of course to keep the volume low, low and secret— and I'd listen fascinated to stations as far away as Pittsburgh, Toronto, Cleveland; there was a hillbilly station broadcasting out of Cleveland, country-and-western music I would never have listened to by day. One by one I got to

know intimately the announcers' voices along the contin-
uum of the glowing dial; hard to believe those strangers
didn't know *me*. But sometimes my room left me short of
breath; it was fresh air I craved: hurriedly I'd dress, pulling
on clothes over my pajamas, and even in rainy or cold
weather I went outside, leaving the house by the kitchen
door so quietly in such stealth no one ever heard, not once
did one of them hear—*I will do it: because I want to do it*—
sleeping their heavy sleep that was like the sleep of mol-
lusks, eyeless. And outside, in the night, the surprise of the
street transformed by the lateness of the hour, the emptiness, the silence: I'd walk to the end of our driveway, staring, listening, my heart beating hard. *So this is—what it is!*
The ordinary sights were made strange: the sidewalks, the
streetlights, the neighboring houses. Yet the fact had no
consciousness of itself except through *me*.

For that has been one of the principles of my life.

And if here and there along the block a window
glowed from within (another insomniac?), or if a lone car
passed in the street casting its headlights before it, or a
train sounded in the distance, or, high overhead, an air-
plane passed, winking and glittering with lights, what happiness swelled my lungs, what gratitude, what conviction; I

was utterly alone for the moment, and invisible, which is identical with being alone.

Come by any time, dear, no need to call first, my grandmother said often. *Come by after school, any time, please!* I tried not to hear the pleading in her voice, tried not to see the soft hurt in her eyes, and the hope.

Grandmother was a "widow": her husband, my step-grandfather, had died of cancer of the liver when I was five years old.

Grandmother had beautiful eyes: deep-set, dark, intelligent, alert. And her hair was a lovely silvery gray, not coarse like others' hair but finespun, silky.

Mother said, "In your grandmother's eyes you can do no wrong." She spoke as if amused but I understood the accusation.

Because Grandmother loved me best of the grandchildren, yes, and she loved me best of all the family; I basked in her love as in the warmth of a private sun. Grandmother loved me without qualification and without criticism, which angered my parents since they understood that so fierce a love made me impervious to their more modulated love, not only impervious but indifferent to the threat of its being withdrawn . . . which is the only true power parents have over their children, isn't it?

We visited Grandmother often, especially now she was alone. She visited us: Sundays, holidays, birthdays. And I would bicycle across the river to her house once or twice a week or drop in after school. Grandmother encouraged me to bring my friends but I was too shy, I never stayed long; her happiness in my presence made me uneasy. Always she would prepare one of my favorite dishes—hot oatmeal with cream and brown sugar, apple cobbler, brownies, fudge, lemon custard tarts—and I sat and ate as she watched, and, eating, I felt hunger; the hunger was in my mouth. To remember those foods brings the hunger back now, the sudden rush of it, the pain. In my mouth.

At home Mother would ask, "Did you spoil your appetite again?"

The river that separated us was the Cassadaga, flowing from east to west, to Lake Ontario, through the small city of Hammond, New York. After I left, aged eighteen, I only returned to Hammond as a visitor. Now that everyone is dead, I never go back.

The bridge that connected us was the Ferry Street

bridge, the bridge we crossed hundreds of times. Grandmother lived south of the river (six blocks south, two blocks west), we lived north of the river (three blocks north, one and a half blocks east); we were about three miles apart. The Ferry Street bridge, built in 1919, was one of those long narrow spiky nightmare bridges; my childhood was filled with such bridges, this one thirty feet above the Cassadaga, with high arches, steep ramps on both sides, six concrete supports, rusted iron grillwork, and neoclassical ornamentation of the kind associated with Chicago commercial architecture, which was the architectural style of Hammond generally.

The Ferry Street bridge. Sometimes in high winds you could feel the bridge sway. I lowered my eyes when my father drove us over; he'd joke as the plank floor rattled and beneath the rattling sound there came something deeper and more sinister, the vibrating hum of the river itself, a murmur, a secret caress against the soles of our feet, our buttocks, and between our legs, so it was an enormous relief when the car had passed safely over the bridge and descended the ramp to land. The Ferry Street bridge was almost too narrow for two ordinary-sized automobiles to pass but only once was my father forced to stop about a quarter of the way out: a gravel truck was bearing down upon us and the driver gave no sign of slowing down so my father braked the car, threw it hurriedly into reverse, and backed up red-faced the way we'd come, and after that the Ferry Street bridge was no joke to him, any more than it was to his passengers.

The other day, that sunny gusty day when I saw Grandmother's face in the mirror, I mean the metallic mirrored surface downtown, I mean the face that had seemed to be Grandmother's face but was not, I began to think of the Ferry Street bridge and since then I haven't slept well; seeing the bridge in my mind's eye the way you do when you're insomniac, the images that should be in dreams are loosed and set careening through the day like lethal bubbles in the blood. I had not known how I'd memorized that bridge, and I'd forgotten why.

The time I am thinking of, I was twelve or thirteen years old; I know I was that age because the Ferry Street bridge was closed for repairs then and it was over the Ferry Street bridge I went, to see Grandmother. I don't remember if it was a conscious decision or if I'd just started walking, not knowing where I was going, or why. It was three o'clock in the morning. No one knew where I was. Beyond the barricade and the DETOUR—BRIDGE OUT signs, the moon was so bright it lit my way like a manic face.

A number of times I'd watched with trepidation certain of the neighborhood boys inch their way out across the steel beams of the skeletal bridge, walking with arms extended for balance, so I knew it could be done without mishap, I knew I could do it if only I had the courage, and it seemed to me I had sufficient courage; now was the time to prove it. Below, the river rushed past slightly higher than usual; it was October, there had been a good deal of rain; but tonight the sky was clear, stars like icy pinpricks, and that bright glaring moon illuminating my way for me so I thought *I will do it*, already climbing up onto what would be the new floor of the bridge when at last it was completed: not planks but a more modern sort of iron mesh, not yet laid into place. But the steel beams were about ten inches wide and there was a grid of them, four beams spanning the river and (I would count them as I crossed; I would never forget that count) fourteen narrower beams at perpendicular angles with the others, and about three feet below these beams there was a complex crisscrossing of cables you might define as a net of sorts if you wanted to think in such terms, a safety net; there was no danger really, *I will do it because I want to do it, because there is no one to stop me.*

And on the other side, Grandmother's house. And even if its windows were darkened, even if I did no more than stand looking quietly at it and then come back home, never telling anyone what I'd done, even so I would have proven something *because there is no one to stop me*, which has been one of the principles of my life. To regret the principle is to regret my entire life.

I climbed up onto one of the beams, trembling with excitement. But how cold it was! I'd come out without my gloves.

And how loud the river below, the roaring like a kind of jeering applause, and it smelled too, of something brackish and metallic. I knew not to glance down at it, steadying myself as a quick wind picked up, teasing tears into my eyes; I was thinking, *There is no turning back: never*, but instructing myself too that the beam was perfectly safe if I was careful for had I not seen boys walking across without slipping? Didn't the workmen walk across too, many times a day? I decided not to stand, though—I was afraid to stand—I remained squatting on my haunches, gripping the edge of the beam with both hands, inching forward in this awkward way, hunched over, right foot and then left foot and then right foot and then left foot, passing the first of the perpendicular beams, and the second, and the third, and the fourth, and so in this clumsy and painful fashion forcing myself to continue until my thigh muscles ached so badly I had to stop and I made the mistake—which even in that instant I knew was a mistake—of glancing down, seeing the river thirty feet below: the way it was flowing so swiftly and with such power and seeming rage, ropy sinuous coils of churning water, foam-flecked, terrible, and its flow exactly perpendicular to the direction in which I was moving.

"Oh, no. Oh, no. Oh, no."

A wave of sharp cold terror shot up into me as if into my very bowels, piercing me between the legs rising from the river itself, and I could not move; I squatted there on the beam unable to move, all the strength drained out of my muscles, and I was paralyzed, knowing, *You're going to die: of course, die,* even as with another part of my mind (there is always this other part of my mind) I was thinking with an almost teacherly logic that the beam *was* safe, it was wide enough, and flat enough, and not damp or icy or greasy, yes certainly it *was* safe. If this was land, for instance in our backyard, if for instance my father had set down a plank flat in the grass, a plank no more than half the width of the beam, couldn't I, Claire, have walked that plank without the lightest tremor of fear? boldly? even gracefully? even blindfolded? without a moment's hesitation? not the flicker of an eyelid, not the most minute leap of a pulse? *You know you aren't going to die: don't be silly,* but it must have been five minutes before I could force myself to move again, my numbed right leg easing forward, my aching foot; I forced my eyes upward too and fixed them resolutely on the opposite shore, or what I took on faith to be the opposite shore, a confusion of sawhorses and barrels and equipment now only fitfully illuminated by the moon.

But I got there; I got to where I meant to go without for a moment exactly remembering why.

Now the worst of it's done: for now.

Grandmother's house, what's called a bungalow, plain stucco, one-story, built close to the curb, seemed closer to the river than I'd expected. Maybe I was running, desperate to get there, hearing the sound of the angry rushing water that was like many hundreds of murmurous voices, and the streets surprised me with their emptiness—so many vacant lots, murky transparencies of space where buildings had once stood—and a city bus passed silently, lit gaily from within, yet nearly empty too, only the driver and single (male) passenger sitting erect and motionless as mannequins, and I shrank panicked into the shadows so they would not see me; maybe I would be arrested: a girl of my age on the street at such an hour, alone, with deep-set frightened eyes, a pale face, guilty mouth, zip-up corduroy jacket, and jeans over her pajamas, disheveled as a runaway. But the bus passed, turned a corner, and vanished. And there was Grandmother's house, not darkened as I'd expected but lighted, and from the sidewalk staring I could see Grandmother inside, or a figure I took to be Grandmother, but why was she awake at such an hour? How remarkable that she should be awake as if awaiting me, and I remembered then—how instantaneously these thoughts came to me, eerie as tiny bubbles that, bursting, yielded riches of a sort that would require a considerable expenditure of time to relate though their duration was in fact hardly more than an instant!—I remembered having heard the family speak of Grandmother's sometimes strange behavior, worrisome behavior in a woman of her age or of any age; the problem was her insomnia unless insomnia was not cause but consequence of a malady of the soul. So it would be reported back to my father, her son, that she'd been seen walking at night in neighborhoods unsafe for solitary women, she'd been seen at a midnight showing of a film in downtown Hammond, and even when my step-grandfather was alive (he worked on a lake freighter, he was often gone) she might spend time in local taverns, not drinking heavily but drinking, and this was behavior that might lead to trouble, or so the family worried, though there was never any specific trouble so far as anyone knew, and Grandmother smoked too, smoked on the street, which "looks cheap," my mother said, my mother too smoked but never on the street. The family liked to tell and retell the story of a cousin of my father's coming to Hammond on a Greyhound bus, arriving at the station at about six in the morning, and there in the waiting room was my grandmother in her old fox-fur coat sitting there with a book in her lap, a cigarette in one hand, just sitting there placidly and with no mind for the two or three others, distinctly odd, near-derelict men, in the room with her, just sitting there reading her book (Grandmother was always reading, poetry, biographies of great men like Lincoln, Mozart, Julius Caesar, Jesus of Nazareth), and my father's cousin came in, saw her, said, "Aunt Tina, what on earth are you doing here?" and Grandmother had looked up calmly and said, "Why not? It's for waiting, isn't it?"

Another strange thing Grandmother had done—it had nothing to do with her insomnia that I could see, unless all our strangenesses, as they are judged in others' eyes, are morbidly related—was arranging for her husband's body to be cremated, not buried in a cemetery plot but cremated, which means burned to mere ash, which means annihilation, and though cremation had evidently been my stepgrandfather's wish it had seemed to the family that Grandmother had complied with it too readily, and so immediately following her husband's death that no one had a chance to dissuade her. "What a thing," my mother said, shivering, "to do to your own husband!"

I was thinking of this now, seeing through one of the windows a man's figure, a man talking with Grandmother in her kitchen; it seemed to me that perhaps my stepgrandfather had not yet died, thus was not cremated, and some of the disagreement might be resolved; but I must have already knocked at the door since Grandmother was there opening it. At first she stared at me as if scarcely recognizing me; then she laughed, she said, "What are *you* doing here?" and I tried to explain but could not, the words failed to come; my teeth were chattering with cold and fright and the words failed to come, but Grandmother led me inside, she was taller than I remembered and younger, her hair dark, wavy, falling to her shoulders, and her mouth red with lipstick; she laughed, leading me into the kitchen where a man, a stranger, was waiting. "Harry, this is my granddaughter Claire," Grandmother said, and the man stepped forward, regarding me with interest yet speaking of me as if I was somehow not present: "She's your granddaughter?" "She is." "I didn't know you had a granddaughter." "You don't know lots of things."

And Grandmother laughed at us both, who gazed in perplexity and doubt at each other. Laughing, she threw her head back like a young girl, or a man, and bared her strong white teeth.

I was then led to sit at the kitchen table in my usual place, Grandmother went to the stove to prepare something for me, and I sat quietly, not frightened yet not quite at ease though I understood I was safe now, Grandmother would take care of me now, and nothing could happen. I saw that the familiar kitchen had been altered; it was very brightly lit, almost blindingly lit, yet deeply shadowed in the corners; the rear wall where the sink should have been dissolved into what would have been the backyard but I had a quick flash of the backyard, where there were flower and vegetable beds. Grandmother loved to work in the yard, she brought flowers and vegetables in the summer wherever she visited; the most beautiful of her flowers were peonies, big gorgeous crimson peonies, and the thought of the peonies was confused with the smell of the oatmeal Grandmother was stirring on the stove for me to eat. Oatmeal was the first food of my childhood, the first food I can remember, but Grandmother made it her own way, her special way, stirring in brown sugar, cream, a spoonful of dark honey so just thinking of it I felt my mouth water violently; almost it hurt, the saliva flooded so, and I was embarrassed that a trickle ran down my chin and I couldn't seem to wipe it off and Grandmother's friend Harry was watching me, but finally I managed to wipe it off on my fingers, and Harry smiled.

The thought came to me, not a new thought but one I'd had for years, but now it came with unusual force, like the saliva flooding my mouth, that when my parents died I would come live with Grandmother—of course, I would come live with Grandmother—and Grandmother at the stove stirring my oatmeal in a pan must have heard my thoughts, for she said, "Claire, why don't you come live with me, it's time, isn't it?" and I said, "Oh, yes," and Grandmother didn't seem to have heard for she repeated her question, turning now to look at me, to smile, her eyes shining and her mouth so amazingly red, two delicate spots of rouge on her cheeks so my heart caught, seeing how beautiful she was, as young as my mother or younger, and she laughed, saying, "Claire, why don't you come live with me, it's time, isn't it?" and again I said, "Oh, yes, Grandmother," nodding and blinking tears from my eyes; they were tears of infinite happiness, and relief: "Oh, Grandmother, *yes.*"

Grandmother's friend Harry was a navy radio operator, he said, or had been; he wore no uniform and he was no age I could have guessed, with silvery-glinting hair in a crew cut, muscular shoulders and arms, but maybe his voice was familiar? maybe I'd heard him over the radio? Grandmother was urging him to tell me about the universe, distinctly she said those odd words, "Why don't you tell Claire about the universe," and Harry stared at me frowning and said, "Tell Claire what about the universe?" and Grandmother laughed and said, "Oh—anything!" and Harry said, shrugging, "Hell, I don't know," then, raising his voice, regarding me with a look of compassion: "The universe goes back a long way, I guess. Ten billion years? Twenty billion? Is there a difference? They say it got started with an explosion, and in a second—well, really a fraction of a second—a tiny bit of tightness got flung out; it's fly-ing out right now, expanding"—he drew his hands, broad stubby hands, dramatically apart—"and most of it is emptiness, I guess, whatever 'emptiness' is. It's still expand-ing, all the pieces flying out; there's a billion galaxies like ours, or maybe a billion billion galaxies like ours, but don't worry, it goes on forever even when we die—" but at this Grandmother turned sharply; sensing my reaction, she said, "Oh, dear, don't tell the child *that*, don't frighten poor little Claire with *that*."

"You told me to tell her about the—"

"Oh, just *stop*."

Quickly Grandmother came to hug me, settled me into my chair as if I was a much smaller child sitting there at the kitchen table, my feet not touching the floor; and there was my special bowl, the bowl Grandmother kept for me, sparkling yellow with lambs running around the rim; yes, and my special spoon too, a beautiful silver spoon with the initial C engraved on it which Grandmother kept polished, so I understood I was safe, nothing could harm me; Grandmother would not let anything happen to me so long as I was there. She poured my oatmeal into my dish; she was saying, "It's true we must all die one day, darling, but not just yet, you know, not tonight, you've just come to visit, haven't you, dear? and maybe you'll stay? maybe you won't ever leave? *now it's time?*"

The words *it's time* rang with a faint echo.

I can hear them now: *it's time: time.*

Grandmother's arms were shapely and attractive, her skin pale and smooth and delicately translucent as a candled egg, and I saw that she was wearing several rings, the wedding band that I knew but others, sparkling with light, and there so thin were my arms beside hers, my hands that seemed so small, sparrow sized, and my wrists so bony, and it came over me, the horror of it, that meat and bone should define my presence in the universe; the point of entry in the universe that was *me* that was *me* that was *me*, and no other, yet of a fragile materiality that any fire could consume. "Oh, Grandmother—I'm so afraid!" I whimpered, seeing how I would be burned to ash, and Grandmother comforted me, and settled me more securely into the chair, pressed my pretty little spoon between my fingers, and said, "Darling, don't think of such things, just *eat*. Grandmother made this for *you*."

I was eating the hot oatmeal, which was a little too hot, but creamy as I loved it; I was terribly hungry, eating like an infant at the breast so blindly my head bowed and eyes nearly shut, rimming with tears, and Grandmother asked, *Is it good? Is it good?*—she'd spooned in some dark honey too—*Is it good?* and I nodded mutely; I could taste grains of brown sugar that hadn't melted into the oatmeal, stark as bits of glass, and I realized they were in fact bits of glass, some of them large as grape pits, and I didn't want to hurt Grandmother's feelings but I was fearful of swallowing the glass so as I ate I managed to sift the bits through the chewed oatmeal until I could maneuver it into the side of my mouth into a little space between my lower right gum and the inside of my cheek, and Grandmother was watching, asking *Is it good?* and I said, "Oh, yes," half choking and swallowing, "oh, *yes*."

A while later when neither Grandmother nor Harry

was watching I spat out the glass fragments into my hand but I never knew absolutely, I don't know even now, if they were glass and not for instance grains of sand or fragments of eggshell or even bits of brown sugar crystalized into such a form not even boiling oatmeal could dissolve it.

I was leaving Grandmother's house; it was later, time to leave. Grandmother said, "But aren't you going to stay?" and I said, "No, Grandmother, I can't," and Grandmother said, "I thought you were going to stay, dear," and I said, "No, Grandmother, I can't," and Grandmother said, "But why?" and I said, "I just can't," and Grandmother said, laughing so her laughter was edged with annoyance, "Yes, but *why?*" Grandmother's friend Harry had disappeared from the kitchen, there was no one in the kitchen but Grandmother and me, but we were in the street too, and the roaring of the river was close by, so Grandmother hugged me a final time and gave me a little push, saying, "Well, good night, Claire," and I said apologetically, "Good night, Grandmother," wondering if I should ask her not to say anything to my parents about this visit in the middle of the night, and she was backing away, her dark somber gaze fixed upon me half in reproach. "Next time you visit Grandmother you'll stay, won't you? Forever?" and I said, "Yes, Grandmother," though I was very frightened, and as soon as I was out of Grandmother's sight I began to run.

At first I had a hard time finding the Ferry Street bridge. Though I could hear the river close by; I can always hear the river close by.

Eventually, I found the bridge again. I know I found the bridge; otherwise how did I get home? That night?

LIFE AFTER HIGH SCHOOL

"Sunny? Sun-ny?"

On that last night of March 1959, in soiled sheepskin parka, unbuckled overshoes, but bare-headed in the lightly falling snow, Zachary Graff, eighteen years old, six feet one and a half inches tall, weight 203 pounds, IQ 160, stood beneath Sunny Burhman's second-story bedroom window, calling her name softly, urgently, as if his very life depended upon it. It was nearly midnight: Sunny had been in bed for a half hour, and woke from a thin dissolving sleep to hear her name rising mysteriously out of the dark, low, gravelly, repetitive as the surf. "*Sun*-ny—?" She had not spoken with Zachary Graff since the previous week, when she'd told him, quietly, tears shining in her eyes, that she did not love him; she could not accept his engagement ring, still less marry him. This was the first time in the twelve weeks of Zachary's pursuit of her that he'd dared to come to the rear of the Burhmans' house, by day or night; the first time, as Sunny would say afterward, he'd ever appealed to her in such a way.

They would ask, In what way?

Sunny would hesitate, and say, So—emotionally. In a way that scared me.

So you sent him away?

She did. She'd sent him away.

It was much talked of, at South Lebanon High School, how, in this spring of their senior year, Zachary Graff, who had never to anyone's recollection asked a girl out before, let alone pursued one so publicly and with such clumsy devotion, seemed to have fallen in love with Sunny Burhman.

Of all people—Sunny Burhman.

Odd too that Zachary should seem to have discovered Sunny, when the two had been classmates in the South Lebanon, New York, public schools since first grade, back in 1947.

Zachary, whose father was Homer Graff, the town's

preeminent physician, had, since ninth grade, cultivated a clipped, mock-gallant manner when speaking with female classmates: his Clifton Webb style. He was unfailingly courteous, but unfailingly cool; measured; formal. He seemed impervious to the giddy rise and ebb of adolescent emotion, moving, clumsy but determined, like a grizzly bear on its hind legs, through the school corridors, rarely glancing to left or right: *his* gaze, its myopia corrected by lenses encased in chunky black plastic frames, was firmly fixed on the horizon. Dr. Graff's son was not unpopular so much as feared, thus disliked.

If Zachary's excellent academic record continued uninterrupted through final papers, final exams, and there was no reason to suspect it would not, Zachary would be valedictorian of the Class of 1959. Barbara ("Sunny") Burhman, later to distinguish herself at Cornell, would graduate only ninth, in a class of eighty-two.

Zachary's attentiveness to Sunny had begun, with no warning, immediately after Christmas recess, when classes resumed in January. Suddenly, a half dozen times a day, in Sunny's vicinity, looming large, eyeglasses glittering, there Zachary *was*. His Clifton Webb pose had dissolved, he was shy, stammering, yet forceful, even bold, waiting for the advantageous moment (for Sunny was always surrounded by friends) to push forward and say, "Hi, Sunny!" The greeting, utterly commonplace in content, sounded, in Zachary's mouth, like a Latin phrase tortuously translated.

Sunny, so named for her really quite astonishing smile, that dazzling white Sunny smile that transformed a girl of conventional freckled snub-nosed prettiness to true beauty, might have been surprised, initially, but gave no sign, saying, "Hi, Zach!"

In those years, the corridors of South Lebanon High School were lyric crossfires of *Hi!* and *H'lo!* and *Good to see ya!* uttered hundreds of times daily by the golden girls, the popular, confident, good-looking girls, club officers, prom queens, cheerleaders like Sunny Burhman and her friends, tossed out indiscriminately, for that was the style.

Most of the students were in fact practicing Christians, of Lutheran, Presbyterian, Methodist stock.

Like Sunny Burhman, who was, or seemed, even at the time of this story, too good to be true.

That's to say—*good*.

So, though Sunny soon wondered why on earth Zachary Graff was hanging around her, why, again, at her elbow, or lying in wait for her at the foot of a stairs, why, for the nth time that week, *him,* she was too *good* to indicate impatience, or exasperation; too *good* to tell him, as her friends advised, to get lost.

He telephoned her too. Poor Zachary. Stammering over the phone, his voice lowered as if he was in terror of being overheard, "Is S-Sunny there, Mrs. B-Burhman? May I speak with her, please?" And Mrs. Burhman, who knew Dr. Graff and his wife, of course, since everyone in South Lebanon, population 3,800, knew everyone else or knew of them, including frequently their family histories and facts about them of which their children were entirely unaware, hesitated, and said, "Yes, I'll put her on, but I hope you won't talk long—Sunny has homework tonight." Or, apologetically but firmly: "No, I'm afraid she isn't here. May I take a message?"

"N-no message," Zachary would murmur, and hurriedly hang up.

Sunny, standing close by, thumbnail between her just perceptibly gap-toothed front teeth, expression crinkled in dismay, would whisper, "Oh Mom. I feel so *bad.* I just feel so—*bad.*"

Mrs. Burhman said briskly, "You don't have time for all of them, honey."

Still, Zachary was not discouraged, and with the swift passage of time it began to be observed that Sunny engaged in conversations with him—the two of them sitting, alone, in a corner of the cafeteria, or walking together after a meeting of the Debate Club, of which Zachary was president and Sunny a member. They were both on the staff of the South Lebanon High *Beacon*, and the South Lebanon High Yearbook 1959, and the South Lebanon *Torch* (the literary magazine). They were both members of the National Honor Society and the Quill & Scroll Society. Though Zachary Graff in his aloofness and impatience with most of his peers would be remembered as antisocial, a "loner," in fact, as his record of activities suggested, printed beneath his photograph in the yearbook, he had time, or made time, for things that mattered to him.

He shunned sports, however. High school sports, at least.

His life's game, he informed Sunny Burhman, unaware of the solemn pomposity with which he spoke, would be *golf*. His father had been instructing him, informally, since his twelfth birthday.

Said Zachary, "I have no natural talent for it, and I find it profoundly boring, but golf will be my game." And he pushed his chunky black glasses roughly against the bridge of his nose, as he did countless times a day, as if they were in danger of sliding off.

Zachary Graff had such a physical presence, few of his contemporaries would have described him as unattractive, still less homely, ugly. His head appeared oversized, even for his massive body; his eyes were deep-set, with a look of watchfulness and secrecy; his skin was tallow colored, and blemished, in wavering patches like topographical maps. His big teeth glinted with filaments of silver, and his breath, oddly for one whose father was a doctor, was stale, musty, cobwebby—not that Sunny Burhman ever alluded to this fact, to others.

Her friends began to ask of her, a bit jealously, reproachfully, "What do you two talk about so much?— you and *him*?" and Sunny replied, taking care not to hint, with the slightest movement of her eyebrows, or rolling of her eyes, that, yes, she found the situation peculiar too, "Oh—Zachary and I talk about all kinds of things. *He* talks, mainly. He's brilliant. He's"—pausing, her forehead delicately crinkling in thought, her lovely brown eyes for a moment clouded—"well, *brilliant*."

In fact, at first, Zachary spoke, in his intense, obsessive

way, of impersonal subjects: the meaning of life, the future of Earth, whether science or art best satisfies the human hunger for self-expression. He said, laughing nervously, fixing Sunny with his shyly bold stare, "Just to pose certain questions is, I guess, to show your hope they can be answered."

Early on, Zachary seemed to have understood that, if he expressed doubt, for instance about "whether God exists" and so forth, Sunny Burhman would listen seriously; and would talk with him earnestly, with the air of a nurse giving a transfusion to a patient in danger of expiring for loss of blood. She was not a religious fanatic, but she *was* a devout Christian—the Burhmans were members of the First Presbyterian Church of South Lebanon, and Sunny was president of her youth group, and, among other good deeds, did YWCA volunteer work on Saturday afternoons; she had not the slightest doubt that Jesus Christ, that's to say His spirit, dwelled in her heart, and that, simply by speaking the truth of what she believed, she could convince others.

Though one day, and soon, Sunny would examine her beliefs, and question the faith into which she'd been born; she had not done so by the age of seventeen and a half. She was a virgin, and virginal in all, or most, of her thoughts.

Sometimes, behind her back, even by friends, Sunny was laughed at, gently—never ridiculed, for no one would ridicule Sunny.

Once, when Sunny Burhman and her date and another couple were gazing up into the night sky, standing in the parking lot of the high school, following a prom, Sunny had said in a quavering voice, "It's so big it would be terrifying, wouldn't it?—except for Jesus, who makes us feel at home."

When popular Chuck Crueller, a quarterback for the South Lebanon varsity football team, was injured during a game, and carried off by ambulance to undergo emergency surgery, Sunny mobilized the other cheerleaders, tears fierce in her eyes, "We can do it for Chuck—we can *pray*." And so the eight girls in their short-skirted crimson jumpers and starched white cotton blouses had gripped one another's hands tight, weeping, on the verge of hysteria, had prayed, prayed, *prayed*—hidden away in the depths of the girls' locker room for hours. Sunny had led the prayers, and Chuck Crueller recovered.

So you wouldn't ridicule Sunny Burhman, somehow it wouldn't have been appropriate.

As her classmate Tobias Shanks wrote of her, as one of his duties as literary editor of the 1959 South Lebanon Yearbook: *"Sunny" Burhman!—an all-American girl too good to be true who is nonetheless TRUE!*

If there was a slyly mocking tone to Tobias Shanks's praise, a hint that such goodness was predictable, and superficial, and of no genuine merit, the caption, mere print, beneath Sunny's dazzlingly beautiful photograph, conveyed nothing of this.

Surprisingly, for all his pose of skepticism and superiority, Zachary Graff too was a Christian. He'd been baptized Lutheran, and never failed to attend Sunday services with his parents at the First Lutheran Church. Amid the congregation of somber, somnambulant worshippers, Zachary Graff's frowning young face, the very set of his beefy shoulders, drew the minister's uneasy eye; it would be murmured of Dr. Graff's precocious son, in retrospect, that he'd been perhaps too *serious.*

Before falling in love with Sunny Burhman, and discussing his religious doubts with her, Zachary had often discussed them with Tobias Shanks, who'd been his friend, you might say his only friend, since seventh grade. (But only sporadically since seventh grade, since the boys, each highly intelligent, inclined to impatience and sarcasm, got on each other's nerves.) Once, Zachary confided in Tobias that he prayed every morning of his life—immediately upon waking he scrambled out of bed, knelt, hid his face in his hands, and prayed. For his sinful soul, for his sinful thoughts, deeds, desires. He lacerated his soul the way he'd been taught by his mother to tug a fine-toothed steel comb through his coarse, oily hair, never less than once a day.

Tobias Shanks, a self-professed agnostic since the age of fourteen, laughed, and asked derisively, "Yes, but what do you pray *for*, exactly?" and Zachary had thought a bit, and said, not ironically, but altogether seriously, "To get through the day. Doesn't everyone?"

This melancholy reply Tobias was never to reveal.

Zachary's parents were urging him to go to Muhlenberg College, which was church affiliated; Zachary hoped to go elsewhere. He said, humbly, to Sunny Burhman, "If you go to Cornell, Sunny, I—maybe I'll go there too?"

Sunny hesitated, then smiled. "Oh. That would be nice."

"You wouldn't mind, Sunny?"

"Why would I *mind*, Zachary?" Sunny laughed, to hide her impatience. They were headed for Zachary's car, parked just up the hill from the YM-YWCA building. It was a gusty Saturday afternoon in early March. Leaving the YWCA, Sunny had seen Zachary Graff standing at the curb, hands in the pockets of his sheepskin parka, head lowered, but eyes nervously alert. Standing there, as if accidentally.

It was impossible to avoid him, she had to allow him to drive her home. Though she was beginning to feel panic, like darting tongues of flame, at the prospect of Zachary Graff always *there*.

Tell the creep to get lost, her friends counseled. Even her nice friends were without sentiment regarding Zachary Graff.

Until sixth grade, Sunny had been plain little Barbara Burhman. Then, one day, her teacher had said, to all the class, in one of those moments of inspiration that can alter, by whim, the course of an entire life, "Tell you what, boys and girls—let's call Barbara 'Sunny' from now on—that's what she *is*."

Ever afterward, in South Lebanon, she was "Sunny" Burhman. Plain little Barbara had been left behind, seemingly forever.

So, of course, Sunny could not tell Zachary Graff to get lost. Such words were not part of her vocabulary.

Zachary owned a plum-colored 1956 Plymouth, which other boys envied—it seemed to them distinctly unfair that Zachary, of all people, had his own car, when so few of them, who loved cars, did. But Zachary was oblivious of their envy, as, in a way, he seemed oblivious of his own good fortune. He drove the car as if it was an adult duty, with middle-aged fussiness and worry. He drove the car as if he was its own chauffeur. Yet, driving Sunny home, he talked—chattered—continuously. Speaking of college, and of religious "obligations," and of his parents' expectations of him; speaking of medical school; the future; the life—"beyond South Lebanon."

He asked again, in that gravelly, irksomely humble voice, if Sunny would mind if he went to Cornell. And Sunny said, trying to sound merely reasonable, "Zachary, it's a *free world*."

Zachary said, "Oh no it isn't, Sunny. For some of us, it isn't."

This enigmatic remark Sunny was determined not to follow up.

Braking to a careful stop in front of the Burhmans'

house, Zachary said, with an almost boyish enthusiasm, "So—Cornell? In the fall? We'll both go to Cornell?"

Sunny was quickly out of the car before Zachary could put on the emergency brake and come around, ceremoniously, to open her door. Gaily, recklessly, infinitely relieved to be out of his company, she called back over her shoulder, "Why not?"

Sunny's secret vanity must have been what linked them.

For several times, gravely, Zachary had said to her, "When I'm with you, Sunny, it's possible for me to believe."

He meant, she thought, in God. In Jesus. In the life hereafter.

The next time Zachary maneuvered Sunny into his car, under the pretext of driving her home, it was to present the startled girl with an engagement ring.

He'd bought the ring at Stern's Jewelers, South Lebanon's single good jewelry store, with money secretly withdrawn from his savings account; that account to which, over a period of more than a decade, he'd deposited modest sums with a painstaking devotion. This was his "college fund," or had been—out of the $3,245 saved, only $1,090 remained. How astonished, upset, furious his parents would be when they learned—Zachary hadn't allowed himself to contemplate.

The Graffs knew nothing about Sunny Burhman. So far as they might have surmised, their son's frequent absences from home were nothing out of the ordinary—he'd always spent time at the public library, where his preferred reading was reference books. He'd begin with Volume One of an encyclopedia and make his diligent way through each successive volume, like a horse grazing a field, rarely glancing up, uninterested in his surroundings.

"Please—will you accept it?"

Sunny was staring incredulously at the diamond ring, which was presented to her, not in Zachary's big clumsy fingers, with the dirt-edged nails, but in the plush-lined little box, as if it might be more attractive that way, more like a gift. The ring was 24-karat gold and the diamond was small but distinctive, and coldly glittering. A beautiful ring, but Sunny did not see it that way.

She whispered, "Oh. Zachary. Oh *no*—there must be some misunderstanding."

Zachary seemed prepared for her reaction, for he said, quickly, "Will you just try it on?—see if it fits?"

Sunny shook her head. No she couldn't.

"They'll take it back to adjust it, if it's too big," Zachary said. "They promised."

"Zachary, no," Sunny said gently. "I'm so sorry."

Tears flooded her eyes and spilled over onto her cheeks.

Zachary was saying, eagerly, his lips flecked with spittle, "I realize you don't l-love me, Sunny, at least not yet, but—you could wear the ring, couldn't you? Just—wear it?" He continued to hold the little box out to her, his hand visibly shaking. "On your right hand, if you don't want to wear it on your left? Please?"

"Zachary, no. That's impossible."

"Just, you know, as a, a gift—? Oh Sunny—"

They were sitting in the plum-colored Plymouth, parked, in an awkwardly public place, on Upchurch Avenue three blocks from Sunny's house. It was four twenty-five P.M., March 26, a Thursday: Zachary had lingered after school in order to drive Sunny home after choir practice. Sunny would afterward recall, with an odd haltingness, as if her memory of the episode was blurred with tears, that, as usual, Zachary had done most of the talking. He had not argued with her, nor exactly begged, but spoke almost formally, as if setting out the basic points of his debating strategy: If Sunny did not love him, he could love enough for both; and, If Sunny did not want to be "officially" engaged, she could wear his ring anyway, couldn't she?

It would mean so much to him, Zachary said.

Life or death, Zachary said.

Sunny closed the lid of the little box, and pushed it from her, gently. She was crying, and her smooth pageboy was now disheveled. "Oh Zachary, I'm *sorry*. I *can't*."

Sunny knelt by her bed, hid her face in her hands, prayed.

Please help Zachary not to be in love with me. Please help me not to be cruel. Have mercy on us both O God.

O God help him to realize he doesn't love me—doesn't know me.

Days passed, and Zachary did not call. If he was absent from school, Sunny did not seem to notice.

Sunny Burhman and Zachary Graff had two classes together, English and physics; but, in the busyness of

Sunny's high school life, surrounded by friends, mesmerized by her own rapid motion as if she was lashed to the prow of a boat bearing swiftly through the water, she did not seem to notice.

She was not a girl of secrets. She was not a girl of stealth. Still, though she had confided in her mother all her life, she did not tell her mother about Zachary's desperate proposal; perhaps, so flattered, she did not acknowledge it as desperate. She reasoned that if she told either of her parents they would telephone Zachary's parents immediately. I can't betray him, she thought.

Nor did she tell her closest girl friends, or the boy she was seeing most frequently at the time, knowing that the account would turn comical in the telling, that she and her listeners would collapse into laughter, and this too would be a betrayal of Zachary.

She happened to see Tobias Shanks, one day, looking oddly at *her*. That boy who might have been twelve years old, seen from a short distance. Sunny knew that he was, or had been, a friend of Zachary Graff's; she wondered if Zachary confided in him; yet made no effort to speak with him. He didn't like her, she sensed.

No, Sunny didn't tell anyone about Zachary and the

engagement ring. Of all sins, she thought, betrayal is surely the worst.

"Sunny? Sun-ny?"

She did not believe she had been sleeping but the low, persistent, gravelly sound of Zachary's voice penetrated her consciousness like a dream voice—felt, not heard.

Quickly, she got out of bed. Crouched at her window without turning on the light. Saw, to her horror, Zachary down below, standing in the shrubbery, his large head uplifted, face round like the moon, and shadowed like the moon's face. There was a light, damp snowfall; blossomlike clumps fell on the boy's broad shoulders, in his matted hair. Sighting her, he began to wave excitedly, like an impatient child.

"Oh. Zachary. My God."

In haste, fumbling, she put on a bulky-knit ski sweater over her flannel nightgown, kicked on bedroom slippers, hurried downstairs. The house was already darkened; the Burhmans were in the habit of going to bed early. Sunny's only concern was that she could send Zachary away without her parents knowing he was there. Even in her distress she was not thinking of the trouble Zachary might make for her: she was thinking of the trouble he might make for himself.

Yet, as soon as she saw him close up, she realized that something was gravely wrong. Here was Zachary Graff—yet not Zachary.

He told her he had to talk with her, and he had to talk with her now. His car was parked in the alley, he said.

He made a gesture as if to take her hand, but Sunny drew back. He loomed over her, his breath steaming. She could not see his eyes.

She said no she couldn't go with him. She said he must go home, at once, before her parents woke up.

He said he couldn't leave without her, he had to talk with her. There was a raw urgency, a forcefulness, in him, that Sunny had never seen before, and that frightened her.

She said no. He said yes.

He reached again for her hand, this time taking hold of her wrist.

His fingers were strong.

"I told you—I can love enough for both!"

Sunny stared up at him, for an instant mute, paralyzed, seeing not Zachary Graff's eyes but the lenses of his glasses, which appeared, in the semidark, opaque. Large snowflakes were falling languidly, there was no wind. Sunny saw Zachary Graff's face, which was pale and clenched as a muscle, and she heard his voice, which was the voice of a stranger, and she felt him tug at her so roughly her arm was strained in its very socket, and she cried, "No! no! go away! no!"—and the spell was broken, the boy gaped at her another moment, then released her, turned, and ran.

No more than two or three minutes had passed since Sunny unlocked the rear door and stepped outside, and Zachary fled. Yet afterward, she would recall the encounter as if it had taken a very long time, like a scene in a protracted and repetitive nightmare.

It would be the last time Sunny Burhman saw Zachary Graff alive.

Next morning, all of South Lebanon talked of the death of Dr. Graff's son Zachary: he'd committed suicide by parking his car in a garage behind an unoccupied house on Upchurch Avenue, and letting the motor run until the gas tank was emptied. Death was diagnosed as the result of carbon monoxide poisoning, the time estimated at approximately four thirty A.M. of April 1, 1959.

Was the date deliberate?—Zachary had left only a single note behind, printed in firm block letters and taped to the outside of the car windshield:

APRIL FOOL'S DAY 1959

TO WHOM IT MAY (OR MAY NOT) CONCERN:

I, ZACHARY A. GRAFF, BEING OF SOUND
MIND & BODY, DO HEREBY DECLARE THAT
I HAVE TAKEN MY OWN LIFE OF MY OWN
FREE WILL & I HEREBY DECLARE ALL
OTHERS GUILTLESS AS THEY ARE
IGNORANT OF THE DEATH OF THE
AFOREMENTIONED & THE LIFE.

(SIGNED)
ZACHARY A. GRAFF

Police officers, called to the scene at seven forty-five A.M., reported finding Zachary, lifeless, stripped to his underwear, in the rear seat of the car; the sheepskin parka was oddly draped over the steering wheel, and the interior of the car was, again oddly, for a boy known for his fastidious habits, littered with numerous items: a Bible, several high school textbooks, a pizza carton and some uneaten crusts of pizza, several empty Pepsi bottles, an empty bag of M&M's candies, a pair of new, unlaced gym shoes (size eleven), a ten-foot length of clothesline (in the glove compartment), and the diamond ring in its plush-lined little box from Stern's Jewelers (in a pocket of the parka).

Sunny Burhman heard the news of Zachary's suicide before leaving for school that morning, when a friend telephoned. Within earshot of both her astonished parents, Sunny burst into tears, and sobbed, "Oh my God—it's my fault."

So the consensus in South Lebanon would be, following the police investigation, and much public speculation, not that it was Sunny Burhman's fault, exactly, not that the girl was to blame, exactly, but, yes, poor Zachary Graff, the doctor's son, had killed himself in despondency over her: her refusal of his engagement ring, her rejection of his love.

That was the final season of her life as "Sunny" Burhman.

She was out of school for a full week following Zachary's death, and, when she returned, conspicuously paler, more subdued, in all ways less sunny, she did not speak, even with her closest friends, of the tragedy; nor did anyone bring up the subject with her. She withdrew her name from the balloting for the senior prom queen, she withdrew from her part in the senior play, she dropped out of the school choir, she did not participate in the annual statewide debating competition—in which, in previous years, Zachary Graff had excelled. Following her last class of the day she went home immediately, and rarely saw her friends on weekends. Was she in mourning?—or was she simply ashamed? Like the bearer of a deadly virus, herself unaffected, Sunny knew how, on all sides, her classmates and her teachers were regarding her: She was the girl for whose love a boy had thrown away his life, she was an unwitting agent of death.

Of course, her family told her that it wasn't her fault that Zachary Graff had been mentally unbalanced.

Even the Graffs did not blame her—or said they didn't.

Sunny said, "Yes. But it's my fault he's dead."

The Presbyterian minister, who counseled Sunny, and

prayed with her, assured her that Jesus surely understood, and that there could be no sin in *her*—it wasn't her fault that Zachary Graff had been mentally unbalanced. And Sunny replied, not stubbornly, but matter-of-factly, sadly, as if stating a self-evident truth, "Yes. But it's my fault he's dead."

Her older sister, Helen, later that summer, meaning only well, said, in exasperation, "Sunny, when are you going to cheer *up?*" and Sunny turned on her with uncharacteristic fury, and said, "Don't call me that idiotic name ever again!—I want it *gone!*"

When in the fall she enrolled at Cornell University, she was "Barbara Burhman."

She would remain "Barbara Burhman" for the rest of her life.

Barbara Burhman excelled as an undergraduate, concentrating on academic work almost exclusively; she went on to graduate school at Harvard, in American studies; she taught at several prestigious universities, rising rapidly through administrative ranks before accepting a position, both highly paid and politically visible, with a well-known research foundation based in Manhattan. She was the author of numerous books and articles; she was married, and the mother of three children; she lectured widely, she was frequently interviewed in the popular press, she lent her name to good causes. She would not have wished to think of herself as extraordinary—in the world she now inhabited, she was surrounded by similarly active, energetic, professionally engaged men and women—except in recalling as she sometimes did, with a mild pang of nostalgia, her old, lost self, sweet "Sunny" Burhman of South Lebanon, New York.

She hadn't been queen of the senior prom. She hadn't even continued to be a Christian.

The irony had not escaped Barbara Burhman that, in casting away his young life so recklessly, Zachary Graff had freed her for hers.

With the passage of time, grief had lessened. Perhaps in fact it had disappeared. After twenty, and then twenty-five, and now thirty-one years, it was difficult for Barbara, known in her adult life as an exemplar of practical sense, to feel a kinship with the adolescent girl she'd been, or that claustrophobic high school world of the late 1950s. She'd never returned for a single reunion. If she thought of

Zachary Graff—about whom, incidentally, she'd never told her husband of twenty-eight years—it was with the regret with which we think of remote acquaintances, lost to us by accidents of fate. Forever, Zachary Graff, the most brilliant member of the class of 1959 of South Lebanon High, would remain a high school boy, trapped, aged eighteen.

Of that class, the only other person to have acquired what might be called a national reputation was Tobias Shanks, now known as T. R. Shanks, a playwright and director of experimental drama; Barbara Burhman had followed Tobias' career with interest, and had sent him a telegram congratulating him on his most recent play, which went on to win a number of awards, dealing, as it did, with the vicissitudes of gay life in the 1980s. In the winter of 1990 Barbara and Tobias began to encounter each other socially, when Tobias was playwright-in-residence at Bard College, close by Hazelton-on-Hudson where Barbara lived. At first they were strangely shy of each other; even guarded; as if, in even this neutral setting, their South Lebanon ghost-selves exerted a powerful influence. The golden girl, the loner. The splendidly normal, the defiantly "odd." One night Tobias Shanks, shaking Barbara Burhman's hand, had smiled wryly, and said, "It *is*

Sunny, isn't it?" and Barbara Burhman, laughing nervously, hoping no one had overheard, said, "No, in fact it isn't. It's Barbara."

They looked at each other, mildly dazed. For one saw a small-boned but solidly built man of youthful middle age, sweet-faced, yet with ironic, pouched eyes, thinning gray hair, and a close-trimmed gray beard; the other saw a woman of youthful middle age, striking in appearance, impeccably well-groomed, with fading hair of no distinctive color and faint, white, puckering lines at the edges of her eyes. Their ghost-selves *were* there—not aged, or not aged merely, but transformed, as the genes of a previous generation are transformed by the next.

Tobias stared at Barbara for a long moment, as if unable to speak. Finally he said, "I have something to tell you, Barbara. When can we meet?"

Tobias Shanks handed the much-folded letter across the table to Barbara Burhman, and watched as she opened it, and read it, with an expression of increasing astonishment and wonder.

"*He* wrote this? Zachary? To you?"

"He did."

"And you—? Did you—?"

Tobias shook his head.

His expression was carefully neutral, but his eyes swam suddenly with tears.

"We'd been friends, very close friends, for years. Each other's only friend, most of the time. The way kids that age can be, in certain restricted environments—kids who aren't what's called 'average' or 'normal.' We talked a good deal about religion—Zachary was afraid of hell. We both liked science fiction. We both had very strict parents. I suppose I might have been attracted to Zachary at times—I knew I was attracted to other guys—but of course I never acted upon it; I wouldn't have dared. Almost no one dared, in those days." He laughed, with a mild shudder. He passed a hand over his eyes. "I couldn't have *loved* Zachary Graff as he claimed he loved me, because—I couldn't. But I could have allowed him to know that he wasn't sick, crazy, 'perverted' as he called himself in that letter." He paused. For a long painful moment Barbara thought he wasn't going to continue. Then he said, with that same mirthless shuddering laugh, "I could have made him feel less lonely. But I didn't. I failed him. My only friend."

Barbara had taken out a tissue, and was dabbing at her eyes.

She felt as if she'd been dealt a blow so hard she could not gauge how she'd been hurt—if there was hurt at all.

She said, "Then it hadn't ever been 'Sunny'—she was an illusion."

Tobias said thoughtfully, "I don't know. I suppose so. There was the sense, at least as I saw it at the time, that, yes, he'd chosen you; decided upon you."

"As a symbol."

"Not just a symbol. We all adored you—we were all a little in love with you." Tobias laughed, embarrassed. "Even me."

"I wish you'd come to me and told me, back then. After—it happened."

"I was too cowardly. I was terrified of being exposed, and, maybe, doing to myself what he'd done to himself. Suicide is so very attractive to adolescents." Tobias paused, and reached over to touch Barbara's hand. His fingertips were cold. "I'm not proud of myself, Barbara, and I've tried to deal with it in my writing, but—that's how I was, back then." Again he paused. He pressed a little harder against Barbara's hand. "Another thing—after Zachary went to you, that night, he came to me."

"To you?"

"To me."

"And—?"

"And I refused to go with him too. I was furious with him for coming to the house like that, risking my parents discovering us. I guess I got a little hysterical. And he fled."

"He fled."

"Then, afterward, I just couldn't bring myself to come forward. Why I saved that letter, I don't know—I'd thrown away some others that were less incriminating. I suppose I figured—no one knew about me, everyone knew about you. 'Sunny' Burhman."

They were at lunch—they ordered two more drinks— they'd forgotten their surroundings—they talked.

After an hour or so Barbara Burhman leaned across the table, as at one of her professional meetings, to ask, in a tone of intellectual curiosity, "What do you think Zachary planned to do with the clothesline?"

CAPRICORN

This guy shows up at the tennis courts late Friday afternoon, I figure he must be Capricorn. My cousin Steff is unaware of him, she's in her crouch waiting for me to serve, saying, with that nervous giggle of hers, "Don't serve so hard, Melanie? Please?" The idea is I'm helping Steff learn tennis while she's visiting this summer, not beating her. It's just that sometimes I forget, my racquet takes on a life of its own.

So I'm demonstrating to Steff how to serve. This part of tennis is her weakness: she messes up, gets demoralized, messes up more, wants to quit, I have to cajole her into trying again, and maybe she does okay for a while, and then she messes up again. . . . "Practice. All you need is practice." (Maybe this is true, and maybe not. But Steff is eager to believe.) But I'm nervous, now. Seeing this guy watching us. Third day this week I've seen him drifting by to watch Steff and me play, I mean I think it's the same guy. In the chat room last night I inquired *Capricorn I: was that you today you-know-where?* and his reply was *Capricorn II: if you ask you already know.* Which gave me a shiver, it was so cool. I mean, it said everything and it said nothing, right?

Eight weeks, six days Capricorn I and Capricorn II have been corresponding on the Internet. Some of our exchange has been pretty serious (about whether life has any actual meaning or just what people try to tell you), and some of it is more fun (our favorite bands, movies this summer, all-time movie-best lists, things we hate, people in our lives we wish we could kill!, etc.), and for me it's educational, you can learn so much from an older, smart, and thoughtful guy like Capricorn, things you can't from anybody your own age. But meeting Capricorn, that's something different. I guess I'm a little scared, or anyway nervous. If Steff wasn't here, I'd run away. (I think.) On the Web I have this cool, calm attitude, but in actual life I can get excited pretty easily and say the wrong thing. So I try to be extra-cool, in my actual life. Like now. Trying not to choke having to serve with not only Steff staring at me with her face crinkled like a child's, fearful I will slam the ball directly at her (which I guess I have done a few times, but not on purpose), but this Brad Pitt–cool guy in dark sunglasses, this utter stranger from Land's End, Long Island (which was how Capricorn identified himself online back in March, though there is no Land's End at the tip of the Island, I checked), watching me, too. Twining his fingers through the wire mesh of the fence.

Not that I'm looking at him of course. But I'm aware of him in the corner of my eye like something throbbing there.

My first serve, I'm shaky, I connect with the ball too hard and too high and it flies over Steff's head and bounces harmlessly off the fence. Embarrassing! My second serve is better, it's dynamite, like my dad taught me, a low serve but damn it skims the top of the net, falls and bounces in the most vulnerable way, and only poor Steff lunging and swinging her racquet wildly could mess up the return. So it's my point, but my face is burning. I'm ashamed.

Steff calls out the score, like a good pupil. "Fifteen-love."

I call over to her, "Okay. Let's get serious."

Earlier in the week when this guy showed up at the tennis courts, I mean I think he's the same person (about five foot nine, sort of ropey-muscled, dark hair, and those sexy dark glasses and a white T-shirt and khakis), he only just watched Steff and me for maybe ten minutes, then turned and walked away abruptly. (I felt so bad. I guess we bored him.) I wasn't even sure if he was Capricorn I. He gave me no sign, or signal. Of course, I ignored him, too. I mean, I'd been ignoring him all along. Like I had no idea who he was or even if anybody was standing there. See, it was never definite that Capricorn I would show up at the park. It was more like a dare. I never provided an actual address. I mean, Capricorn I knows the suburb I live in. And he knows there's a Juniper Hills Memorial Park. And at the park there are tennis courts. And I'd be playing about this time with my girl cousin on one of those courts. I didn't tell Capricorn I my actual name of course, you never tell your name, but for some reason (who knows why, online I do lots of weird things) I said *Maybe I'm Ponytail. Or maybe not.* I did hint I was a "big busty girl" mature for my age, sixteen-going-on-nineteen with "yellow hair" and "long legs." And "other hidden attributes" too.

In fact I am fourteen, with ordinary brown hair, pretty

ordinary features, five foot four, not-long legs. But I am unusually mature for my age, you could say I am fourteen-going-on-nineteen.

It's my cousin Stephanie Klaff who's the big busty blonde, with the ponytail halfway down her back, sort of a messy straggly ponytail today, but Steff herself is good-looking, almost you might say gorgeous, with a heart-shaped face and large blue eyes guys are always gaping at, but Steff is so shy, or so unaware, she never looks back. She's fifteen, and immature for her age. She's from Plattsburgh, upstate New York, near the Canadian border and even talks funny: some words, like "car"—"far"— "house"—you can hardly comprehend, it's like her nose is stuffed up. Steff's mother—at least this is my mom's theory—has made her think she's clumsy, even homely. She does have big feet she's self-conscious of: size 11C, which in white tennis shoes is, well, *big*. (My feet are size 6.) Steff stammers a little, sometimes. If she sees you're listening, she gets red in the face and forgets what she's saying. Steff is okay, don't misunderstand. She's not my type but she's definitely okay to visit for a few weeks while her mom, who is my mom's messed-up former-alcoholic older sister, tries to straighten out marital problems in godforsaken Plattsburgh, New York, where they live. My real friends are mostly away for the summer so this is fine. I've known my cousin since we were little, but never well until the past few years when she came sometimes to stay with us during the summer. She's so sweet and slow sometimes you'd think she was mildly retarded but she isn't. Her grades in school are okay. Steff is just kind of clumsy, a blonde of that type you expect to be dumb and usually is. She must weigh 135 pounds, her bra size is 36C. Her body, which guys practically drool over, she tries to hide in clothes like the loose tank top she's wearing and the white sailcloth shorts at least two sizes too big. Even my mom smiled at Steff, saying her clothes looked a little large compared to what other girls wore, and poor Steff just blushed in that way of hers and couldn't think of a reply so I stepped in quick like I have a way of doing and said, "That's the way they dress in Canada, Mom. It's cool." And Steff never caught on this was a joke, and probably Mom didn't either.

"Okay, Steff. Your turn."

So Steff serves, and her balls are easy to return, so I can glance over at this guy leaning against the fence looking cool, giving nothing away. I keep my face tight as a mask so he can't guess. (Which of us, Steff or Melanie, is Capricorn II? He's looking mostly at Steff.) On the Web when I was LONELYGIRL and first met Capricorn I had the idea from something he said he was born in the mid-1970s (which would make him about twenty-six) but I don't think so. He's older.

Anyway I prefer older men. And older men prefer me. My vocabulary, my sense of humor. My "attitude" and "philosophy of life." *Wise beyond your years* Capricorn I praised me just the other night. *You must be lonely there. Nobody to talk to. I know what that is.*

Later Capricorn I said, *When the stars are in conjunction these two lone Capricorns must meet.*

So I said yes, maybe. At the tennis courts. Maybe.

(I know, people say not to hook up with individuals on the Web. As if you couldn't figure out a creep or a con man for yourself. I know I can.)

So Steff is serving, and I'm returning the ball nice and easy so Steff can hit it back, swinging and lunging and managing to connect. Frankly this is more fun than winning, for me. Steff is like a beautiful big sheep dog or something I've trained, and am showing off for Capricorn I. *See? I'm in control here. Not Ponytail.*

(He's watching. Gripping the fence with both hands, and his chin pressed against the wire mesh. Mostly I can see just the sunglasses, covering half his face.)

"Good shot, Steff," I call to her, when Steff surprises me and makes me run to the back left corner of the court, and miss her lucky shot. Steff is embarrassed to make the point, saying, "Oh, well. The sun's in your eyes, Melanie. I'm sorry."

I'm almost sarcastic, saying, "Sorry, why? You didn't put the sun in the sky, did you?"

But definitely Steff is improving. I'm proud of my accomplishment. By the time she returns to Plattsburgh she'll be an okay tennis player.

It's then I realize, seeing her eyes shift, *She sees him. He's watching her so hard, she sees him too.*

"Hey girls: terrific game."

When we take a break, hot and sweaty, right away he comes over. My heart gives a kick but I don't let on. I have a kind of closed-in sulky look, my mom calls my bulldog look, that comes over me when I'm nervous. Steff reacts to being nervous by smiling which is what she does now, when this dark-haired stranger comes up to us and compliments us on our game. (He's kidding of course. "Terrific game"!) Steff stammers something about just learning, like she has to explain at once why she isn't a better player, almost she's apologizing, and Capricorn comes up close to her, like he already knows her. He's casual, as if he's only just walking through the park, happening to see us play tennis. I was right about his height, he's just a little taller than Steff, and definitely he's older than twenty-five. Steff is smiling and blinking at him as if (I can see her mind working) this friendly individual is someone associated with the tennis courts, or the park, and he's someone known to me, Melanie. Because he's wearing what looks like some kind of photo I.D. on his belt. And the way I look at him, sort of unsurprised by him, sidelong, with a little smile. (See, I don't smile at strangers. I'm not all that friendly to the general populace, Steff knows.) Capricorn talks to us about tennis and his voice is low, gravelly, sexy. His white T-shirt is spotless, and dazzling in the hot sun. You can see he works out: he's got arm, shoulder, chest muscles, not ugly and bulgy like some guys but hard like a rock. His eyes are hidden behind the dark wraparound glasses but I can imagine them: very dark eyes, intelligent, warm, with curly lashes. His hair is very black, like (maybe) it's dyed. But I don't know, his skin is olive-dark, and slightly coarse. He's good-looking, though. There's something keyed-up, edgy about him. An excited feeling. I'd like to touch his arm like a kid would do saying *Hi! I'm Capricorn II. I'm your psychic twin.*

He's saying, mostly to Steff, "I used to coach tennis, summer camp. I'd like to take you two on, two against one, if I had my racquet with me. If I had the time right now." Capricorn says this with a sly smile so maybe he means something other than tennis. So you can interpret it as a joke, or you can interpret it straight. I laugh, kind of loud, I'm quick to take it as a joke, while Steff, staring and blinking at him, this good-looking stranger who has stepped out of nowhere to speak to us like an old friend, takes it straight. Steff stammers, "Oh gosh—Melanie's the one—the real tennis player—she's my cousin—she's teaching me." Capricorn says, "And what's your name, Ponytail?" kind of aggressively, ignoring me, and Steff says, not knowing she doesn't have to reply to such a question, "Stephanie." Capricorn says, smiling a little harder, "I thought you were Ponytail." Steff is confused, laughing and blushing and looking to me for help. Capricorn says, "One thing I already know about you, 'Stephanie,'" and

Steff stammers, "Wha-at?" and Capricorn says, "You're not from around here. Upstate? Or maybe Toronto?" Steff is really blushing now. Saying, "I t-told you my name, now—what's your name?" Unconsciously Steff is swinging her ponytail. Moving her shoulders. She's giggling nervously, licking her lips. Capricorn smiles at her saying, "My name? Well, now. Maybe you know my name. I'm Cap. 'Cap E. Corn the First.'"

He's hoping that Steff will give in and confess she's Cap E. Corn the Second. Though by this time he must have figured out, Steff just isn't getting it, therefore she isn't Capricorn II, and therefore I must be Capricorn II.

I want to punch this guy in the arm. *Me! Look at me. I'm the one.*

Instead I go, "How's the weather at Land's End, Long Island, Cap?" and Capricorn turns to me, has to acknowledge me, shrugs and says, "It's there. One fact about weather, it's always there." He's trying to figure out what this is. His mind is working, how'd he get so confused? There's big busty blond Steff and there's me, the brown-haired girl, not the girl he's been expecting, what's going on here? Obviously he's trying not to let on he's disappointed. Eyeing me now, and maybe I'm not so bad: sort

of plain-pretty, with intelligent/ironic/Capricorn eyes; pug
nose, plum-colored mouth; average weight, kind of small-
breasted, with boyish hips and lean muscled legs. We talk a
little more about Land's End, how maybe it doesn't exist,
and Steff can't follow any of this, glancing back and forth
between us like she's watching a tennis game between two
really good, well-matched players. I'm feeling so excited! I
am Capricorn II, and this is Capricorn I, and he knows
now, and I know that he knows, there's a kind of current
passing between us and poor Steff hasn't a clue. With a shy
girl's eagerness, blundering on not knowing that nobody's
listening, she says yes she doesn't live here, she's from
Plattsburgh on Lake Champlain, does he know where that
is? Capricorn says no, but he'd like to know. Maybe he'll
come visit, someday.

"In the meantime you girls look pretty dehydrated.
How's about a Coke?"

It's only a couple hundred yards to the Pagoda
Restaurant, so we go there with Capricorn, whom Steff is
calling "Cap," the three of us have Diet Cokes sitting on
the terrace by the pond watching ducks, geese, swans being
fed bread crusts by mostly older people. We talk, joke
around and laugh a lot. I'm feeling dazed, almost I can't

believe this. The first time ever, somebody from the Web has become *real*. I do a lot of living in my head, I guess. Capricorn I was sort of in my head, and now he's here buying my cousin and me Cokes, and we're getting along like we've known each other for a long time. Steff is more relaxed, too. She surprises me by accepting a cigarette from Capricorn, I never knew Steff smoked. Capricorn pays attention to Steff and me both, now he knows who I am. Turns out he's a day trader, self-employed, with a business degree from the Wharton School, ever hear of the Wharton School?—he's addressing me now because he has glommed onto the fact that sweet Stephanie probably wouldn't know the Wharton School from a local grade school, and I tell him yes, I have definitely heard of the Wharton School, it's in Philadelphia. An older cousin of mine went there, I say, and this seems to impress Capricorn, but he doesn't ask my cousin's name, and changes the subject. He asks Steff about life in Plattsburgh, how cold does it get, what's she studying, easy things Steff can answer without becoming tongue-tied, and I'd be a little jealous except I know that Capricorn knows me, his psychic twin. *The bond between us. Under the sign of Capricorn.*

Capricorn says suddenly as if he's just thought of it, "Stephanie and Melanie—you need a ride home? My car's parked right over there." Steff exchanges a glance with me, and I say that my mom is coming to pick us up in a half hour, which is true. Hearing this, Capricorn stubs out his cigarette and stands. Sort of brusque and laughing mumbling, "Well, then! It's O voir for today, my friends." Without a backward glance he walks away knowing we're gaping after him.

I caught a glimpse of what he was wearing on his belt: not an I.D. badge but a shiny plastic button depicting a horned goat on its hind legs, and the words CAPRICORNS HAVE MORE FUN.

Capricorn I and Capricorn II bonded in friendship under the tenth sign of the Zodiac: The Goat. His birthday is December 23, mine is January 6. On the Web I was LONELYGIRL until I became Capricorn II.

And now I am not lonely any longer.

It's said of Capricorns that we are *practical, cautious, self-sufficient personalities. Highly motivated. Brooding and secretive. Cold, unforgiving, egoistic. Loyal friends and fierce enemies.*

The key phrase for Capricorns is *I use*.

Later, when we're back at the house and Mom is out of earshot, Steff says, giggling, "That mustache! I kind of don't like mustaches, even little neat ones, do you?"

"Mustache? He didn't have any mustache."

"Yes he did. A little narrow one. I guess it's kind of sexy, like that rapper what's-his-name, the kind of light-skinned guy that looks like an Italian? Like him."

I'm incredulous, staring at Steff like she's putting me on.

"Steff, what? Capricorn did not have any mustache, for God's sake."

Steff blinks at me, confused. "What'd you call him? 'Capricorn'?"

Quickly I say, "I called him—what his name is, what he told us." I'm trying not to sound impatient with Steff, she's so easily wounded. "Didn't he say it was—'Cap C. Corn'?"

Steff says slowly, "'Cap E. Corn.' Like, the zodiac? Capricorn? I didn't get it. God, I'm stupid. How'd you catch on?"

I shrug and indicate I just did.

Steff is biting the end of her ponytail in that maddening way of hers, a worse habit than biting her thumbnail,

"'Capricorn.' He's kind of good-looking, I guess. He's maybe about—twenty-five? The sunglasses and the mustache make him look older. But *sexy*."

"Steff, Capricorn didn't have any mustache."

(And he isn't twenty-five. He's maybe ten years older.)

"He did have a mustache, he *did*."

We're like kid sisters, bickering. I tell her, "Wait and see, Steff, you're wrong. No mustache."

Steff's eyes widen. "We're going to see Cap again, you think?"

"Maybe."

"He's somebody you know?"

"Maybe."

"Oh come on, Melanie! Tell me."

Steff regards me with wondering blue eyes. She's like a little girl sometimes, you want to shield her from harm. She knows that I'm more than a year younger than she is, and exaggerates how much more I know than she does. I guess she attributes my superiority to me living forty minutes from sophisticated Manhattan and her living practically in Canada.

"How'd you meet a guy like that? Have you—gone out with him?"

For the third time I say, like this is my secret at least for right now, "Maybe."

. . . the first time, so long ago I have no memory of myself. My memory is of a brilliant blue sky splotched with sun, sudden angry rain, and again sun, and steamy glittering canals and gondoliers in shiny black boats and the alley I turned into, Mommy and Daddy behind me calling after me *Melanie, come back* and I didn't hear, I was four years old and believed myself a big girl, running and giggling and confident that Daddy would run after me but suddenly I was lost, the alleys were so narrow and there were so many people I couldn't see behind me, I couldn't see past their legs, I ran back the way I'd come, I thought it was the way I'd come, but there was no Daddy, and there was no Mommy, and a man squatting on a doorstep reached out to me as I came near, he had olive-dark skin, soft dark shining eyes, black curly hair lush as a girl's, and his fingers wriggled at me in play, or in menace, he laughed, he bared his very white teeth in low throaty laughter and murmured to me in words I couldn't understand, I turned to run the other way, I was sobbing, I collided with the legs of strangers, a couple caught me saying in a language I could understand *It's a little girl, where are her parents* and so I was saved. And another time in my grandmother's old house in Nantucket where we were visiting he was hiding squatting behind dusty old trunks and boxes in the attic and they thought it was wasps I ran from gasping and panicked. And another time, so many years ago it might have happened to another child, a very small child, I was crawling on my hands and knees in my parents' bedroom that was semi-darkened and in another part of the house a TV was turned up and I lifted the edge of the bedspread, I peeked under the bed and blood rushed into my face, I saw him there, lying very still, his face hidden at first then I saw it, a face with just holes for eyes, a hole for his nose and a grinning hole for his mouth, I tried to scream but the blood pounded so hard in my throat I could not and afterward they were saying *Melanie? Honey? What is it? What has scared you so? Did you have a bad dream, honey?* and to each other they said *It must have been a nightmare, feel her pulse!*

Next day, Mom takes us to the swim club.

No Juniper Park. No tennis.

This is my decision. I'm thinking *Make him wait. He prefers Ponytail. And I am his twin, not her.*

Nor did I log on to my computer to check out messages for Capricorn II.

Steff is possibly disappointed but doesn't say anything, with Mom and me she's always cheerful, upbeat. Comparing our household, I guess, with hers. Always she's saying how lucky I am. And I go, *Oh, sure!* But I guess I am, I mean obviously I am. Only just I get bored with being lucky. And I get lonely for my own psychic kind.

Still, I'm staying away from Juniper Park for a day or two.

Steff is hesitant to bring up the subject of "Cap" having come to the conclusion I guess that he's some kind of boyfriend of mine.

Poor Steff! It demonstrates how naive she is, imagining that an adult man like that, a day trader with a degree from the Wharton School, somewhere in his thirties and good-looking as he is, would be dating *me*.

That night, though I'm pretty worn out from swimming laps like, one of the lifeguards said, a demented fish, I can't sleep. My eyes feel like they're burning in my head. I'm trying to see Capricorn's eyes behind those dark wraparound glasses, and I'm trying to read Capricorn's I.D. at his belt. I'm trying to see if he has a mustache (though I'm positive that he does not). A sound in the room like a baby whimpering wakes me (so I guess I've been asleep after all).

When Steff comes to stay with us, she always stays in my room in the twin bed. We're almost too old to "room" together but Steff would be hurt I guess if I suggested to Mom that she stay in our guest room, which is a large beautiful room with its own sun porch. I can't risk hurting Steff's feelings. She's the closest thing to a sister I have. Most nights she sleeps sound as a baby, though turning in her sleep and sometimes grinding her teeth, moaning softly. I suppose it's bad dreams. She wakes herself, goes "Huh?" in the middle of the night and I pretend not to hear. Then she falls back asleep again and in the morning she won't remember anything. I've overheard Steff (I was not eavesdropping) on the phone talking with her mother, it's surprising to hear my cousin say things like *Oh Mom I just don't believe you* and even once *I hate you Mom I'm never coming back there!* Another time, I heard Steff say, practically crying, *Mom I want to come home, everybody is real nice to me here but I'm lonely.*

If I slip from my bed and sit at my computer in the dark, if I'm very quiet and the screen is turned away from Steff's side of the room, she never hears me. And so in the dark of the night I log on with excited fingers, it's three eighteen A.M. when I click onto my e-mail and my heart kicks, yes there is a message from *cap 1*.

cap 2/missed you

Rapidly I type in

cap 1/maybe Thurs.

(Thursday is day after tomorrow. No, tomorrow is already here. Thursday is tomorrow.)

At the park, Thursday afternoon. In the heat of mid-summer only a few of the tennis courts are in use. The net on our court is beginning to fray, there are cracks in the asphalt. Steff keeps glancing around, alert and edgy. Neither of us has said a word about Capricorn. But Steff has shampooed and brushed her hair so it's silky, shining in the ponytail falling halfway down her back. Describing this hair to Capricorn I I'd called it "yellow" but it isn't yellow, it's pale gleaming gold.

I'm edgy, too, and hot. Helping Steff with her serve. She's trying but she's distracted, fumbling the ball. I see her glancing over my head. When she hits the ball well, I praise her like you'd praise a child: "Excellent, Steff!" But she keeps glancing around, toward the sidelines. Every guy who walks by, swinging a racquet or otherwise, Steff's eyes swing onto him.

All this day I have refused to check my e-mail. It's beginning to mean too much. A clenching sensation in my stomach, at just the thought of logging on.

Steff fumbles the ball again. Giggling and apologizing and glancing over my head.

"Steff, damn it! Forget him."

"Oh, Melanie. You're so critical all the time."

Steff is pouty, wiping sweat from her upper lip. I notice she's wearing lipstick today. Her eyes look bigger, more vividly defined. In even her loose tank top you can see the outline of her breasts. She's wearing denim cut-offs that fit her better than the white sailcloth shorts. Her legs are firm, strong-looking. She tosses the ball into the air to serve it as I've coached her, swings her racquet at a quirky angle, has a few lucky shots then begins to fumble again, and mutters under her breath, "Oh damn. I hate this."

I'm shocked to hear these words. I almost can't believe I've heard them from my cousin.

"Hate what, Steff? Tennis? I thought—"

Quickly Steff says, "Oh gosh, I don't hate tennis. Or these lessons. I—I hate being clumsy. You're such a good player it makes me worse."

Her eyes shift over my head, beyond the tennis court.

Steff says, "You make me nervous, Melanie. Like you're always—judging me."

"Steff, no. I'm not judging you. I'm impressed with how much you've learned. Your serve—"

Steff laughs, blushing. "Oh, 'my serve.' Like I'll ever be playing tennis back home."

I see Steff's widened blue eyes shifting past me again. There's a quick little frown between her eyebrows that signals *He's here.*

And when I turn, Capricorn has appeared.

My heart kicks, too. Like my cousin's.

This time Capricorn waves to us and settles on a

bench to watch us play. Leans back, crosses his muscled legs, smiles at us, and watches.

"Oh, Melanie! You're mean."

"Steff, it's just tennis."

We're excited and nervous playing tennis with Capricorn so intently observing from his bench. I'm proud of my backhand, and my dynamite serve that makes poor Steff squeal and hide behind her racquet. I try to breathe through my nose, not my mouth. Steff is panting like a horse. I'm deliberately placing my balls to make her lunge and run, back to the farthest corner of the court, forward to the net where she practically charges into it. When we have a good volley, Capricorn applauds. "Terrific, girls! Olympic class."

He's so funny, he makes us snort with laughter. We're attacked by giggles like phantom fingers running up and down our sides. You'd think we were children, not the age we are. Steff's ponytail is swishing, swirling. "Hey, I want to change sides," she says, "the sun is in my eyes *again*."

Capricorn calls over, affectionate and chiding, "Be a good sport, Ponytail. You're fantastic win, lose, or draw."

I'm waiting for Capricorn to praise me for my dynamite serves. But mostly he just winces, sympathetic with
(unless he's mocking) Steff as she lunges to hit a return she
can't reach. I'm playing pretty well, I think. After I make
another point, Capricorn says in mock alarm, "Ooooh!
Ain't that Cap 2 *mean*."

He's said it! My secret name. My face burns with
pleasure.

Luckily Steff doesn't hear. And if she did, she wouldn't
have a clue what *Cap 2* could possibly mean.

We play three games under the watchful eye of
Capricorn the Goat. Steff is erratic and choppy but when
she connects with the ball, she definitely connects. Of
course, I win each of our games but Steff scores points and
our last game is embarrassingly close.

Steff cries, "Wow! Enough." Lifting her tank top at the
midriff to wipe her forehead, ducking her head in a quick,
childlike gesture. I wonder if Capricorn, strolling over to
join us, catches a glimpse of her breasts in her pink satin
bra. Steff's eyes are shining from the exercise. I'm breathless, too. I have to concede that beating my cousin at
tennis is getting harder all the time.

Capricorn offers us a white terrycloth towel he found

somewhere and wetted at the drinking fountain. You'd think, seeing the three of us from the edge of the court, that this handsome dark-haired man in sunglasses, T-shirt, and shorts, with a tight-muscled upper body, is one of our fathers, picking us up after our game.

Capricorn says, "There's a risk of dehydration, playing in the hot sun like this. You both need drinks."

Capricorn speaks sincerely. He's truly concerned.

It's then I see: *he has a mustache.*

So Steff was right. I was wrong. Capricorn has a narrow little trimmed mustache on his upper lip. Suave and sexy and inconspicuous.

The other day, out of shyness, I must not have looked at him too closely.

I'm dreading Steff nudging me in the ribs, laughing at me for being so blind and sure of myself. But Steff takes no notice of me at all, dabbing fastidiously at her face with the damp towel and telling Capricorn in this sweet thrilled voice she'd love something to drink. Steff is pouting, showing off. Capricorn can't take his eyes off her.

Capricorn isn't wearing the goat button today. Just for our first meeting, I guess.

• • •

Capricorn is jingling his car keys, asks if we'd like to drive out to a place he noticed on the lake, a higher-class café than the Pagoda Restaurant. Steff smiles at the suggestion but I hesitate, it runs through my mind my mom wouldn't like it if we went in a car with a man we didn't know, and before we can answer Capricorn catches my look and says, "Well, then! We'll stay in the park. This is a great park."

So we walk over to the Pagoda Restaurant and sit at almost the same table we'd been sitting at the other day. The waitress smiles at us, remembering us. You can surmise that Capricorn left her a generous tip, she certainly remembers him and is smiling at him like he's some kind of local celebrity. In his stylish dark wraparound glasses, and his gleaming black hair that sort of lifts from his head like it's been air-blown, Capricorn does look like somebody special. He talks and acts like a TV broadcaster, his voice mellow and words carefully chosen. He orders Diet Cokes for "my girls" and a beer for himself and a platter of chips and Tex-Mex sauce that he and Steff mostly eat, I'm not hungry. Also, I hate eating between meals and getting my teeth all gummy and not being able to brush them.

What were the things he said to you it will afterward be asked.

Who were witnesses, who saw him with you.

Mostly we're laughing, saying silly things. Watching the noisy mallards on the pond, beating their wings and pecking at one another as people toss them bread crusts. ("Family life, girls. Be forewarned," Capricorn says.) Steff makes Capricorn laugh describing some of the losers her mother has been dating, including a mailman who was arrested for hiding away five thousand pieces of undelivered mail in his cellar. When I ask Capricorn about the stock market, day trading, etc., he becomes more serious, explaining such terms as *stock*, *dividend*, *capital gain*, what *stock market* actually means. Capricorn explains he isn't in the stock market per se, he's in the *options market*, and sometimes the *futures market*. You can play the options market, Capricorn says, without ever owning an actual stock and you can make a lot of money, and the futures market is even more of a crapshoot, not for timid souls. Mostly he's talking now to Steff, though I'm the one who's really interested and can follow what he's saying, and Steff is nodding and flinging her ponytail around in that maddening way. "See, you're buying and selling contracts for future delivery," Capricorn says, "not actual deliveries, of anything. Basically you're buying and selling the rights to buy and sell. The product doesn't exist, but the money is real. See, Ponytail"—he takes hold of Steff's ponytail and strokes it—"you can win big and lose big without ever owning a stock."

Steff says, with a little shiver, watching Capricorn through her pale-blond eyelashes, "Are you serious, or is that some joke?"

Capricorn says, tugging at Steff's ponytail, "Stephanie, I am always serious, and never more than when I'm joking."

When Capricorn is turned to Steff I try to see his eyes behind the sunglasses but can't very well. I do see his narrow little mustache and wonder how I could have missed it. I notice how he fusses dipping his taco chips into the hot sauce, twirling each chip one, two, three times before lifting it to his mouth. I notice how he pats his mouth with a paper napkin, his lips and his mustache, every time he takes a bite. His teeth are very white, and damp. There are fine almost invisible creases in his face like cobwebs. But his skin looks warm and healthy like it's cared for, like he rubs something into it, oil, shaving cream. His hair is so black, it has a bluish cast. Nothing about Capricorn isn't cared for, premeditated.

I am the one, not Ponytail. Your psychic twin.

When I excuse myself to use the rest room, they hardly notice me. Steff is asking about the "futures market" with this earnest, little-girl face, and Capricorn is explaining, jotting figures down on a napkin with a ballpoint pen. My heart is beating hard in resentment but I'm trying to see the humor of the situation. There's logic in humor: I'm a true Capricorn, which means I believe in logic, caution, self-sufficiency. Also brooding, secrecy. Enmity.

Of course he prefers Ponytail. If you were a man, you would prefer Ponytail, too. Cap 2 exists only on the Web. Cap 2 is just words typed onto a flat glass screen to be read and erased.

When I return from the rest room, Capricorn and Stephanie are standing close together on the terrace steps, conferring about something. When they see me, Capricorn says casually, "Melanie. How's about joining Ponytail and me on a cool drive around the lake? It's only three miles, we'll be back way before six."

Steff must have told Capricorn that my mother is coming to pick us up at six. It's four twenty P.M. now.

I'd thought we would be playing more tennis. I would

be instructing my cousin, while Capricorn looked on.

I'm wondering how, if Capricorn lives somewhere else (Long Island?), he knows about our lake. I'm wondering if he has cruised around our suburban village, if he has planned this. What he has planned.

Capricorn says, smiling, "It's a hot day. We can cool off. We can watch the sailboats from that café. Stephanie says she's never driven all the way around the lake."

This isn't true. My family has driven us around the lake more than once when Steff has visited.

I tell them I'll just wait for them. Back by the tennis courts. My mother might come early to pick us up.

It isn't likely that Mom would come early. Ever.

I just want to get away from them. I want them to get away from me. I'm not going to cry. Capricorns don't cry.

Steff says, sort of embarrassed, "Cap says there's a really nice café out there on the lake. You can rent boats and canoes. C'mon, Melanie! I don't want to play tennis anymore today, it's too hot."

"You go on, Steff. I'll wait by the courts."

Capricorn says, with forced enthusiasm, "We could get ice cream. There's a Tastee Freez out there. You'd like that, wouldn't you?"

"Actually, no. That's for Stephanie, not me. She's crazy for ice cream." I hate it that my voice sounds resentful, and I know my face is bulldog-sulky.

Capricorn is edgy but polite. He isn't going to try to talk me into joining them. His car keys are jingling in his hand.

"Okay, Melanie. We'll be back within the hour."

Steff leaves her tennis gear with me, making a face like she's bored with it, can't wait to slip away. I watch the two of them walk side by side, almost the same height. Steff's ponytail is bouncing like pale fire. Capricorn is laughing about something, nudging her in the arm. They make their way along the edge of the pond, toward the parking lot and out of sight.

His license plate number. I should try to see it.

But I don't follow after them. I would be ashamed to follow after them. I remain on the terrace and finish my lukewarm Coke. Capricorn has paid our bill, with a five-dollar tip. This is almost exactly a fifty percent tip. The napkin with the numbers on it is gone, though. And I don't know Capricorn's name.

I toss the remainder of the taco chips into the pond for the mallards to squabble over.

• • •

At six P.M. I'm waiting by the tennis courts for Steff.

By six ten P.M. she still isn't here.

By six fifteen P.M. Mom drives up. "Where's Stephanie?"

I hear myself tell Mom that Steff is in the women's room, but after five minutes, ten minutes, when Steff doesn't appear, and Mom is anxious that something must be wrong with Steff and asks me to go check, I have to say, not meeting Mom's eye, "Steff went for a ride around the lake, I guess. She'll be back any minute."

Mom says, "A ride? A ride with who?"

"Some guy she met."

Mom stares at me. She removes her pale-tinted sunglasses, and I'm fearful of her eyes. "What guy, Melanie? Who?"

"Just—a guy. At the tennis court. He's a tennis player, I guess. A coach, he said. He was watching us play, and we got to talking. He bought us Cokes." Saying this, about the Cokes, I hear my voice crack.

Mom climbs out of her car, clumsy in haste. Her ignition keys are in her hand and she drops them. She's looking around, shading her eyes.

"When did they leave?"

My mind is blank. I'm nervous, confused. I hear myself say, "I don't know, maybe an hour ago . . ."

"Did you say this person is someone you know? One of the tennis coaches here?"

"No, Mom. I didn't say that."

"Somebody from your high school?"

"I don't think so. . . . He was older."

"Older? How much older?"

"Maybe . . . twenty-five?"

"And you don't know his name."

"No."

"You saw his car?"

"No."

Mom interrogates me like somebody on TV but I only repeat what I've told her. She's anxious, and making me anxious. There is nothing scarier than an adult who is beginning to realize he or she isn't in control of a situation. Mom takes hold of my arm, squeezing it. She says, like she's pleading, "Melanie, you're saying—you and Stephanie met a man at the tennis court, he bought you Cokes, and—Stephanie got into his car with him and—they're gone?"

I hear myself say, stammering, "Steff isn't real late,

Mom—only a few minutes late. She—"

It's almost six thirty P.M. They left at four thirty P.M. Capricorn said *Back within the hour.*

Mom starts thinking aloud in this way of hers that means she's upset and is trying to remain calm: saying maybe she should drive around the lake herself, I could ride with her and maybe we'd see the car Steff is in, I could recognize the car; but I interrupt Mom to say no, I don't know the guy's car, I told her I hadn't seen it. Mom hardly seems to hear me. She changes her mind saying no, I'd better stay right here at the tennis courts in case Steff returns, and she'll drive around the lake by herself. By this time Mom is talking sort of wildly. She's pressing her fingertips against her eyelids and I see her lips working silently like she's praying (but my mom doesn't pray) before she says, "Oh Melanie, we'd better call the police. I think we'd better call the police," and I say quickly, "But Mom, Steff is only a few minutes late, maybe it's too soon," and Mom says, confused, "She's only—a few minutes late? I thought you said she was an hour late," and I'm laughing angrily, "Mom. I never said that. You always exaggerate everything." In the confusion of the moment I don't know what I'm saying, and I don't think that Mom does, either. Mom has grabbed my arm, she's squeezing so it hurts. We're breathless and staring at each other and our eyes are bright with tears so almost there's the consolation, we're having one of our quick flare-up arguments, that's all this is.

Nothing to do with my cousin Stephanie. Just Mom and me, one of our "misunderstandings."

So Mom waits, and I wait. We're pacing around the car, looking up every time a figure appears, especially a tall blond girl. By this time, most of the tennis courts are in use. There are plenty of people here, predominantly adults. I see men who resemble Capricorn, at a distance: he's a physical type I guess, wearing sunglasses, T-shirt, khaki shorts or pants. Black-haired men, with tight-muscled torsos.

I'm wondering are they all Capricorns? Born under the sign of the Goat.

There's a sick cold sensation in the pit of my belly. I'm trying not to panic. I wish I could tell Mom this isn't her fault, not to blame herself, but Mom would say *Then who is to blame?*

Then, this happens: I see Steff before Mom does, and she's coming out of the women's rest room, the same rest room I'd told Mom she had gone into, behind the tennis courts. Steff is smoking a cigarette, it looks like. I wave and shout, "Steff!" and she stares at me for a long moment like she hardly recognizes me, then drops the cigarette and hurries in our direction. Steff's blond ponytail is crooked and her face is flushed and mottled as if she has just stepped off the tennis court.

Steff has returned just in time. Mom is talking with a park attendant, describing her niece Stephanie Klaff who's "missing."

Mom hurries to Steff to hug her. Mom is so relieved she's almost laughing. "Honey, where on earth have you been? Are you—all right?"

Steff stands stiffly, taller than Mom by several inches, not returning Mom's anxious hug. There's an expression on her face like she's just enduring this. Our eyes catch: a weird look passes between us. "I'm fine, Aunt Em. Sorry I'm so late." Her voice is flat. Steff doesn't sound sorry. She doesn't sound much like herself. Her lips are pale and raw-looking, her lower face looks swollen. Over Mom's shoulder she continues to stare at me. She says in a slow, sullen voice, "We got lost. The lake drive doesn't go all the way around the lake, there's all kinds of inlets and dead ends. You should've told us, Melanie."

My cousin's voice is so resentful, I'm shocked.

After Stephanie returns to Plattsburgh I won't speak with her again for years. I won't see her again for even longer.

After that day, Capricorn I disappears from the Web. Capricorn II disappears. No trace.

Driving home from the park Mom tries to question Steff, where was she, who was the man, but Steff cuts her off short saying he was just a guy, nobody special, and our lake isn't so special either—"Not compared to Lake Champlain."

Steff hardly speaks to me. Her eyes shift through me like I'm invisible. If I try to talk to her about anything she cuts me off, too.

That evening Steff doesn't eat dinner with us. Usually she's in the kitchen helping Mom before I come downstairs, and always at the table she's very hungry, but this evening she remains upstairs in our room saying she has a migraine headache, even the smell of food nauseates her.

Mom is in a state of confused panic. I guess you could

call it that. Clutching at me, squeezing my arm. Like I must know more than I've told her: she knows! But she doesn't know. "Stephanie has been hurt. She's been . . ." Mom pauses, searching for the right word, the word she dares utter aloud. ". . . taken advantage of. We have to get help for her." But Steff is calm and indifferent to Mom's appeals. Steff has an air of not hearing Mom's appeals. Several times when Mom knocked on the door of my room, entered almost shyly and tried to speak with Steff, Steff cut her off almost rudely, insisting that no nothing had happened, please Aunt Em can we change the subject.

But that night, after midnight, at a time when Steff would ordinarily be deeply asleep, I hear her in her bed breathing quick and hard like she's trying not to cry. At first I pretend to be asleep. Then I whisper, "Steff . . . ? Is something wrong?" After a moment Steff says furiously, "Nothing is wrong! Leave me alone." I'm scared and sick with guilt. I wish Mom was here, Mom would know what to do. Steff says, beginning to cry openly, "I want to go home. I don't like it here. I want to go home tomorrow." In the dark I stumble to Steff's bed, I try to hold her, at first she pushes me away like she hates me then it's okay, I hold Steff as she cries, cries like her heart is broken, sobs herself to sleep like a little girl. I'm crying, too. I'm thinking that Steff is my sister, I love my sister. I'm thinking *What have I done, why when I love my sister?*

THE VISIT

I tell Mom *I am not going*.

I tell Mom *no I am not*.

Please don't ask me again, Mom!

And Mom says, like she hasn't heard a word, "Lisanne. Grandma misses you so. She's always asking after you, what can I tell her?"

Tell her anything you want to tell her.

"Honey, I know it's hard. It's hard on all of us. But you can't just pretend"—Mom pauses, fearful of becoming emotional. Since Mom is the adult it's her role to be rational; since I'm the adolescent daughter, it's my role to be emotional so that I can then be scolded. Mom's voice slip slides between outright threat and subtle coercion—

"whatever it is you think you're pretending."

No I said. *No.*

Grandma has been in Unit A (Alzheimer's Unit) of Assisted Living Facilities at Pendlebrook Manor for eleven weeks. I have not been counting but I know it's eleven weeks. Because it's been at least eleven times Mom has asked me to accompany her. Mom visits Grandma often, after work. Three times a week at least. She'd call Grandma on the phone except the telephone makes Grandma nervous now, and gets her confused. But Grandma is Mom's actual mother, Mom is supposed to be devoted like that, isn't she? I'm just a granddaughter.

I said *I am not going to that place.*

Pendlebrook Manor looks like an upscale condo village, about twelve miles from our town. Like it's been built on a golf course, that kind of sculpted green lawn. Tall trees, evergreen shrubs, flower beds and flagstone paths and white lawn furniture, like something in a storybook. Except you don't want to live in this story.

I think the style is "Colonial": white clapboards, dark-green shutters and trim, brick chimneys. "Peaceful

Country Living for Senior Citizens on a 60-Acre Campus Overlooking Scenic Pendlebrook Creek with Provisions for 24-Hour Personal Care Assistance and On-Site Health Care as Needed."

The place they've locked Grandma in. The place Grandma will never leave for the rest of her life.

"Lisanne? I'll be leaving in about ten minutes. If—"

This time I don't say a word. And I'm not hearing a word.

"—you're a little afraid, honey, that's all right. I'm afraid, too. I mean, when I set out. It's still such a shock. But when I get there, and see Grandma, it's different somehow. And I—I'm happy I'm there. And I believe you would be, too. If—"

(Mom, I hate you sometimes. I wish wish wish you would leave me alone.)

"—if you came along, you could just wait in the car, or walk around outside, if you didn't want to—you know, come inside with me. And maybe when you get there, you'll change your mind. How's about giving it a try? You know you're always changing your mind, honey. That's the good, healthy thing about you. . . ."

(Calling me "honey"! You're just manipulating me. You

want me to cry. Well, I won't cry. And I'm not going to fucking Pendlebrook Manor I've told you.)

"Just through here, Lisanne. We have to be buzzed in."

Buzzed in! This part of the Manor is like a prison for God's sake. Big double doors with Plexiglas windows, TV monitors, electronic locks, codes to punch in, buzzers, alarms . . .

"Well, the patients in this unit have to be protected, Lisanne. Some of them get confused easily. They can't be allowed to wander off and hurt themselves."

Wander off home, Mom means.

The lobby of Unit A is all right, I guess. I mean, it looks normal enough. Like the lobby of an upscale hotel like Marriott. There are sofas, chairs, potted plants. Even classical music piped in. Mom knows the routine so well by this time, she doesn't need anyone to escort her to Grandma's residence hall. We just walk along this corridor, Mom a few feet ahead of me. I'm breathing kind of funny. It's like just before a swim meet, when I'm so tense I can hardly breathe and start to feel light-headed. *Why am I here? I don't want to be here.* It's like a baby voice inside my head. But something always happens, I get calmer, I seem to come alive, adrenaline rushes to my heart, I guess it must be, and I'm okay. *You're here because you chose to be here* the voice counsels me.

(I guess that's right. Somehow, I changed my mind and told Mom all right, I'd come with her to see Grandma. But only once, maybe. I'm making no promises for the future.)

Mom punches in a code beside a set of big double doors. Above the doors is just the letter *A.* I'm thinking how, once a patient is admitted through those doors, he or she can never step outside again alone. They've been "committed" to a mental health facility. It's a life sentence is what I'm thinking, and I start to feel panicked again.

"Lisanne, come on. Grandma's room is this way. She might be in the lounge, too. Or outside."

Suddenly, we're in the Hot Zone. The big double doors shut behind us with a hiss.

My first impression is kind of confused, surprised. I don't know what I was expecting, but not this. We're in an open lounge area with round tables, six chairs apiece. It's flooded with light from tall windows. There's a smell of something sweet, or maybe yeasty, like baking bread. Pastries. Mom says, "This is where Grandma and the other patients have their meals. It's attractive, isn't it?" Mom is speaking casually but I know that she's pleading with me to say yes. So I mumble something that sounds like *yes*. I'm trying not to think of Grandma and Grandpa's house that I always loved to visit, and stayed overnight in for as long as I can remember; I'm trying not to compare this impersonal place to what I remember of that house. . . .

The dining area is mostly empty now, in the late afternoon. There are glass doors overlooking a terrace, flower beds, and a garden where a few elderly individuals appear to be gardening. (Is Grandma one of these? She always loved her garden at home.) Mom is pulling gently at my arm, even as a heavyset older woman leaning on a walker calls out urgently to us from across the room. "Hello? Hello? Hello? *Hello?*" I'm so surprised, I stare at this woman who's older than Grandma, with flattened yellowish-white hair, round eyeglasses that give her an alert-owl look, and a necklace of striking coral shells around her neck. The way she speaks to Mom and me, it seems that she knows us. "Are you coming to see me, dear?" She's looking at me, now. Her voice has become hopeful, almost childlike. Mom whispers to me to say *no I'm sorry* so I stammer, "N-No, I'm sorry, I'm—" and Mom smiles at the woman and pulls me along. "Don't linger. Don't look at her, and the others. It isn't necessary. Look straight ahead, Lisanne." Close by, stationed near a birdcage we have to pass, is an elderly man with a handsome, sunken face, and he too looks at us eagerly, as if we've come to visit him. At first, in my confusion, I think he must be the husband of the woman wearing the coral shell necklace. He stares at me mumbling urgent pleading words I can't decipher. Mom seems to know him, she smiles brightly and murmurs *Hello!* but doesn't make eye contact, and keeps moving. My heart is beating hard, I can't help thinking we're being rude. *It's a different place here. A different dimension. Even the air is different.* The elderly man shuffles after us, but can't keep up with our pace. I feel that I should explain who we are, where we're going, I should apologize for our indifference to him, but his tone changes abruptly, he's angry and scolding, "Is that what you do . . . walk right past . . . Come back here! . . . I'm talking to you. Ashley!"

At least I think the name is Ashley. I can't be sure.

There's a faint roaring in my ears. I'm conscious of eyes moving eagerly onto Mom and me. Several aides in pale-blue uniforms smile and greet Mom by name, which is reassuring. "Mrs. Janeway, good evenin'." Mom asks an aide named Cella where Grandma is, and the young woman says, "Lorine is in the dayroom."

The sound of Grandma's first name "Lorine" on this stranger's lips is disconcerting. It's as if the young aide has become acquainted with my grandmother in a way I never have.

Mom leads me along a corridor past rooms (some of the doors are open, most are not) and into a lounge area where a number of elderly individuals are sitting. A large TV is on, but virtually no one is watching. There's a sand-colored, long-haired, fattish mixed-breed dog being vigorously petted and cooed over. When I see Grandma with the dog, something hits me in the chest and I almost start crying. It's so weird to see Grandma here, with strangers. The dog sees Mom and me, barks excitedly, and runs waddling to Mom to be petted. Mom calls out, "Mother! Hello. Look who's come to see you." My eyes are misted over with tears, I'm trying to smile, going to Grandma to hug her, and to be hugged. *She doesn't know me. That scared look in Grandma's eyes.* Mom is saying loudly, "Lisanne has come to see you, Mother. Isn't that nice?" Grandma hugs me tight as I lean over her, she's murmuring, "Lis-anne, Lis-anne," like she can't believe it, I am such a wonderful surprise. If she didn't seem to recognize me for a fraction of a second, she is over that now.

Grandma's hair is whiter than I remember, and seems thinner, and her face is thinner. She is a beautiful woman, eighty-six years old (I only just learned this fact recently) who has never looked old; her face isn't wrinkled much, just the skin is pale and soft and in little creases and folds, and her eyes are sort of a pale washed-out blue, sunken, blinking. Grandma is wearing a flower-print smock and loose-fitting blue slacks and there are rings on four of her fingers, which catches my eye, it's so unusual. And Grandma wearing not one but two wristwatches, one on each thin wrist. When she leans back to squint at me, I see that there's a fresh-looking cut, like a scab that's been picked at, on her forehead. Again she says, smiling happily, "Lisanne. I knew you would come."

I hear myself stammer, "Grandma, I—I love you."

I can't help it. I'm crying helplessly now, can hardly catch my breath.

Mom and I help Grandma up. She's a little stiff, she says, from arthritis. Grandma, standing, is shorter than I remember. At first she seems uncertain on her feet, leaning against Mom and me. Then she slips her hand into mine, and squeezes it, like there's a secret between us. This is a gesture Grandma used to make, a long time ago when I was a little girl. Mom has slipped her arm through Grandma's to help her walk.

All this while the sand-colored dog is nudging our legs, licking joyfully at our hands. "Isn't Frisky the friendliest dog?" Mom says. Grandma says, "Frisky is my best friend here. Frisky came with me here. Sometimes they let her sleep in my room." We spend some minutes stroking Frisky's ears, petting Frisky's panting sides, admiring Frisky's big thumping tail and all-around personality. In her former life, Grandma never especially liked dogs; or maybe she was afraid of them, not wanting a dog to leap up on her, or slavishly lick her hands. (Grandma would have rushed off to wash her hands thoroughly if any dog had ever dared lick her hands like this. She would have made a show of elaborately brushing her clothes free of real or imagined dog hairs.) How grateful we are for Frisky! As we make our slow way along the corridor, Frisky accompanies us importantly, trotting just ahead of Grandma. I feel a surge of gratitude for the dog, and affection. I'm thinking *She loves them all.*

Loves us all. Frisky doesn't judge.

My face is burning, I'm still shaky from my sudden, wholly unexpected outburst of tears. At least no one stared at me. Or even took much notice. Evidently breaking down and bawling isn't unusual in Unit A. I see that Mom is trying to smile, talking to Grandma. For the first time I realize how hard this is for her, what a strain Mom is under. She works at a demanding, full-time job as a CPA, and she takes care of our household, my dad and me; she was exhausted and depressed after Grandpa's death, from heart failure, last year; then Grandma began to fail, almost immediately after Grandpa died, and the responsibility of taking care of her, and eventually finding a place for her, was all Mom's. Selling my grandparents' house, clearing and cleaning it; settling my grandparents' estate, and making financial arrangements for Grandma . . . For eleven weeks I've been angry with Mom, I've been disapproving and disgusted, and now I feel ashamed of myself. *You'll find Grandma a little changed, Lisanne. But she's still Grandma.* So Mom has been preparing me.

I realize that Mom is worried about me, too. Lisanne is another of Mom's responsibilities.

I seem to see myself from a distance, a tall slender

fourteen-year-old girl with long straight wheat-colored hair, a face splotched from crying, a shaky-smiling mouth.

Grandma taught me to stand back and "see" myself at crucial times. *The I behind the eyes* Grandma called it. The first time, I was nine or ten, and crying over something the way it seemed I was always crying over something. As a child, I was either very happy or I was weepy, sulky, or furious. (What was always so crucial? I can't imagine.) Grandma said there's a way of detaching yourself from the "storm" of emotions, to get a clearer view of yourself, alone and with other people. It's a way of overcoming childishness. It's a way of helping other people.

And so I try. Sometimes I forget, I guess I am an emotional person, but I try.

Mom leads us outside, into the garden. It's sundazzled, almost too warm. "Isn't it lovely here!" Mom says, as if she has never seen it before. Evidently there's a bench—a gnarly-looking wooden bench—that is Grandma's favorite, so we head for this, a slow, stiff but pleasant walk in the sunshine. Mom and I are commenting on the beautiful flowers, which are mostly zinnias, asters, and black-eyed Susans, and Grandma is thanking us, as if the flowers are hers. "I started those from seed. The"—she's frowning, not able to think of the word *zinnia*—"you can't trust the nursery, for colors. All the roses died." In her former life, Grandma was known as a fierce perfectionist of a gardener. She had many, maybe too many, flowers she fussed over, including roses, which were beautiful when they were healthy and in bloom but often sickened with black spot and other rose ailments, or succumbed to Grandma's great scourge, the Japanese beetle. Grandma's lavish flower beds were a source of both pleasure and anguish to her; they'd become a kind of joke in the family. Now, at Pendlebrook Manor, all the flowers in these beds appear to be healthy, and blooming. (No roses.)

Seated on the gnarly bench, Grandma turns suddenly to me. "Lisanne. Were you away at school?"

"No, Grandma."

"You were away."

"No . . ."

Grandma knows I don't go away to school. This is so weird!

"You were gone for years. You're a big girl now."

"Oh no, Grandma," I say, hurt, "it's just been a few weeks. I mean, since—"

Grandma is clutching at me with her fingers like talons. As if she's losing her balance. She seems confused suddenly, frightened. Mom comes to my rescue and says something plausible, if untrue, yes Lisanne has been visiting cousins in New Jersey. Luckily at this moment Frisky trots panting to us, a soiled red Frisbee in her jaws, so there's the need for Mom, then me, then Grandma to toss the Frisbee to Frisky, and this deflects the issue of whether I have been away for years or not.

I remember now that Mom warned me on the way over: Don't disagree with Grandma, no matter what she says. Don't seem to be criticizing her for not remembering as well as you do, and don't criticize the Manor. "Oh, God: why not?" I asked, and Mom said, embarrassed, "Because Grandma seems to think sometimes that the Manor is home. If you say something even slightly critical about the place, she will feel bad, as if you'd said it about her own house." For some reason, this incensed me. "Mom, that's just crazy."

I didn't mean crazy, though. I meant tragic.

We sit on the bench for a while longer, then continue walking around the garden area, in a loop. We spend some time examining the vegetable garden where (Mom has told me) Grandma helped put in the tomato plants, which are staked, heavy with fat, reddening tomatoes, grown to a height of more than five feet. Both Mom and I compliment Grandma on the tomatoes and she says quickly, "Oh, Dad put most of these in. I just weed." I'm shocked by this, and say, before I can think clearly, "He did? G-Grandpa?" Grandma points at a wing of the Manor. "Dad lives over there. He'll be so happy to see you, dear."

I'm stunned. I don't know where to look. Don't dare look at Mom.

Grandpa has been dead for eighteen months.

"That sun! It's nice, but you can get too much sun."

Mom says this; and Grandma says, as if this is a conversation they have had numerous times, "Yes. You can get too much sun."

Back inside the Manor, Mom continues walking with Grandma and me, ostensibly showing me things but really, I can see, using the occasion to exercise Grandma, who needs to walk frequently each day, with Mom or with aides. I gather that Mom has a certain itinerary, a route she takes; Grandma seems to feel comfortable with routine, and anticipates each aspect of the walk with a little smile.

"These are our birds, aren't they pretty? I love our birds."
We admire a pair of beautifully feathered lovebirds in a
cage and, in another cage, a half dozen small fluttering,
chirping Australian finches. Mom tells me, in a voice just
subtly altered so that, I can sense, Grandma doesn't hear,
though she's standing between us, "The residents here take
care of the birds, those who can. They take care of Frisky,
and there's a resident cat, too, Silky. There's a small aquar-
ium, over there." Grandma says, with a mischievous little
laugh, "Dad doesn't like birds! He says they're dirty and
noisy. But he doesn't know about these." I hear myself say,
with a conspiratorial smile, "That's good, Grandma! These
birds are your secret."

Mom walks us quite a distance along a carpeted open
area, past the dining tables again, where we avoid making
eye contact with the heavyset woman wearing the coral
necklace; or maybe the woman has drifted off into a light
doze, seated on a sofa in the sun. Luckily, the elderly man
who scolded "Ashley" is nowhere in sight.

As we walk, we pass rooms: I can't resist glancing into
some of them, and am impressed and reassured by how
attractively they've been furnished, obviously with private
items of furniture, wall hangings, carpets, curtains. We

pass a piano, which provokes me to say, "Grandma, you can play piano here," but Grandma seems not to hear me, and Mom shakes her head at me. (What did I say wrong? Grandma used to play piano, didn't she? But not for a long time, I guess. And her finger joints are arthritic now.) After a few minutes Grandma says, "Where is my room? We're walking too . . . we walked too far. . . . Where is . . .?" She seems anxious suddenly. Mom says, "We're going to your room right now, Mother. See? There's your door. With your name on it." Affixed to the door is a large heart made of pink construction paper with the name LORINE block-printed on it, in red crayon. It's like something a kinder-garten pupil might have done. I block the thought that Grandma must have made this in one of the Unit's therapy classes.

Grandma, who'd been a high school teacher for several years before she quit to raise her family.

Grandma, who gave me books for Christmas and my birthday, starting when I was a year old.

That's the main reason that Grandma is at Pendle-brook Manor, Mom has said. The facility has an intensive Alzheimer's program. . . . She has to be kept active. Her mind. Otherwise, Alzheimer's patients lose their ability to interact with others. They lapse into apathy, staring into space. They even lose their will to eat sometimes.

I block the thought that Grandma will end up like that. I'm just not thinking of it at all.

I mean, maybe I was. Before this visit. Now I see time differently. It's like there is no "time" in Unit A as there is in the outside world. There is no "future" and not much of a "past." Just the present day, the hour.

One visit at a time.

One breath at a time.

Now that Grandma is returned to her room, she's almost, for a few minutes, her old self. Except for the scab on her forehead, and her thinned hair and cheeks. She eases free of Mom's and my hands and invites us inside. Grandma's quarters are very attractive, which is a relief. Everything is neat, spotlessly clean. There's a faint odor of furniture polish, disinfectant. We admire Grandma's things, which are familiar to our eyes: the bright chintz bedspread, the rocking chair with a matching chintz cushion, the hooked rug, framed photographs and watercolors (painted by Grandma herself, as a girl), end tables, chairs, potted plants. Repeatedly Grandma says, "I love it here, I love this room. Isn't this nice?"—

she's pointing to a needlepoint cushion—"and this"—
she's pointing to an African violet plant, profuse with
flowers—"Oh! See who's here."

It's Silky, Unit A's long-haired white Persian, napping
on the carpet beside Grandma's bed. Silky seems unsurprised by us. She yawns luxuriantly, allows herself to be
petted and fussed over, purrs loudly, sniffs for a treat
from us; being given no treat, Silky turns languidly and
leaves the room. (Where is Frisky? Somehow the sand-
colored dog has drifted off in the wake of another resident.) "Isn't she beautiful? I love her so. I just love her to
death." Grandma speaks vehemently, as she would never
have spoken of a cat, any cat, in her former life. She's
staring at the doorway through which the fickle Silky
departed as if, for a moment, she has forgotten that Mom
and I are still here.

Grandma sits in her rocking chair, and Mom moves
familiarly about her quarters, checking things. She waters
Grandma's plants. She flushes the toilet in the bathroom.
She runs water briskly, briefly into the tub, as if washing
something away. Grandma and I are admiring the
photos and paintings on the walls, curious to me in this
new place as in a teasing, subtly taunting riddle. And I

think *Nothing of Grandpa's is here. Except for the photos he's in, Grandpa has vanished.* We're admiring a skillfully executed watercolor of a scene in the Adirondacks, a view of mountains from our family's Lake Placid lodge, and I hear myself say, "You painted that, Grandma—remember?" Grandma laughs uneasily and says, "I did? I did not."

I start to protest *Yes, yes you did*; then catch myself.

"It's beautiful anyway. Whoever painted it."

Grandma smiles at me quizzically. "You painted it? In school?"

Next, we admire Grandma's rings. Except for an opal in a white gold setting, these rings are new to me. And the wristwatches? One of them is Grandma's watch, I guess, though it's loose on her wrist; the other, even looser, appears to be a man's watch. These are strange items, which Grandma examines as I do, smiling and admiring. Mom returns to the room and next examines Grandma's bureau top and drawers, and Grandma's closet. For the first time during the visit, Mom's voice reflects annoyance, distress. "Oh, Mother, what did you do with . . . What happened to . . ." Things seem to be missing from Grandma's room: items of clothing Mom has recently bought for

Grandma, a single bedroom slipper, Grandma's favorite brand of shampoo, a straw gardening hat. Grandma is vague about what has become of these things, though she smiles and puckers her face and gives the appearance of trying to recall. "Did you look in the . . ." Grandma points in the direction of the bathroom, having misplaced the word. She blinks guiltily and absentmindedly picks at the scab on her forehead.

"Grandma? Don't." Gently, I take Grandma's hand.

Mom summons a passing aide to complain of these "pilferings"—"thefts." The aide tells Mom that residents of Unit A are always in and out of one another's rooms. They take things assuming they have the right, wherever they find them. Most of the residents have the idea that the unit is their home, and the other residents are visitors. She says, "Lorine, now, you see she's wearing those rings?—somebody gave her those, or she found them. Lorine always has the prettiest things. One of those wristwatches her man friend gave her. And Lorine is always giving things away. Somebody says, 'Oh, isn't that pretty!'—'Oh, I like that!'—Lorine takes it right off and gives it away. She's a real generous lady, Mrs. Janeway. First thing she told me, when we met, she said I'd been her 'star pupil,' so she wanted to give me a 'star'—tried to give me her opal ring, right then. It'd be gone by now, except it's too tight for her knuckle. See, Lorine is real popular here. But try to keep her from giving her nice things away, or wandering into people's rooms and taking their things—well, that can't be done. You got to understand this, Mrs. Janeway, didn't the director tell you?"

The aide speaks patiently, as if Mom should know these facts.

Mom rarely stays more than forty minutes with Grandma, who becomes quickly tired from these visits, so we prepare to leave. Grandma walks with us to the door of her room, hesitates, seems not to know if she should be coming with us or staying behind. Mom says carefully, "Lisanne and I are leaving for now, Mother. It's almost your dinnertime." Mom hugs and kisses Grandma, not once but several times, as if each time is a fresh good-bye unrelated to the others. When it's time for me to say good-bye to Grandma, I start to choke up, my face begins to crumple like a baby's on the brink of crying. Grandma seems confused, asking where are we going, and we say, "We're going home, Grandma, but we'll be back soon. . . . It's almost your dinnertime now."

I say, "I love you, Grandma." Grandma hugs me tight, I can smell her hair, her body, a sweet, slightly stale fragrance like crushed rose petals. Grandma says, "Honey, why are you crying? There's nothing to cry about. . . ." Behind Grandma's frail back I feel this weird, wet sensation on my fingers, I look and it's Frisky, saying good-bye to me, too.

"Leaving her there. That's . . . Oh God."

In our car, Mom begins to cry. I can see she's been holding this off for the past forty minutes. The kind of helpless crying, a deep hurt, yet without emotion, it tears your heart to hear in your mother especially. I would hug Mom except I'm shy of touching her. "Mom? It's okay, Mom." I feel shaky, too. I will have so much to think about, back home; for hours, days. For the rest of my life. "Grandma is happy, Mom. She really is. It's a good place, Mom. You chose a really good place. You had to do it, Mom: Grandma couldn't live by herself anymore, and she couldn't stay with us, she needs a place like this. Mom, don't cry. I'm sorry I was so . . ."

Next time I visit Grandma, the following Sunday, Grandma is wearing the coral shell necklace.

The scab on her forehead hasn't healed. She seems vague about when she saw me last. But she recognizes me at once. She knows me. I'm her granddaughter, I'm Lisanne.

THE MODEL

1. THE APPROACH OF MR. STARR

Had he stepped out of nowhere, or had he been watching her for some time, even more than he'd claimed, and for a different purpose?—she shivered to think that, yes, probably, she had many times glimpsed him in the village, or in the park, without really seeing him: him, and the long gleaming black limousine she would not have known to associate with him even had she noticed him: the man who called himself Mr. Starr.

As, each day, her eyes passed rapidly and lightly over any number of people both familiar to her and strangers, blurred as in the background of a film in which the foreground is the essential reality, the very point of the film.

She was seventeen. It was in fact the day after her

birthday, a bright gusty January day, and she'd been running in the late afternoon, after school, in the park overlooking the ocean, and she'd just turned to head toward home, pausing to wipe her face, adjust her damp cotton headband, feeling the accelerated strength of her heartbeat and the pleasant ache of her leg muscles: and she glanced up, shy, surprised, and there he stood, a man she had never knowingly seen before. He was smiling at her, his smile broad and eager, hopeful, and he stood in such a way, leaning lightly on a cane, as to block her way on the path; yet tentatively too, with a gentlemanly, deferential air, so as to suggest that he meant no threat. When he spoke, his voice sounded hoarse as if from disuse. "Excuse me!—Hello! Young lady! I realize that this is abrupt, and an intrusion on your privacy, but I am an artist, and I am looking for a model, and I wonder if you might be interested in posing for me? Only here, I mean, in the park—in full daylight! I am willing to pay, per hour—"

Sybil stared at the man who might have been in his forties, or well into his fifties. His thin, lank hair was the color of antique silver—perhaps he was even older. His skin was luridly pale, grainy, and rough; he wore glasses with lenses so darkly tinted as to suggest the kind of glasses worn by the blind; his clothes were plain, dark, conservative—a tweed jacket that fitted him loosely, a shirt buttoned tight to the neck, and no tie, highly polished black leather shoes in an outmoded style. There was something hesitant, even convalescent in his manner, as if, like numerous others in this coastal Southern California town with its population of the retired, the elderly, and the infirm, he had learned by experience to carry himself with care; he could not entirely trust the earth to support him. His features were refined, but worn; subtly distorted, as if seen through wavy glass, or water.

Sybil didn't like it that she couldn't see the man's eyes. Except to know that he was squinting at her, hard. The skin at the corners of his eyes was whitely puckered as if, in his time, he'd done a good deal of squinting and smiling.

Quickly, but politely, Sybil murmured, "No, thank you, I can't."

She was turning away, but still the man spoke, apologetically, "I realize this is a—surprise, but, you see, I don't know how else to make inquiries. I've only just begun sketching in the park, and—"

"Sorry!"

Sybil turned, began to run, not hurriedly, by no means

in a panic, but at her usual measured pace, her head up and her arms swinging at her sides. She was, for all that she looked younger than her seventeen years, not an easily frightened girl, and she was not frightened now; but her face burned with embarrassment. She hoped that no one in the park who knew her had been watching—Glencoe was a small town, and the high school was about a mile away. Why had that preposterous man approached *her*!

He was calling after her, probably waving his cane after her—she didn't dare look back. "I'll be here tomorrow! My name is Starr! Don't judge me too quickly—please! I'm true to my word! My name is Starr! I'll pay you, per hour—" and here he cited an exorbitant sum, nearly twice what Sybil made baby-sitting or working as a librarian's assistant at the branch library near her home, when she could get hired.

She thought, astonished, "He must be mad!"

2. THE TEMPTATION

No sooner had Sybil Blake escaped from the man who called himself Starr, running up Buena Vista Boulevard to Santa Clara, up Santa Clara to Meridian, and so to home, than she began to consider that Mr. Starr's offer was, if preposterous, very tempting. She had never modeled of course but, in art class at the high school, some of her classmates had modeled, fully clothed, just sitting or standing about in ordinary poses, and she and others had sketched them, or tried to—it was really not so easy as it might seem, sketching the lineaments of the human figure; it was still more difficult, sketching an individual's face. But modeling, in itself, was effortless, once you overcame the embarrassment of being stared at. It was, you might argue, a morally neutral activity.

What had Mr. Starr said—*Only here, in the park, in full daylight! I'm true to my word!*

And Sybil needed money, for she was saving for college; she was hoping, too, to attend a summer music institute at U.C. Santa Barbara. (She was a voice student, and she'd been encouraged by her choir director at the high school to get good professional training.) Her aunt Lora Dell Blake, with whom she lived, and had lived since the age of two years eight months, was willing to pay her way—was determined to pay her way—but Sybil felt uneasy about accepting money from Aunt Lora, who worked as a physical therapist at a medical facility in Glencoe, and whose salary, at the top of the pay structure available to her as a state employee, was still modest by California standards. Sybil reasoned that her aunt Lora Dell could not be expected to support her forever.

A long time ago, Sybil had lost her parents, both of them together, in one single cataclysmic hour, when she'd been too young to comprehend what Death was, or was said to be. They had died in a boating accident on Lake Champlain, Sybil's mother at the age of twenty-six, Sybil's father at the age of thirty-one, very attractive young people, a "popular couple" as Aunt Lora spoke of them, choosing her words with care, and saying very little more. *For why ask,* Aunt Lora seemed to be warning Sybil—*you will only make yourself cry.* As soon as she could manage the move, and as soon as Sybil was placed permanently in her care, Aunt Lora had come to California, to this sun-washed coastal town midway between Santa Monica and Santa Barbara. Glencoe was less conspicuously affluent than either of these towns, but, with its palm-lined streets, its sunny placidity, and its openness to the ocean, it was the very antithesis, as Aunt Lora said, of Wellington, Vermont, where the Blakes had lived for generations. (After their move to California, Lora Dell Blake had formally adopted Sybil as her child: thus Sybil's name was

"Blake," as her mother's had been. If asked what her father's name had been, Sybil would have had to think before recalling, dimly, "Conte.") Aunt Lora spoke so negatively of New England in general and Vermont in particular, Sybil felt no nostalgia for it; she had no sentimental desire to visit her birthplace, not even to see her parents' graves. From Aunt Lora's stories, Sybil had the idea that Vermont was damp and cold twelve months of the year, and frigidly, impossibly cold in winter; its wooded mountains were unlike the beautiful snow-capped mountains of the West, and cast shadows upon its small, cramped, depopulated and impoverished old towns. Aunt Lora, a transplanted New Englander, was vehement in her praise of California—"With the Pacific Ocean to the west," she said, "it's like a room with one wall missing. Your instinct is to look out, not back; and it's a good instinct."

Lora Dell Blake was the sort of person who delivered statements with an air of inviting contradiction. But tall, rangy, restless, belligerent, she was not the sort of person most people wanted to contradict.

Indeed, Aunt Lora had never encouraged Sybil to ask questions about her dead parents, or about the tragic accident that had killed them; if she had photographs, snapshots, mementos of life back in Wellington, Vermont, they were safely hidden away, and Sybil had not seen them. "It would just be too painful," she told Sybil, "—for us both." The remark was both a plea and a warning.

Of course, Sybil avoided the subject.

She prepared carefully chosen words, should anyone happen to ask her why she was living with her aunt, and not her parents; or, at least, one of her parents. But—this was Southern California, and very few of Sybil's classmates were living with the set of parents with whom they'd begun. No one asked.

An orphan?—I'm not an orphan, Sybil would say. I was never an orphan because my aunt Lora was always there.

I was two years old when it happened, the accident.

No, I don't remember.

But no one asked.

Sybil told her aunt Lora nothing about the man in the park—the man who called himself Starr—she'd put him out of her mind entirely and yet, in bed that night, drifting into sleep, she found herself thinking suddenly of him, and seeing him again, vividly. That silver hair, those gleaming black shoes. His eyes hidden behind dark glasses. How tempting, his offer!—though there was no question of Sybil accepting it. Absolutely not.

Still, Mr. Starr seemed harmless. Well-intentioned. An eccentric, of course, but *interesting*. She supposed he had money, if he could offer her so much to model for him. There was something *not contemporary* about him. The set of his head and shoulders. That air about him of gentlemanly reserve, courtesy—even as he'd made his outlandish request. In Glencoe, in the past several years, there had been a visible increase in homeless persons and derelicts, especially in the oceanside park, but Mr. Starr was certainly not one of these.

Then Sybil realized, as if a door, hitherto locked, had swung open of its own accord, that she'd seen Mr. Starr before . . . somewhere. In the park, where she ran most afternoons for an hour? In downtown Glencoe? On the street? In the public library? In the vicinity of Glencoe Senior High School? In the school itself, in the auditorium? Sybil summoned up a memory as if by an act of physical exertion: the school choir, of which she was a member, had been rehearsing Handel's *Messiah* the previous month for their annual Christmas pageant, and Sybil had sung her solo part, a demanding part for contralto voice, and the choir director had praised her in front of the others . . . and she'd seemed to see, dimly, a man, a stranger, seated at the very rear of the auditorium, his features indistinct but his gray hair striking, and wasn't this man miming applause, clapping silently? *There. At the rear, on the aisle.* It frequently happened that visitors dropped by rehearsals—parents or relatives of choir members, colleagues of the music director. So no one took special notice of the stranger sitting unobtrusively at the rear of the auditorium. He wore dark, conservative clothes of the kind to attract no attention, and dark glasses hid his eyes. But there he was. *For Sybil Blake. He'd come for Sybil.* But at the time, Sybil had not seen.

Nor had she seen the man leave. Slipping quietly out of his seat, walking with a just perceptible limp, leaning on his cane.

3. THE PROPOSITION

Sybil had no intention of seeking out Mr. Starr, nor even of looking around for him, but the following afternoon, as she was headed home after her run, there, suddenly, the man was—taller than she recalled, looming large, his dark glasses winking in the sunlight, and his pale lips stretched in a tentative smile. He wore his clothes of the previous day except he'd set on his head a sporty plaid golfing cap that gave him a rakish yet wistful air, and he'd tied, as if in haste, a rumpled cream-colored silk scarf around his neck. He was standing on the path in approximately the same place as before, and leaning on his cane; on a bench close by were what appeared to be his art supplies, in a canvas duffel bag of the sort students carried. "Why, hello!" he said, shyly but eagerly, "—I didn't dare hope you would come back, but"—his smile widened as if on the verge of desperation, the puckered skin at the corners of his eyes tightened—"I *hoped*."

After running, Sybil always felt good: strength flowed into her legs, arms, lungs. She was a delicate-boned girl, since infancy prone to respiratory infections, but such vigorous exercise had made her strong in recent years; and with physical confidence had come a growing confidence in herself. She laughed, lightly, at this strange man's words, and merely shrugged, and said, "Well—this *is* my park, after all." Mr. Starr nodded eagerly, as if any response from her, any words at all, were of enormous interest. "Yes, yes," he said, "—I can see that. Do you live close by?"

Sybil shrugged. It was none of his business, was it,

where she lived? "Maybe," she said.

"And your—name?" He stared at her, hopefully, adjusting his glasses more firmly on his nose. "—My name is Starr."

"My name is—Blake."

Mr. Starr blinked, and smiled, as if uncertain whether this might be a joke. "Blake—? An unusual name for a girl," he said.

Sybil laughed again, feeling her face heat. She decided not to correct the misunderstanding.

Today, prepared for the encounter, having anticipated it for hours, Sybil was distinctly less uneasy than she'd been the day before: the man had a business proposition to make to her, that was all. And the park *was* an open, public, safe place, as familiar to her as the small neat yard of her aunt Lora's house.

So, when Mr. Starr repeated his offer, Sybil said, yes, she was interested after all; she did need money, she was saving for college. "For college?—really? So young?" Mr. Starr said, with an air of surprise. Sybil shrugged, as if the remark didn't require any reply. "I suppose, here in California, young people grow up quickly," Mr. Starr said. He'd gone to get his sketch pad, to show Sybil his work,

THE MODEL • 323

and Sybil turned the pages with polite interest, as Mr. Starr chattered. He was, he said, an "amateur artist"—the very epitome of the "amateur"—with no delusions regarding his talent, but a strong belief that the world is redeemed by art—"And the world, you know, being profane, and steeped in wickedness, requires constant, ceaseless redemption." He believed that the artist "bears witness" to this fact; and that art can be a "conduit of emotion" where the heart is empty. Sybil, leafing through the sketches, paid little attention to Mr. Starr's tumble of words; she was struck by the feathery, uncertain, somehow *worshipful* detail in the drawings, which, to her eye, were not so bad as she'd expected, though by no means of professional quality. As she looked at them, Mr. Starr came to look over her shoulder, embarrassed, and excited, his shadow falling over the pages. The ocean, the waves, the wide rippled beach as seen from the bluff—palm trees, hibiscus, flowers—a World War II memorial in the park— mothers with young children—solitary figures huddled on park benches—cyclists—joggers—several pages of joggers: Mr. Starr's work was ordinary, even commonplace, but certainly earnest. Sybil saw herself amid the joggers, or a figure she guessed must be herself, a young girl with shoulder-length dark hair held off her face by a headband, in jeans and a sweatshirt, caught in mid stride, legs and swinging arms caught in motion—it *was* herself, but so clumsily executed, the profile so smudged, no one would have known. Still, Sybil felt her face grow warmer, and she sensed Mr. Starr's anticipation like a withheld breath.

Sybil did not think it quite right for her, aged seventeen, to pass judgment on the talent of a middle-aged man, so she merely murmured something vague and polite and positive; and Mr. Starr, taking the sketch pad from her, said, "Oh, I *know*—I'm not very good, yet. But I propose to try." He smiled at her, and took out a freshly laundered white handkerchief, and dabbed at his forehead, and said, "Do you have any questions about posing for me, or shall we begin? We'll have at least three hours of daylight, today."

"Three hours!" Sybil exclaimed. "That long?"

"If you get uncomfortable," Mr. Starr said quickly, "—we'll simply stop, wherever we are." Seeing that Sybil was frowning, he added, eagerly, "We'll take breaks every now and then, I promise. And, and"—seeing that Sybil was still indecisive—"I'll pay you a full hour's fee for any part of an hour." Still Sybil stood, wondering if, after all, she should be agreeing to this, without her aunt Lora, or anyone, knowing; wasn't there something just faintly odd about Mr. Starr, and about his willingness to pay her so much for doing so little? And wasn't there something troubling (however flattering) about his particular interest in her? Assuming Sybil was correct, and he'd been watching her . . . aware of her . . . for at least a month. "I'll be happy to pay you in advance, Blake."

The name "Blake" sounded very odd, in this stranger's mouth. Sybil had never before been called by her last name only.

Sybil laughed nervously and said, "You don't have to pay me in advance—thanks!"

So Sybil Blake, against her better judgment, became a model, for Mr. Starr.

And, despite her self-consciousness, and her intermittent sense that there was something ludicrous in the enterprise, as about Mr. Starr's intense, fussy, self-important manner as he sketched her (he was a perfectionist, or wanted to give that impression: crumpling a half dozen sheets of paper, breaking out new charcoal sticks, before he began a sketch that pleased him), the initial session was easy, effortless. "What I want to capture," Mr. Starr said,

"—is, beyond your beautiful profile, Blake—and you *are* a beautiful child!—the brooding quality of the ocean. That look to it, d'you see?—of it having consciousness of a kind, actually thinking. Yes, *brooding*!"

Sybil, squinting down at the white-capped waves, the rhythmic crashing surf, the occasional surfers riding their boards with their remarkable amphibian dexterity, thought that the ocean was anything but *brooding*.

"Why are you smiling, Blake?" Mr. Starr asked, pausing. "Is something funny?—am *I* funny?"

Quickly Sybil said, "Oh, no, Mr. Starr, of course not."

"But I *am*, I'm sure," he said happily. "And if you find me so, please *do* laugh!"

Sybil found herself laughing, as if rough fingers were tickling her. She thought of how it might have been . . . had she had a father, and a mother: her own family, as she'd been meant to have.

Mr. Starr was squatting now on the grass close by, and peering up at Sybil with an expression of extreme concentration. The charcoal stick in his fingers moved rapidly. "The ability to *laugh*," he said, "is the ability to *live*—the two are synonymous. You're too young to understand that right now, but one day you will." Sybil shrugged, wiping at her eyes. Mr. Starr was talking grandly. "The world is fallen and profane—the opposite of 'sacred,' you know, *is* 'profane.' It requires ceaseless vigilance—ceaseless redemption. The artist is one who redeems by restoring the world's innocence, where he can. The artist gives, but does not take away, not even supplant."

Sybil said, skeptically, "But you want to make money with your drawings, don't you?"

Mr. Starr seemed genuinely shocked. "Oh, my, no. Adamantly, *no*."

Sybil persisted, "Well, most people would. I mean, most people need to. If they have any talent"—she was speaking with surprising bluntness, an almost childlike audacity—"they need to sell it, somehow."

As if he'd been caught out in a crime, Mr. Starr began to stammer apologetically, "It's true, Blake, I—I am not like most people, I suppose. I've inherited some money—not a fortune, but enough to live on comfortably for the rest of my life. I've been traveling abroad," he said, vaguely, "—and, in my absence, interest accumulated."

Sybil asked doubtfully, "You don't have any regular profession?"

Mr. Starr laughed, startled. Up close, his teeth were

chunky and irregular, slightly stained, like aged ivory piano keys. "But dear child," he said, "*this* is my profession— 'redeeming the world'!"

And he fell to sketching Sybil with renewed enthusiasm.

Minutes passed. Long minutes. Sybil felt a mild ache between her shoulder blades. A mild uneasiness in her chest. *Mr. Starr is mad. Is Mr. Starr "mad"?* Behind her, on the path, people were passing by, there were joggers, cyclists—Mr. Starr, lost in a trance of concentration, paid them not the slightest heed. Sybil wondered if anyone knew her, and was taking note of this peculiar event. Or was she, herself, making too much of it? She decided she would tell her aunt Lora about Mr. Starr that evening, tell Aunt Lora frankly how much he was paying her. She both respected and feared her aunt's judgment: in Sybil's imagination, in that unexamined sphere of being we call the imagination, Lora Dell Blake had acquired the authority of both Sybil's deceased parents.

Yes, she would tell Aunt Lora.

After only an hour and forty minutes, when Sybil appeared to be growing restless, and sighed several times, unconsciously, Mr. Starr suddenly declared the session over. He had, he said, three promising sketches, and he didn't want to exhaust her, or himself. She *was* coming back tomorrow—?

"I don't know," Sybil said. "Maybe."

Sybil protested, though not very adamantly, when Mr. Starr paid her the full amount, for three hours' modeling. He paid her in cash, out of his wallet—an expensive kid-skin wallet brimming with bills. Sybil thanked him, deeply embarrassed, and eager to escape. Oh, there *was* something shameful about the transaction!

Up close, she was able—almost—to see Mr. Starr's eyes through the dark-tinted lenses of his glasses. Some delicacy of tact made her glance away quickly but she had an impression of kindness—gentleness.

Sybil took the money, and put it in her pocket, and turned, to hurry away. With no mind for who might hear him, Mr. Starr called after her, "You see, Blake?—Starr is true to his word. Always!"

4. IS THE OMISSION OF TRUTH A LIE, OR ONLY AN OMISSION?

"Well!—tell me how things went with *you* today, Sybil!" Lora Dell Blake said, with such an air of bemused exasperation, Sybil understood that, as so often, Aunt Lora had something to say that really couldn't wait—her work at the Glencoe Medical Center provided her with a seemingly inexhaustible supply of comical and outrageous anecdotes. So, deferring to Aunt Lora, as they prepared supper together as usual, and sat down to eat it, Sybil was content to listen, and to laugh.

For it *was* funny, if outrageous too—the latest episode in the ongoing folly at the Medical Center.

Lora Dell Blake, in her late forties, was a tall, lanky, restless woman with close-cropped graying hair; sand-colored eyes, and skin; a generous spirit, but a habit of sarcasm. Though she claimed to love Southern California— "You don't know what paradise is, unless you're from somewhere else"—she seemed in fact an awkwardly transplanted New Englander, with expectations and a sense of personal integrity, or intransigence, quite out of place here. She was fond of saying she did not suffer fools gladly, and so it was. Overqualified for her position at the Glencoe Medical Center, she'd had no luck in finding work elsewhere, partly because she did not want to leave Glencoe, and "uproot" Sybil while she was still in high school; and partly because her interviews were invariably disasters—Lora Dell Blake was incapable of being, or even seeming, docile, tractable, "feminine," hypocritical.

Lora was not Sybil's sole living relative—there were Blakes, and Contes, back in Vermont—but Lora had discouraged visitors to the small stucco bungalow on Meridian Street, in Glencoe, California; she had not in fact troubled to reply to letters or cards since, having been granted custody of her younger sister's daughter, at the time of what she called "the tragedy," she'd picked up and moved across the continent, to a part of the country she knew nothing about—"My intention is to erase the past, for the child's sake," she said, "and to start a new life."

And: "For the child, for poor little Sybil—I would make any sacrifice."

Sybil, who loved her aunt very much, had the vague idea that there had been, many years ago, protests, queries, telephone calls—but that Aunt Lora had dealt with them all, and really had made a new and "uncomplicated" life for them. Aunt Lora was one of those personalities, already strong, who are strengthened, and empowered, by being challenged; she seemed to take pleasure in confrontation, whether with her own relatives or her employers at the Medical Center—anyone who presumed to tell her what to do. She was especially protective of Sybil, since, as she often said, they had no one but each other.

Which was true. Aunt Lora had seen to that.

Though Sybil had been adopted by her aunt, there was never any pretense that she was anything but Lora's niece, not her daughter. Nor did most people, seeing the two together, noting their physical dissimilarities, make that mistake.

So it happened that Sybil Blake grew up knowing virtually nothing about her Vermont background except its general tragic outline; her knowledge of her mother and father, the precise circumstances of their deaths, was as vague and unexamined in her consciousness as a childhood fairy tale. For whenever, as a little girl, Sybil would ask her aunt about these things, Aunt Lora responded with hurt, or alarm, or reproach, or, most disturbingly, anxiety. Her eyes might flood with tears—Aunt Lora, who never cried. She might take Sybil's hands in both her own, and squeeze them tightly, and, looking Sybil in the eyes, say, in a quiet, commanding voice, "But, darling, *you don't want to know.*"

So too, that evening, when, for some reason, Sybil brought up the subject, asking Aunt Lora how, again, exactly, *had* her parents died, Aunt Lora looked at her in surprise; and, for a long moment, rummaging in the pockets of her shirt for a pack of cigarettes that wasn't there (Aunt Lora had given up smoking the previous month, for perhaps the fifth time), it seemed almost that Lora herself did not remember.

"Sybil, honey—why are you asking? I mean, why *now*?"

"I don't know," Sybil said evasively. "I guess—I'm just asking."

"Nothing happened to you at school, did it?"

Sybil could not see how this question related to her own, but she said, politely, "No, Aunt Lora. Of course not."

"It's just that, out of nowhere—I can't help but wonder *why*," Aunt Lora said, frowning, "—you should ask."

Aunt Lora regarded Sybil with worried eyes: a look of such suffocating familiarity that, for a moment, Sybil felt as if a band was tightening around her chest, making it impossible to breathe. *Why is my wanting to know a test of my love for you?—why do you do this, Aunt Lora, every time?* She said, an edge of anger to her voice, "I was seventeen years old last week, Aunt Lora. I'm not a child any longer."

Aunt Lora laughed, startled. "Certainly you're not a child!"

Aunt Lora then sighed, and, in a characteristic gesture, meaning both impatience and a dutiful desire to please, ran both hands rapidly through her hair, and began to speak. She assured Sybil that there was little to know, really. The accident—the tragedy—had happened so long ago. "Your mother, Melanie, was twenty-six years old at the time—a beautiful sweet-natured young woman, with eyes like yours, cheekbones like yours, pale wavy hair. Your father, George Conte, was thirty-one years old—a promising young lawyer, in his father's firm—an attractive, ambitious man—" And here as in the past Aunt Lora paused, as if, in the very act of summoning up this long-dead couple, she had forgotten them, and was simply repeating a story, a family tale, like one of the more extreme of her tales of the Glencoe Medical Center, worn smooth by countless tellings.

"A boating accident—Fourth of July—" Sybil coaxed, "—and I was with you, and—"

"You were with me, and Grandma, at the cottage— you were just a little girl!" Aunt Lora said, blinking tears from her eyes, "—and it was almost dusk, and time for the fireworks to start. Mommy and Daddy were out in Daddy's speedboat—they'd been across the lake, at the Club—"

"And they started back across the lake—Lake Champlain—"

"—Lake Champlain, of course: it's beautiful, but treacherous, if a storm comes up suddenly—"

"And Daddy was at the controls of the boat—"

"—and, somehow, they capsized. And drowned. A rescue boat went out immediately, but it was too late." Aunt Lora's mouth turned hard. Her eyes glistening with tears, as if defiantly. "They drowned."

Sybil's heart was beating painfully. She was certain there must be more, yet she herself could remember nothing—not even herself, that two-year-old child, waiting for Mommy and Daddy who were never to arrive. Her memory of her mother and father was vague, dim, featureless, like a dream that, even as it seems about to drift into consciousness, retreats further into darkness. She said, in a whisper, "It was an accident. *No one* was to blame."

Aunt Lora chose her words with care. "No one was to blame."

There was a pause. Sybil looked at her aunt, who was

not now looking at her. How lined, even leathery, the older woman's face was getting!—all her life she'd been reckless, indifferent, about sun, wind, weather, and now, in her late forties, she might have been a decade older. Sybil said, tentatively, "No one was to blame—?"

"Well, if you must know," Aunt Lora said, "—there was evidence he'd been drinking. They'd been drinking. At the Club."

Sybil could not have been more shocked had Aunt Lora reached over and pinched the back of her hand. "Drinking—?" She had never heard this part of the story before.

Aunt Lora continued, grimly, "But not enough, probably, to have made a difference." Again she paused. She was not looking at Sybil. "Probably."

Sybil, stunned, could not think of anything further to say, or to ask.

Aunt Lora was on her feet, pacing. Her close-cropped hair was disheveled and her manner fiercely contentious, as if she was arguing her case before an invisible audience as Sybil looked on. "What fools! I tried to tell her! 'Popular' couple—'attractive' couple—lots of friends—too many friends! That goddamned Champlain Club, where everyone drank too much! All that money, and privilege! And what good did it do! She—Melanie—so proud of being asked to join—proud of marrying *him*—throwing her life away! That's what it came to, in the end. I'd warned her it was dangerous—playing with fire—but would she listen? Would either of them listen? To Lora?—to *me*? When you're that age, so ignorant, you think you will live forever—you can throw your life away—"

Sybil felt ill, suddenly. She walked swiftly out of the room, shut the door to her own room, stood in the dark, beginning to cry.

So that was it, the secret. The tawdry little secret—drinking, drunkenness—behind the "tragedy."

With characteristic tact, Aunt Lora did not knock on Sybil's door but left her alone for the remainder of the night.

Only after Sybil was in bed, and the house darkened, did she realize she'd forgotten to tell her aunt about Mr. Starr—he'd slipped her mind entirely. And the money he'd pressed into her hand, now in her bureau drawer, rolled up neatly beneath her underwear, as if hidden. . . .

Sybil thought, guiltily, *I can tell her tomorrow.*

5. THE HEARSE

Crouched in front of Sybil Blake, eagerly sketching her likeness, Mr. Starr was saying, in a quick, rapturous voice, "Yes, yes, like that!—yes! Your face uplifted to the sun like a blossoming flower! Just so!" And: "There are only two or three eternal questions, Blake, which, like the surf, repeat themselves endlessly: 'Why are we here?'—'Where have we come from, and where are we going?'—'Is there purpose to the universe, or merely chance?' These questions the artist seems to express in the images he knows." And: "Dear child, I wish you would tell me about yourself. Just a little!"

As if, in the night, some change had come upon her, some new resolve, Sybil had fewer misgivings about modeling for Mr. Starr this afternoon. It was as if they knew each other well, somehow: Sybil was reasonably certain that Mr. Starr was not a sexual pervert, nor even a madman of a more conventional sort; she'd glimpsed his sketches of her, which were fussy, overworked, and smudged, but not bad as likenesses. The man's murmurous chatter was comforting in a way, hypnotic as the surf, no longer quite so embarrassing—for he talked, most of the time, not with her but at her, and there was no need to reply. In a way, Mr. Starr reminded Sybil of her aunt Lora, when she launched into one of her comical anecdotes about the Glencoe Medical Center. Aunt Lora was more entertaining than Mr. Starr, but Mr. Starr was more idealistic.

His optimism was simpleminded, maybe. But it *was* optimistic.

For this second modeling session, Mr. Starr had taken Sybil to a corner of the park where they were unlikely to be disturbed. He'd asked her to remove her headband, and to sit on a bench with her head dropping back, her eyes partly shut, her face uplifted to the sun—an uncomfortable pose at first, until, lulled by the crashing surf below, and Mr. Starr's monologue, Sybil began to feel oddly peaceful, floating.

Yes, in the night some change had come upon her. She could not comprehend its dimensions, nor even its tone. She'd fallen asleep crying bitterly but had wakened feeling—what? Vulnerable, somehow. And wanting to be so. *Uplifted. Like a blossoming flower.*

That morning, Sybil had forgotten again to tell her aunt Lora about Mr. Starr, and the money she was making—such a generous amount, and for so little effort! She shrank from considering how her aunt might respond, for her aunt was mistrustful of strangers, and particularly of men. . . . Sybil reasoned that, when she did tell Aunt Lora, that evening, or tomorrow morning, she would make her understand that there was something kindly and trusting and almost childlike about Mr. Starr. You could laugh at him, but laughter was somehow inappropriate.

As if, though middle-aged, he had been away somewhere, sequestered, protected, out of the adult world. Innocent and, himself, vulnerable.

Today, too, he'd eagerly offered to pay Sybil in advance for modeling, and, another time, Sybil had declined. She would not have wanted to tell Mr. Starr that, were she paid in advance, she might be tempted to cut the session even shorter than otherwise.

Mr. Starr was saying, hesitantly, "Blake?—can you tell me about"—and here he paused, as if drawing a random, inspired notion out of nowhere—"your mother?"

Sybil hadn't been paying close attention to Mr. Starr. Now she opened her eyes, and looked directly at him.

Mr. Starr was perhaps not so old as she'd originally thought, nor as old as he behaved. His face was a handsome face, but oddly roughened—the skin like sandpaper. Very sallow, sickly-pale. A faint scar on his forehead above his left eye, the shape of a fish hook, or a question mark.

Or was it a birthmark?—or, even less romantically, some sort of skin blemish? Maybe his roughened, pitted skin was the result of teenaged acne, nothing more.

His tentative smile bared chunky damp teeth.

Today Mr. Starr was bareheaded, and his thin, fine, uncannily silver hair was stirred by the wind. He wore plain, nondescript clothes, a shirt too large for him, a khaki-colored jacket with rolled-up sleeves. At close range, Sybil could see his eyes through the tinted lenses of his glasses: they were small, deep-set, intelligent, glistening. The skin beneath was pouched and shadowed, as if bruised.

Sybil shivered, peering so directly into Mr. Starr's eyes. As into another's soul, when she was unprepared.

Sybil swallowed, and said, slowly, "My mother is . . . not living."

A curious way of speaking!—for why not say, candidly, in normal usage, *My mother is dead.*

For a long painful moment Sybil's words hovered in the air between them; as if Mr. Starr, discountenanced by his own blunder, seemed not to want to hear.

He said, quickly, apologetically, "Oh—I see. I'm so sorry."

Sybil had been posing in the sun, warmly mesmerized by the sun, the surf, Mr. Starr's voice, and now, as if wakened from a sleep of which she had not been conscious, she felt as if she'd been touched—prodded into wakefulness. She saw, upside down, the fussy smudged sketch Mr. Starr had been doing of her, saw his charcoal stick poised above the stiff white paper in an attitude of chagrin. She laughed, and wiped at her eyes, and said, "It happened a long time ago. I never think of it, really."

Mr. Starr's expression was wary, complex. He asked, "And so—do you—live with your—father?" The words seemed oddly forced.

"No, I don't. And I don't want to talk about this anymore, Mr. Starr, if it's all right with you."

Sybil spoke pleadingly, yet with an air of finality.

"Then—we won't! We won't! We certainly won't!" Mr. Starr said quickly. And fell to sketching again, his face creased in concentration.

And so the remainder of the session passed, in silence.

Again, as soon as Sybil evinced signs of restlessness, Mr. Starr declared she could stop for the day—he didn't want to exhaust her, or himself.

Sybil rubbed her neck, which ached mildly; she stretched her arms, her legs. Her skin felt slightly sun- or wind-burned and her eyes felt seared, as if she'd been staring directly into the sun. Or had she been crying?—she couldn't remember.

Again, Mr. Starr paid Sybil in cash, out of his kidskin wallet brimming with bills. His hand shook just visibly as he pressed the money into Sybil's. (Embarrassed, Sybil folded the bills quickly and put them in her pocket. Later, at home, she would discover that Mr. Starr had given her ten dollars too much: a bonus, for almost making her cry?) Though it was clear that Sybil was eager to get away, Mr. Starr walked with her up the slope, in the direction of the Boulevard, limping, leaning on his cane, but keeping a brisk pace. He asked if Sybil—of course, he called her Blake: "Dear Blake"—would like to have some refreshment with him, in a café nearby?—and, when Sybil declined, murmured, "Yes, yes, I understand—I suppose." He then asked if Sybil would return the following day, and, when Sybil did not say no, added that, if she did, he would like to increase her hourly fee in exchange for asking of her a slightly different sort of modeling—"A slightly modified sort of modeling, here in the park, or perhaps down on the beach, in full daylight of course, as before, and yet, in its way"—Mr. Starr paused nervously, seeking the right word—"experimental."

Sybil asked doubtfully, "'Experimental'—?"

"I'm prepared to increase your fee, Blake, by half."

"What kind of 'experimental'?"

"Emotion."

"What?"

"Emotion. Memory. Interiority."

Now that they were emerging from the park, and more likely to be seen, Sybil was glancing uneasily about: she dreaded seeing someone from school, or, worse yet, a friend of her aunt's. Mr. Starr gestured as he spoke, and seemed more than ordinarily excited. "—'Interiority.' That which is hidden to the outer eye. I'll tell you in more detail tomorrow, Blake," he said. "You *will* meet me here tomorrow?"

Sybil murmured, "I don't know, Mr. Starr."

"Oh, but you must!—please."

Sybil felt a tug of sympathy for Mr. Starr. He *was* kind, and courteous, and gentlemanly; and, certainly, very generous. She could not imagine his life except to see him as a lonely, eccentric man without friends. Uncomfortable as she was in his presence, she yet wondered if perhaps she was exaggerating his eccentricity: what would a neutral observer make of the tall, limping figure, the cane, the canvas duffel bag, the polished black leather shoes that reminded her of a funeral, the fine, thin, beautiful silver hair, the dark glasses that winked in the sunshine . . . ? Would such an observer, seeing Sybil Blake and Mr. Starr together, give them a second glance?

"Look," Sybil said, pointing, "—a hearse."

At a curb close by there was a long sleekly black car with dark-tinted, impenetrable windows. Mr. Starr laughed, and said, embarrassed, "I'm afraid, Blake, that isn't a hearse, you know—it's my car."

"Your car?"

"Yes. I'm afraid so."

Now Sybil could see that the vehicle was a limousine, waiting at the curb. Behind the wheel was a youngish driver with a visored cap on his head; in profile, he appeared Asian. Sybil stared, amazed. So Mr. Starr was wealthy, indeed.

He was saying, apologetically, yet with a kind of boyish pleasure, "I don't drive, myself, you see!—a further handicap. I did, once, long ago, but—circumstances intervened." Sybil was thinking that she often saw chauffeur-driven limousines in Glencoe, but she'd never known anyone who owned one before. Mr. Starr said, "Blake, may I give you a ride home?—I'd be delighted, of course."

Sybil laughed, as if she'd been tickled, hard, in the ribs.

"A ride? In that?" she asked.

"No trouble! Absolutely!" Mr. Starr limped to the rear door and opened it with a flourish, before the driver could get out to open it for him. He squinted back at Sybil, smiling hopefully. "It's the least I can do for you, after our exhausting session."

Sybil was smiling, staring into the shadowy interior of the car. The uniformed driver had climbed out and stood, not quite knowing what to do, watching. He was a Filipino, perhaps, not young after all but with a small, wizened face; he wore white gloves. He stood very straight and silent, watching Sybil.

There was a moment when it seemed, yes, Sybil was going to accept Mr. Starr's offer, and climb into the rear of the long sleekly black limousine, so that Mr. Starr could climb in behind her, and shut the door upon them both; but, then, for some reason she could not have named—it might have been the smiling intensity with which Mr.

Starr was looking at her, or the rigid posture of the white-gloved driver—she changed her mind and called out, "No thanks!"

Mr. Starr was disappointed, and hurt—you could see it in his downturned mouth. But he said, cheerfully, "Oh, I quite understand, Blake—I *am* a stranger, after all. It's better to be prudent, of course. But, my dear, I *will* see you tomorrow—?"

Sybil shouted, "Maybe!" and ran across the street.

6. THE FACE

She stayed away from the park. *Because I want to, because I can.*

Thursday, in any case, was her voice lesson after school. Friday, choir rehearsal; then an evening with friends. On Saturday morning she went jogging, not in the oceanside park but in another park, miles away, where Mr. Starr could not have known to look for her. And, on Sunday, Aunt Lora drove them to Los Angeles for a belated birthday celebration, for Sybil—an art exhibit, a dinner, a play.

So you see, I can do it. I don't need your money, or you.

Since the evening when Aunt Lora had told Sybil

about her parents' boating accident—that it might have been caused by drinking—neither Sybil nor her aunt had cared to bring up the subject again. Sybil shuddered to think of it. She felt properly chastised for her curiosity.

Why do you want to know?—you will only make yourself cry.

Sybil had never gotten around to telling Aunt Lora about Mr. Starr, nor about her modeling. Even during their long Sunday together. Not a word about her cache of money, hidden away in a bureau drawer.

Money for what?—for summer school, for college.

For the future.

Aunt Lora was not the sort of person to spy on a member of her household, but she observed Sybil closely, with her trained clinician's eye. "Sybil, you've been very quiet lately—there's nothing wrong, I hope?" she asked, and Sybil said quickly, nervously, "Oh, no! What could be wrong?"

She was feeling guilty about keeping a secret from Aunt Lora, and she was feeling guilty about staying away from Mr. Starr.

Two adults. Like twin poles. Of course, Mr. Starr was really a stranger—he did not exist in Sybil Blake's life, at all. Why did it feel to her, so strangely, that he did?

Days passed, and, instead of forgetting Mr. Starr, and strengthening her resolve not to model for him, Sybil seemed to see the man, in her mind's eye, ever more clearly. She could not understand why he seemed attracted to her, she was convinced it was not a sexual attraction but something purer, more spiritual, and yet—why? Why *her*?

Why had he visited her high school, and sat in on a choir rehearsal? Had he known she would be there?—or was it simply coincidence?

She shuddered to think of what Aunt Lora would make of this, if she knew. If news of Mr. Starr got back to her.

Mr. Starr's face floated before her. Its pallor, its sorrow. That look of convalescence. Waiting. The dark glasses. The hopeful smile. One night, waking from a particularly vivid, disturbing dream, Sybil thought for a confused moment that she'd seen Mr. Starr, in the room—it hadn't been just a dream! How wounded he'd looked, puzzled, hurt. *Come with me, Sybil. Hurry. Now. It's been so long.* He'd been waiting for her in the park for days, limping, the duffel bag slung over his shoulder, glancing up hopefully at every passing stranger.

Behind him, the elegantly gleaming black limousine, larger than Sybil remembered; and driverless.

Sybil?—Sybil? Mr. Starr called, impatiently.

As if, all along, he'd known her real name. And she had known he'd known.

7. THE EXPERIMENT

So, Monday afternoon, Sybil Blake found herself back in the park, modeling for Mr. Starr.

Seeing him in the park, so obviously awaiting her, Sybil had felt almost apologetic. Not that he greeted her with any measure of reproach (though his face was drawn and sallow, as if he hadn't been sleeping well), nor even questioned her mutely with his eyes *Where have you been?* Certainly not! He smiled happily when he saw her, limping in her direction like a doting father, seemingly determined not to acknowledge her absence of the past four days. Sybil called out, "Hello, Mr. Starr!" and felt, yes, so strangely, as if things were once again right.

"How lovely!—and the day is so fine!—'in full daylight'—as I promised!" Mr. Starr cried.

Sybil had been jogging for forty minutes, and felt very good, strengthened. She removed her damp yellow headband and stuffed it in her pocket. When Mr. Starr repeated the terms of his proposition of the previous week, restating the higher fee, Sybil agreed at once, for of course that was why she'd come. How, in all reasonableness, could she resist?

Mr. Starr took some time before deciding upon a place for Sybil to pose—"It must be ideal, a synthesis of poetry and practicality." Finally, he chose a partly crumbling stone ledge overlooking the beach in a remote corner of the park. He asked Sybil to lean against the ledge, gazing out at the ocean. Her hands pressed flat against the top of the ledge, her head uplifted as much as possible, within comfort. "But today, dear Blake, I am going to record not just the surface likeness of a lovely young girl," he said, "—but *memory*, and *emotion*, coursing through her."

Sybil took the position readily enough. So invigorated did she feel from her exercise, and so happy to be back, again, in her role as model, she smiled out at the ocean as at an old friend. "What kind of memory and emotion, Mr. Starr?" she asked.

Mr. Starr eagerly took up his sketch pad and a fresh

stick of charcoal. It was a mild day, the sky placid and featureless, though, up the coast, in the direction of Big Sur,
massive thunderclouds were gathering. The surf was high,
the waves powerful, hypnotic. One hundred yards below,
young men in surfing gear, carrying their boards lightly as
if they were made of papier-mâché, prepared to enter the
water.

Mr. Starr cleared his throat and said, almost shyly,
"Your mother, dear Blake. Tell me all you know—all you
can remember—about your mother."

"My mother?"

Sybil winced and would have broken her position,
except Mr. Starr put out a quick hand, to steady her. It was
the first time he had touched her in quite that way. He
said, gently, "I realize it's a painful subject, Blake, but—
will you try?"

Sybil said, "No. I don't want to."

"You won't, then?"

"I *can't.*"

"But why can't you, dear?—any memory of your
mother would do."

"*No.*"

Sybil saw that as Mr. Starr was quickly sketching her,

or trying to—his hand shook. She wanted to reach out to snatch the charcoal stick from him and snap it in two. How dare he! Goddamn him!

"Yes, yes," Mr. Starr said hurriedly, an odd, elated look on his face, as if, studying her so intently, he was not seeing her at all, "—yes, dear, like that. Any memory—any! So long as it's yours."

Sybil said, "Whose else would it be?" She laughed, and was surprised that her laughter sounded like sobbing.

"Why, many times innocent children are given memories by adults; contaminated by memories not their own," Mr. Starr said somberly. "In which case the memory is spurious. Inauthentic."

Sybil saw her likeness on the sheet of stiff white paper, upside down. There was something repulsive about it. Though she was wearing her usual jogging clothes Mr. Starr made it look as if she was wearing a clinging, flowing gown; or, maybe, nothing at all. Where her small breasts would have been were swirls and smudges of charcoal, as if she was on the brink of dissolution. Her face and head were vividly drawn, but rather raw, crude, and exposed.

She saw too that Mr. Starr's silver hair had a flat metallic sheen this afternoon; and his beard was faintly visible, metallic too, glinting on his jaws. He was stronger than she'd thought. He had knowledge far beyond hers.

Sybil resumed her position. She stared out at the ocean—the tall, cresting, splendidly white-capped waves. Why was she here, what did this man want of her? She worried suddenly that, whatever it was, she could not provide it.

But Mr. Starr was saying, in his gentle, murmurous voice, "There are people, primarily women!—who are what I call 'conduits of emotion.' In their company, the half dead can come alive. They need not be beautiful women or girls. It's a matter of blood warmth. The integrity of the spirit." He turned the page of his sketch pad and began anew, whistling thinly through his teeth. "Thus an icy-cold soul, in the presence of one so blessed, can regain something of his lost self. Sometimes!"

Sybil tried to summon forth a memory, an image at least, of her mother. *Melanie. Twenty-six at the time. Eyes . . . cheekbones . . . pale wavy hair.* A ghostly face appeared but faded almost at once. Sybil sobbed involuntarily. Her eyes stung with tears.

"—sensed that you, dear Blake—is your name Blake, really?—are one of these. A 'conduit of emotion'—of finer, higher things. Yes, yes! My intuition rarely misguides me!" Mr. Starr spoke as, hurriedly, excitedly, he sketched Sybil's likeness. He was squatting close beside her, on his haunches; his dark glasses winked in the sun. Sybil knew, should she glance at him, she would not be able to see his eyes.

Mr. Starr said, coaxingly, "Don't you remember anything—at all—about your mother?"

Sybil shook her head, meaning she didn't want to speak.

"Her name. Surely you know her name?"

Sybil whispered, "Mommy."

"Ah, yes: 'Mommy.' To you, that would have been her name."

"Mommy—went away. They told me—"

"Yes? Please continue!"

"—Mommy was gone. And Daddy. On the lake—"

"Lake? Where?"

"Lake Champlain. In Vermont, and New York. Aunt Lora says—"

"'Aunt Lora'—?"

"Mommy's sister. She was older. Is older. She took me away. She adopted me. She—"

"And is 'Aunt Lora' married?"

"No. There's just her and me."

"What happened on the lake?"

"—it happened in the boat, on the lake. Daddy was driving the boat, they said. He came for me too but—I don't know if that was that time or some other time. I've been told, but I don't *know*."

Tears were streaming down Sybil's face now; she could not maintain her composure. But she managed to keep from hiding her face in her hands. She could hear Mr. Starr's quickened breath, and she could hear the rasping sound of the charcoal against the paper.

Mr. Starr said gently, "You must have been a little girl when—whatever it was—happened."

"I wasn't little to my*self*. I just *was*."

"A long time ago, was it?"

"Yes. No. It's always—there."

"Always where, dear child?"

"Where I, I—see it."

"See what?"

"I—don't *know*."

"Do you see your mommy? Was she a beautiful woman?—did she resemble you?"

"Leave me alone—I don't know."

Sybil began to cry. Mr. Starr, repentant, or wary, went immediately silent.

Someone —it must have been cyclists—passed behind them, and Sybil was aware of being observed, no doubt quizzically: a girl leaning forward across a stone ledge, face wet with tears, and a middle-aged man on his haunches busily sketching her. An artist and his model. An amateur artist, an amateur model. But how strange, that the girl was crying! And the man so avidly recording her tears!

Sybil, eyes closed, felt herself indeed a conduit of emotion—she *was* emotion. She stood upon the ground but she floated free. Mr. Starr was close beside her, anchoring her, but she floated free. A veil was drawn aside, and she saw a face—Mommy's face—a pretty heart-shaped face—something both affectionate and petulant in that face—how young Mommy was!—and her hair up, brown-blond lovely hair, tied back in a green silk scarf. Mommy hurried to the phone as it rang, Mommy lifted the receiver, Yes? yes? Oh hel*lo*—for the phone was always ringing, and Mommy was always hurrying to answer it, and there was always that expectant note to her voice, that sound of hope, surprise—oh, hel*lo*.

Sybil could no longer maintain her pose. She said, "Mr. Starr, I am through for the day, I am *sorry*." And, as the startled man looked after her, she walked away. He began to call after her, to remind her that he hadn't paid her, but, no, Sybil had had enough of modeling for the day. She broke into a run, she escaped.

8. A LONG TIME AGO . . .

A girl who'd married too young: was that it?

That heart-shaped face, the petulant pursed lips. The eyes widened in mock surprise: Oh, Sybil what have you *done* . . . ?

Stooping to kiss little Sybil, little Sybil giggling with pleasure and excitement, lifting her chubby baby arms to be raised in Mommy's and carried in to bed.

Oh honey, you're too big for that now. Too heavy!

Perfume wafting from her hair, loose to her shoulders, pale golden-brown, wavy. A rope of pearls around her neck. A low-cut summer dress, a bright floral print, like wallpaper. Mommy!

And Daddy, where *was* Daddy?

He was gone, then he was back. He'd come for her, little Sybil, to take her in the boat, the motor was loud, whining, angry as a bee buzzing and darting around your head, so Sybil was crying, and someone came, and Daddy went away again. She'd heard the motor rising, then fading. The churning of the water she couldn't see from where she stood, and it was night too, but she wasn't crying and no one scolded.

She could remember Mommy's face, though they never let her see it again. She couldn't remember Daddy's face.

Grandma said, You'll be all right, poor little darling you'll be all right, and Aunt Lora too, hugging her tight. Forever now you'll be all right, Aunt Lora promised. It was scary to see Aunt Lora crying: Aunt Lora never cried, did she?

Lifting little Sybil in her strong arms to carry her in to bed but it wasn't the same. It would never be the same again.

9. THE GIFT

Sybil is standing at the edge of the ocean.

The surf crashes and pounds about her . . . water streams up the sand, nearly wetting her feet. What a tumult of cries, hidden within the waves! She feels like laughing, for no reason. *You know the reason: he has returned to you.*

The beach is wide, clean, stark, as if swept with a giant broom. A landscape of dreamlike simplicity. Sybil has seen it numberless times but today its beauty strikes her as new. *Your father: your father they told you was gone forever: he has returned to you.* The sun is a winter sun, but warm, dazzling. Poised in the sky as if about to rapidly descend. Dark comes early because, after all, it is winter here, despite the warmth. The temperature will drop twenty degrees in a half hour. *He never died: he has been waiting for you all these years. And now he has returned.*

Sybil begins to cry. Hiding her face, her burning face, in her hands. She stands flat-footed as a little girl and the surf breaks and splashes around her and now her shoes are wet, her feet, she'll be shivering in the gathering chill. *Oh, Sybil!*

When Sybil turned, it was to see Mr. Starr sitting on the beach. He seemed to have lost his balance and fallen— his cane lay at his feet, he'd dropped the sketch pad, his sporty golfing cap sat crooked on his head. Sybil, concerned, asked what was wrong—she prayed he hadn't had a heart attack!—and Mr. Starr smiled weakly and told her quickly that he didn't know, he'd become dizzy, felt the strength go out of his legs, and had had to sit. "I was overcome suddenly, I think, by your emotionl whatever it was," he said. He made no effort to get to his feet but sat there awkwardly, damp sand on his trousers and shoes. Now Sybil stood over him and he squinted up at her, and there passed between them a current of—was it understanding? sympathy? recognition?

Sybil laughed to dispel the moment and put out her hand for Mr. Starr to take, so that she could help him stand. He laughed too, though he was deeply moved, and embarrassed. "I'm afraid I make too much of things, don't I?" he said. Sybil tugged at his hand (how big his hand was! how strong the fingers, closing about hers!) and, as he heaved himself to his feet, grunting, she felt the startling weight of him—an adult man, and heavy.

Mr. Starr was standing close to Sybil, not yet relinquishing her hand. He said, "The experiment was almost too successful, from my perspective! I'm almost afraid to try it again."

Sybil smiled uncertainly up at him. He was about the age her own father would have been—wasn't he? It seemed to her that a younger face was pushing out through Mr. Starr's coarse, sallow face. The hooklike quizzical scar on his forehead glistened oddly in the sun.

Sybil politely withdrew her hand from Mr. Starr's and dropped her eyes. She was shivering—today, she had not been running at all, had come to meet Mr. Starr for purposes of modeling, in a blouse and skirt, as he'd requested. She was bare-legged and her feet, in sandals, were wet from the surf.

Sybil said, softly, as if she didn't want to be heard, "I feel the same way, Mr. Starr."

They climbed a flight of wooden steps to the top of the bluff, and there was Mr. Starr's limousine, blackly gleaming, parked a short distance away. At this hour of the afternoon the park was well populated; there was a gay giggling bevy of high school girls strolling by, but Sybil took no notice. She was agitated, still; weak from crying, yet oddly strengthened, elated too. *You know who he is. You always knew.* She was keenly aware of Mr. Starr limping beside her, and impatient with his chatter. Why didn't he speak directly to her, for once?

The uniformed chauffeur sat behind the wheel of the limousine, looking neither to the right nor the left, as if at attention. His visored cap, his white gloves. His profile like a profile on an ancient coin. Sybil wondered if the chauffeur knew about her—if Mr. Starr talked to him about her. Suddenly she was filled with excitement, that someone else should *know*.

Mr. Starr was saying that, since Sybil had modeled so patiently that day, since she'd more than fulfilled his expectations, he had a gift for her—"In addition to your fee, that is."

He opened the rear door of the limousine and took out a square white box and, smiling shyly, presented it to Sybil. "Oh, what *is* it?" Sybil cried. She and Aunt Lora rarely exchanged presents any longer, it seemed like a ritual out of the deep past, delightful to rediscover. She lifted the cover of the box, and saw, inside, a beautiful purse; a shoulder bag; kidskin, the hue of rich dark honey. "Oh, Mr. Starr—thank you," Sybil said, taking the bag in her hands. "It's the most beautiful thing I've ever seen." "Why don't you open it, dear?" Mr. Starr urged, so Sybil opened the bag, and discovered money inside—fresh-minted bills—the denomination on top was a twenty. "I hope you didn't overpay me again," Sybil said, uneasily, "—I haven't modeled for three hours yet. It isn't fair." Mr. Starr laughed, flushed with pleasure. "Fair to whom?" he asked. "What is 'fair'?—*we* do what *we* like."

Sybil raised her eyes shyly to Mr. Starr's and saw that he was looking at her intently—at least, the skin at the corners of his eyes was tightly puckered. "Today, dear, I insist upon driving you home," he said, smiling. There was a new authority in his voice that seemed to have something to do with the gift Sybil had received from him. "It will soon be getting chilly, and your feet are wet." Sybil hesitated. She had lifted the bag to her face, to inhale the pungent kidskin smell: the bag was of a quality she'd never owned before. Mr. Starr glanced swiftly about, as if to see if anyone was watching; he was still smiling. "Please do climb inside, Blake!—you can't consider me a stranger, now."

Still, Sybil hesitated. Half teasing, she said, "*You* know my name isn't Blake, don't you, Mr. Starr?—how do you know?"

Mr. Starr laughed, teasing too. "*Isn't* it? What is your name, then?"

"Don't you know?"

"Should I know?"

"Shouldn't you?"

There was a pause. Mr. Starr had taken hold of Sybil's

wrist; lightly, yet firmly. His fingers circled her thin wrists with the subtle pressure of a watchband.

Mr. Starr leaned close, as if sharing a secret. "Well, I did hear you sing your solo, in your wonderful Christmas pageant at the high school; I must confess, I'd sneaked into a rehearsal too—no one questioned my presence. And I believe I heard the choir director call you—is it 'Sybil'?"

Hearing her name in Mr. Starr's mouth, Sybil felt a sensation of vertigo. She could only nod, mutely, yes.

"*Is* it?—I wasn't sure if I'd heard correctly. A lovely name, for a lovely girl. And 'Blake'—is 'Blake' your surname?"

Sybil murmured, "Yes."

"Your father's name?"

"No. Not my father's name."

"Oh, and why not? Usually, you know, that's the case."

"Because—" And here Sybil paused, confused, uncertain what to say. "It's my mother's name. Was."

"Ah, really! I see." Mr. Starr laughed. "Well, truly, I suppose I *don't*, but we can discuss it another time. Shall we—?"

He meant, shall we get into the car; he was exerting more pressure on Sybil's wrist, and, though kindly as always, seemed on the edge of impatience. His grip was unexpectedly hard. Sybil stood flat-footed on the sidewalk, wanting to acquiesce; yet, at the same time, uneasily thinking that, no, she should not. Not yet.

So Sybil pulled away, laughing nervously, and Mr. Starr had to release her, with a disappointed downturning of his mouth. Sybil thanked him, saying she preferred to walk. "I hope I will see you tomorrow, then?—'Sybil'?" Mr. Starr called after her. "Yes?"

But Sybil, hugging her new bag against her chest, as a small child might hug a stuffed animal, was walking quickly away.

Was the black limousine following her, at a discreet distance?

Sybil felt a powerful compulsion to look back, but did not.

She was trying to recall if, ever in her life, she'd ridden in such a vehicle. She supposed there had been hired, chauffeur-driven limousines at her parents' funerals, but she had not attended those funerals; had no memory of anything connected with them, except the strange behavior of her grandmother, her aunt Lora, and other adults—

their grief, but, underlying that grief, their air of profound and speechless shock.

Where is Mommy, she'd asked, *where is Daddy,* and the replies were always the same: *Gone away.*

And crying did no good. And fury did no good. Nothing little Sybil could do, or say, or think did any good. That was the first lesson, maybe.

But Daddy isn't dead, you know he isn't. You know, and he knows, why he has returned.

10. "POSSESSED"

Aunt Lora was smoking again!—back to two packs a day. And Sybil understood guiltily that she was to blame.

For there was the matter of the kidskin bag. The secret gift. Which Sybil had hidden in the farthest corner of her closet, wrapped in plastic, so the smell of it would not permeate the room. (Still, you could smell it—couldn't you? A subtle pervasive smell, rich as any perfume?) Sybil lived in dread that her aunt would discover the purse, and the money; though Lora Dell Blake never entered her niece's room without an invitation, somehow, Sybil worried, it *might* happen. She had never kept any important secret from her aunt in her life, and this secret both filled her with a sense of excitement and power, and weakened her, in childish dread.

What most concerned Lora, however, was Sybil's renewed interest in *that*—as in, "Oh, honey, are you thinking about *that* again. *Why?*"

That was the abbreviated euphemism for what Lora might more fully call "the accident"—"the tragedy"—"your parents' deaths."

Sybil, who had never shown more than passing curiosity about *that* in the past, as far as Lora could remember, was now in the grip of what Lora called "morbid curiosity." That mute, perplexed look in her eyes! That tremulous, sometimes sullen, look to her mouth! One evening, lighting up a cigarette with shaking fingers, Lora said, bluntly, "Sybil, honey, this tears my heart out. What *is* it you want to know?"

Sybil said, as if she'd been waiting for just this question, "Is my father alive?"

"What?"

"My father. George Conte. *Is* he—maybe—alive?"

The question hovered between them, and, for a long, pained moment, it seemed almost that Aunt Lora might snort in exasperation, jump up from the table, walk out of the room. But then she said, shaking her head adamantly, dropping her gaze from Sybil's, "Honey, no. The man is not alive." She paused. She smoked her cigarette, exhaled smoke vigorously through her nostrils; seemed about to say something further; changed her mind; then said, quietly, "You don't ask about your mother, Sybil. Why is that?"

"I—believe that my mother is dead. But—"

"But—?"

"My—my father—"

"—isn't?"

Sybil said, stammering, her cheeks growing hot, "I just want to *know*. I want to see a, a—grave! A death certificate!"

"I'll send to Wellington for a copy of the death certificate," Aunt Lora said slowly. "Will that do?"

"You don't have a copy here?"

"Honey, why would I have a copy here?"

Sybil saw that the older woman was regarding her with a look of pity, and something like dread. She said, stammering, her cheeks warm, "In your—your legal things. Your papers. Locked away—"

"Honey, no."

There was a pause. Then Sybil said, half sobbing, "I

was too young to go to their funeral. So I never saw. Whatever it was—I never *saw*. Is that it? They say that's the reason for the ritual—for displaying the dead."

Aunt Lora reached over to take Sybil's hand. "It's one of the reasons, honey," she said. "We meet up with it all the time, at the medical center. People don't believe that loved ones are dead—they know, but can't accept it; the shock is just too much to absorb at once. And, yes, it's a theory, that if you don't see a person actually dead—if there isn't a public ceremony to define it—you may have difficulty accepting it. You may"—and here Aunt Lora paused, frowning—"be susceptible to fantasy."

Fantasy! Sybil stared at her aunt, shocked. *But I've seen him, I know. I believe him and not you!*

The subject seemed to be concluded for the time being. Aunt Lora briskly stubbed out her cigarette and said, "I'm to blame—probably. I'd been in therapy for a couple of years after it happened and I just didn't want to talk about it any longer, so when you'd asked me questions, over the years, I cut you off; I realize that. But you see, there's so little to say—Melanie is dead, and *he* is dead. And it all happened a long time ago."

That evening, Sybil was reading in a book on memory she'd taken out of the Glencoe Public Library: *It is known that human beings are "possessed" by an unfathomable number of dormant memory traces, of which some can be activated under special conditions, including excitation by stimulating points in the cortex. Such traces are indelibly imprinted in the nervous system and are commonly activated by mnemonic stimuli—words, sights, sounds, and especially smells. The phenomenon of déjà vu is closely related to these experiences, in which a "doubling of consciousness" occurs, with the conviction that one has lived an experience before. Much of human memory, however, includes subsequent revision, selection, and fantasizing. . . .*

Sybil let the book shut. She contemplated, for the dozenth time, the faint red marks on her wrist, where Mr. Starr—the man who called himself Mr. Starr—had gripped her, without knowing his own strength.

Nor had Sybil been aware, at the time, that his fingers were so strong; and had clasped so tightly around her wrist.

11. "MR. STARR"—OR "MR. CONTE"

She saw him, and saw that he was waiting for her. And her impulse was to run immediately to him, and observe,

with childish delight, how the sight of her would illumi-
nate his face. *Here! Here I am!* It was a profound power that
seemed to reside in her, Sybil Blake, seventeen years old—
the power to have such an effect upon a man whom she
scarcely knew, and who did not know her.

Because he loves me. Because he's my father. That's why.

And if he isn't my father—

It was late afternoon of a dull, overcast day. Still, the
park was populated at this end: joggers were running,
some in colorful costumes. Sybil was not among them,
she'd slept poorly the previous night, thinking of—what?
Her dead mother who'd been so beautiful?—her father
whose face she could not recall (though, yes surely, it was
imprinted deep, deep in the cells of her memory)?—her
aunt Lora who was, or was not, telling her the truth, and
who loved her more than anyone on earth? And Mr. Starr
of course.

Or Mr. Conte.

Sybil was hidden from Mr. Starr's gaze as, with an air
of smiling expectancy, he looked about. He was carrying
his duffel bag and leaning on his cane. He wore his plain,
dark clothes; he was bareheaded, and his silvery hair shone;
if Sybil had been closer, she would have seen light winking

in his dark glasses. She had noticed the limousine, parked up on the boulevard a block away.

A young woman jogger ran past Mr. Starr, long-legged, hair flying, and he looked at her, intently—watched her as she ran out of sight along the path. Then he turned back, glancing up toward the street, shifting his shoulders impatiently. Sybil saw him check his wristwatch.

Waiting for you. You know why.

And then, suddenly—Sybil decided not to go to Mr. Starr, after all. The man who called himself Starr. She changed her mind at the last moment, unprepared for her decision except to understand that, as, she quickly walked away, it must be the right decision: her heart was beating erratically, all her senses alert, as if she had narrowly escaped great danger.

12. THE FATE OF "GEORGE CONTE"

On Mondays, Wednesdays, and Fridays Lora Dell Blake attended an aerobics class after work, and on these evenings she rarely returned home before seven o'clock. Today was a Wednesday, at four: Sybil calculated she had more than enough time to search out her aunt's private papers, and to put everything back in order, well before her aunt came home.

Aunt Lora's household keys were kept in a top drawer of her desk, and one of these keys, Sybil knew, was to a small aluminum filing cabinet beside the desk, where confidential records and papers were kept. There were perhaps a dozen keys, in a jumble, but Sybil had no difficulty finding the right one. "Aunt Lora, please forgive me," she whispered. It was a measure of her aunt's trust of her that the filing cabinet was so readily unlocked.

For never in her life had Sybil Blake done such a thing, in violation of the trust between herself and her aunt. She sensed that, unlocking the cabinet, opening the sliding drawers, she might be committing an irrevocable act.

The drawer was jammed tight with manila folders, most of them well-worn and dog-eared. Sybil's first response was disappointment—there were hundreds of household receipts, financial statements, Internal Revenue records dating back for years. Then she discovered a packet of letters dating back to the 1950s, when Aunt Lora would have been a young girl. There were a few snapshots, a few formally posed photographs—one of a strikingly beautiful, if immature-looking, girl in a high school graduation cap and gown, smiling at the camera with glossy lips. On the rear was written "Melanie, 1969." Sybil stared at this like ness of her mother—her mother long before she'd become her mother—and felt both triumph and dismay: for, yes, here was the mysterious "Melanie," and, yet, *was* this the "Melanie" the child Sybil knew?—or, simply, a high school girl, Sybil's own approximate age, the kind who, judging from her looks and self-absorbed expression, would never have been a friend of Sybil's?

Sybil put the photograph back, with trembling fingers. She was half grateful that Aunt Lora had kept so few mementos of the past—there could be fewer shocks, reve-lations.

No photographs of the wedding of Melanie Blake and George Conte. Not a one.

No photographs, so far as Sybil could see, of her father "George Conte" at all.

There was a single snapshot of Melanie with her baby daughter, Sybil, and this Sybil studied for a long time. It had been taken in summer, at a lakeside cottage; Melanie was posing prettily, in a white dress, with her baby snug in the crook of her arm, and both were looking toward the camera, as if someone had just called out to them, to make them laugh—Melanie with a wide, glamorous, yet sweet smile, little Sybil gaping open-mouthed. Here Melanie looked only slightly more mature than in the graduation photograph: her pale-brown hair, many shades of brown and blond, was shoulder-length, and upturned; her eyes were meticulously outlined in mascara, prominent in her heart-shaped face.

In the foreground, on the grass, was the shadow of a man's head and shoulders—"George Conte," perhaps? The missing person.

Sybil stared at this snapshot, which was wrinkled and faded. She did not know what to think, and, oddly, she felt very little: for was the infant in the picture really herself, Sybil Blake, if she could not remember?

Or did she in fact remember, somewhere deep in her brain, in memory traces that were indelible?

From now on, she would "remember" her mother as the pretty, self-assured young woman in this snapshot. This image, in full color, would replace any other.

Reluctantly, Sybil slid the snapshot back in its packet. How she would have liked to keep it!—but Aunt Lora would discover the theft, eventually. And Aunt Lora must be protected against knowing that her own niece had broken into her things, violated the trust between them.

The folders containing personal material were few, and quickly searched. Nothing pertaining to the accident, the "tragedy"?—not even an obituary? Sybil looked in adjacent files, with increasing desperation. There was not only the question of who her father was, or had been, but the question, nearly as compelling, of why Aunt Lora had eradicated all trace of him, even in her own private files. For a moment Sybil wondered if there had ever been any "George Conte" at all: maybe her mother had not married, and that was part of the secret? Melanie had died in some terrible way, terrible at least in Lora Dell Blake's eyes, thus the very fact must be hidden from Sybil, after so many years? Sybil recalled Aunt Lora saying, earnestly, a few years ago, "The only thing you should know, Sybil, is that your mother—and your father—would not want you to grow up in the shadow of their deaths. They would have wanted you—your mother especially—to be *happy*."

Part of this legacy of happiness, Sybil gathered, had been for her to grow up as a perfectly normal American girl, in a sunny, shadowless place with no history, or, at any rate, no history that concerned her. "But I don't want to be *happy*, I want to *know*," Sybil said aloud.

But the rest of the manila files, jammed so tightly

together they were almost inextricable, yielded nothing.

So, disappointed, Sybil shut the file drawer, and locked it.

But what of Aunt Lora's desk drawers? She had a memory of their being unlocked, thus surely containing nothing of significance; but now it occurred to her that, being unlocked, one of these drawers might in fact contain something Aunt Lora might want to keep safely hidden. So, quickly, with not much hope, Sybil looked through these drawers, messy, jammed with papers, clippings, further packets of household receipts, old programs from plays they'd seen in Los Angeles—and, in the largest drawer, at the very bottom, in a wrinkled manila envelope with MEDICAL INSURANCE carefully printed on its front, Sybil found what she was looking for.

Newspaper clippings, badly yellowed, some of them spliced together with aged cellophane tape—

Wellington, Vt., Man Shoots Wife, Self
Suicide Attempt Fails

Area Man Kills Wife in July 4 Quarrel

Attempts Suicide on Lake Champlain

George Conte, 31, Arrested for Murder
Wellington Lawyer Held in Shooting Death of Wife, 26

Conte Trial Begins
Prosecution Charges "Premeditation"
Family Members Testify

So Sybil Blake learned, in the space of less than sixty seconds, the nature of the tragedy from which her aunt Lora had shielded her for nearly fifteen years.

Her father was indeed a man named George Conte, and this man had shot her mother, Melanie, to death, in their speedboat on Lake Champlain, and pushed her body overboard. He had tried to kill himself too but had only critically wounded himself with a shot to the head. He'd undergone emergency neurosurgery, and recovered; he was arrested, tried, and convicted of second-degree murder; and sentenced to between twelve and nineteen years in prison, at the Hartshill State Prison in northern Vermont.

Sybil sifted through the clippings, her fingers numb.

So this was it! This! Murder, attempted suicide!—not mere drunkenness and an "accident" on the lake.

Aunt Lora seemed to have stuffed the clippings in an envelope in haste, or in revulsion; with some, photographs had been torn off, leaving only their captions—"Melanie and George Conte, 1975," "Prosecution witness Lora Dell Blake leaving courthouse." Those photographs of George Conte showed a man who surely did resemble "Mr. Starr": younger, dark-haired, with a face heavier in the jaws and an air of youthful self-assurance and expectation. *There. Your father. "Mr. Starr." The missing person.*

There were several photographs, too, of Melanie Conte, including one taken for her high school yearbook and one of her in a long, formal gown with her hair glamorously upswept—"Wellington woman killed by jealous husband." There was a wedding photograph of the couple looking very young, attractive, and happy; a photograph of the "Conte family at their summer home"; a photograph of "George Conte, lawyer, after second-degree murder verdict"—the convicted man, stunned, downlooking, being taken away handcuffed between two grim sheriff's men. Sybil understood that the terrible thing that had happened in her family had been of enormous public interest in Wellington, Vermont, and that this was part of its terribleness, its shame.

What had Aunt Lora said?—she'd been in therapy for some time afterward, thus did not want to relive those memories.

And she'd said, *It all happened a long time ago.*

But she'd lied, too. She had looked Sybil full in the face and lied, lied. Insisting that Sybil's father was dead when she knew he was alive.

When Sybil herself had reason to believe he was alive.

My name is Starr! Don't judge me too quickly!

Sybil read, and reread, the aged clippings. There were perhaps twenty of them. She gathered two general things: that her father, George Conte, was from a locally prominent family, and that he'd had a very capable attorney to defend him at his trial; and that the community had greatly enjoyed the scandal, though, no doubt, offering condolences to the grieving Blake family. The spectacle of a beautiful young wife murdered by her "jealous" young husband, her body pushed from an expensive speedboat to sink in Lake Champlain—who could resist? The media had surely exploited this tragedy to its fullest.

Now you see, don't you, why your name had to be

changed. Not "Conte," the murderer, but "Blake," the victim, is your parent.

Sybil was filled with a child's rage, a child's inarticulate grief—Why, why! This man named George Conte had, by a violent act, ruined everything!

According to the testimony of witnesses, George Conte had been "irrationally" jealous of his wife's friendship with other men in their social circle; he'd quarreled publicly with her upon several occasions, and was known to have a drinking problem. On the afternoon of July Fourth, the day of the murder, the couple had been drinking with friends at the Lake Champlain Club for much of the afternoon, and had then set out in their boat for their summer home, three miles to the south. Midway, a quarrel erupted, and George Conte shot his wife several times with a .32 caliber revolver, which, he later confessed, he'd acquired for the purpose of "showing her I was serious." He then pushed her body overboard and continued on to the cottage where, in a "distraught state," he tried to take his two-year-old daughter, Sybil, with him, back to the boat—saying that her mother was waiting for her. But the child's grandmother and aunt, both relatives of the murdered woman, prevented him from taking her, so he returned to the boat alone, took it out a considerable distance onto the lake, and shot himself in the head. He collapsed in the idling boat and was rescued by an emergency medical team and taken to a hospital in Burlington where his life was saved.

Why, why did they save *his* life?—Sybil thought bitterly.

She'd never felt such emotion, such outrage, as she felt for this person George Conte: "Mr. Starr." He'd wanted to kill her too, of course—that was the purpose of his coming home, wanting to get her, saying her mother wanted her. Had Sybil's grandmother and Aunt Lora not stopped him, he would have shot her too, and dumped her body into the lake, and ended it all by shooting himself—but not killing himself. A bungled suicide. And then, after recovering, a plea of "not guilty" to the charge of murder.

A charge of second-degree murder, and a sentence of only between twelve and nineteen years. So, he was out. George Conte was out. As "Mr. Starr," the amateur artist, the lover of the beautiful and the pure, he'd found her out, and he'd come for her.

And you know why.

13. "YOUR MOTHER IS WAITING FOR YOU"

Sybil Blake returned the clippings to the envelope so

conspicuously marked MEDICAL INSURANCE, and returned the envelope to the very bottom of the unlocked drawer in her aunt's desk. She closed the drawer carefully, and, though she was in an agitated state, looked about the room, to see if she'd left anything inadvertently out of place; any evidence that she'd been in here at all.

Yes, she'd violated the trust Aunt Lora had had in her. Yet Aunt Lora had lied to her too, these many years. And so convincingly.

Sybil understood that she could never again believe anyone, fully. She understood that those who love us can, and will, lie to us; they may act out of a moral conviction that such lying is necessary, and this may in fact be true—but, still, they *lie*.

Even as they look into our eyes and insist they are telling the truth.

Of the reasonable steps Sybil Blake might have taken, this was the most reasonable: she might have confronted Lora Dell Blake with the evidence she'd found and with her knowledge of what the tragedy had been, and she might have told her about "Mr. Starr."

But she hated him so. And Aunt Lora hated him. And,

hating him as they did, how could they protect themselves against him, if he chose to act? For Sybil had no doubt, now, her father had returned to her, to do her harm.

If George Conte had served his prison term, and been released from prison, if he was free to move about the country like any other citizen, certainly he had every right to come to Glencoe, California. In approaching Sybil Blake, his daughter, he had committed no crime. He had not threatened her, he had not harassed her, he had behaved in a kindly, courteous, generous way; except for the fact (in Aunt Lora's eyes this would be an outrageous, unspeakable fact) that he had misrepresented himself.

"Mr. Starr" was a lie, an obscenity. But no one had forced Sybil to model for him, nor to accept an expensive gift from him. She had done so willingly. She had done so gratefully. After her initial timidity, she'd been rather eager to be so employed.

For "Mr. Starr" had seduced her—almost.

Sybil reasoned that, if she told her aunt about "Mr. Starr," their lives would be irrevocably changed. Aunt Lora would be upset to the point of hysteria. She would insist upon going to the police. The police would rebuff her, or, worse yet, humor her. And what if Aunt Lora went to confront "Mr. Starr" herself?

No, Sybil was not going to involve her aunt. Nor implicate her, in any way.

"I love you too much," Sybil whispered. "You are all I have."

To avoid seeing Aunt Lora that evening, or, rather, to avoid being seen by her, Sybil went to bed early, leaving a note on the kitchen table explaining that she had a mild case of the flu. Next morning, when Aunt Lora looked in Sybil's room, to ask her worriedly how she was, Sybil smiled wanly and said she'd improved; but, still, she thought she would stay home from school that day.

Aunt Lora, ever vigilant against illness, pressed her hand against Sybil's forehead, which did seem feverish. She looked into Sybil's eyes, which were dilated. She asked if Sybil had a sore throat, if she had a headache, if she'd had an upset stomach or diarrhea, and Sybil said no, no, she simply felt a little weak, she wanted to sleep. So Aunt Lora believed her, brought her Bufferin and fruit juice and toast with honey, and went off quietly to leave her alone.

Sybil wondered if she would ever see her aunt again.

But of course she would: she had no doubt she could

force herself to do what must be done.

Wasn't her mother waiting for her?

A windy, chilly afternoon. Sybil wore warm slacks and a wool pullover sweater and her jogging shoes. But she wasn't running today. She carried her kidskin bag, its strap looped over her shoulder.

Her handsome kidskin bag, with its distinctive smell.

Her bag, into which she'd slipped, before leaving home, the sharpest of her aunt's several finely honed steak knives.

Sybil Blake hadn't gone to school that day but she entered the park at approximately three forty-five, her usual time. She'd sighted Mr. Starr's long elegantly gleaming black limousine parked on the street close by, and there was Mr. Starr himself, waiting for her.

How animated he became, seeing her!—exactly as he'd been in the past. It seemed strange to Sybil that, somehow, to him, things were unchanged.

He imagined her still ignorant, innocent. Easy prey.

Smiling at her. Waving. "Hello, Sybil!"

Daring to call her that—"Sybil."

He was hurrying in her direction, limping, using his

cane. Sybil smiled. There was no reason not to smile, thus she smiled. She was thinking with what skill Mr. Starr used that cane of his, how practiced he'd become. Since the injury to his brain?—or had there been another injury, suffered in prison?

Those years in prison, when he'd had time to think. Not to repent—Sybil seemed to know he had not repented—but, simply, to think.

To consider the mistakes he'd made, and how to unmake them.

"Why, my dear, hello!—I've missed you, you know," Mr. Starr said. There was an edge of reproach to his voice but he smiled to show his delight. "—I won't ask where *were* you, now you're *here*. And carrying your beautiful bag—"

Sybil peered up at Mr. Starr's pale, tense, smiling face. Her reactions were slow at first, as if numbed; as if she were, for all that she'd rehearsed this, not fully wakened—a kind of sleepwalker.

"And—you *will* model for me this afternoon? Under our new, improved terms?"

"Yes, Mr. Starr."

Mr. Starr had his duffel bag, his sketch pad, his charcoal

sticks. He was bareheaded, and his fine silver hair blew in the wind. He wore a slightly soiled white shirt with a navy-blue silk necktie and his old tweed jacket; and his gleaming black shoes that put Sybil in mind of a funeral. She could not see his eyes behind the dark lenses of his glasses but she knew by the puckered skin at the corners of his eyes that he was staring at her intently, hungrily. She was his model, he was the artist, when could they begin? Already, his fingers were flexing in anticipation.

"I think, though, we've about exhausted the possibilities of this park, don't you, dear? It's charming, but rather common. And so *finite*," Mr. Starr was saying, expansively. "Even the beach, here in Glencoe. Somehow it lacks—amplitude. So I was thinking—I was hoping—we might today vary our routine just a bit, and drive up the coast. Not far—just a few miles. Away from so many people, and so many distractions." Seeing that Sybil was slow to respond, he added, warmly, "I'll pay you double, Sybil—of course. You know you can trust me by now, don't you? Yes?"

That curious, ugly little hook of a scar in Mr. Starr's forehead—its soft pale tissue gleamed in the whitish light. Sybil wondered if that was where the bullet had gone in.

Mr. Starr had been leading Sybil in the direction of the curb, where the limousine was waiting, its engine idling almost soundlessly. He opened the rear door. Sybil, clutching her kidskin bag, peered inside, at the cushioned, shadowy interior. For a moment, her mind was blank. She might have been on a high board, about to dive into the water, not knowing how she'd gotten to where she was, or why. Only that she could not turn back.

Mr. Starr was smiling eagerly, hopefully. "Shall we? Sybil?"

"Yes, Mr. Starr," Sybil said, and climbed inside.

ACKNOWLEDGMENTS

Many of the stories included in this volume originally appeared in the following publications, often in slightly different forms:

"Where Are You Going, Where Have You Been?" and
"How I Contemplated the World . . ." in *The Wheel of Love*

"The Sky Blue Ball" in *The Collector of Hearts*

"Small Avalanches" in *The Goddess and Other Women*

"Haunted" and "The Model" in *Haunted: Tales of the Grotesque*

"Bad Girls" in *New Plays* (as a full-length play)

"'Shot'" in *Where Is Here?*

"Why Don't You Come Live With Me It's Time" in *Heat*

"Life After High School" in *Will You Always Love Me?*